Lieut-Colonel Walter Rowley
Lancs in 1913. Following the f
Army, he was commissioned in
and spent the Second World Wai ... . , ...
From 1945 to 1961 his service took him to Germany, Hong
Kong (the background to his first novel *48 Hour Pass – Hong
Kong*) Singapore and Malaya, and included a 6-month attach-
ment to the American Army based in Chicago USA. This, his
second novel, reflects the impact of real-life on a young man
of the Fifties.

Walter Rowley was appointed an Officer of the Military
Division of the order of the British Empire in Her Majesty's
Honours List of June 1960.

Retiring from the Army in 1961 his life continued its strong
connections with travel, but this time with Pontins Holidays,
where he gained further Managerial experience with them in
the UK, Majorca, Spain, Morocco, Greece and Yugoslavia. He
is still retained by Holiday Club Pontins as a Consultant.

A man who has always thrived on activity, he is a Founder-
Member of the Under-privileged Childrens' Charity formed in
1975 in Bristol, and is Secretary of the Parochial Church
Council of St Bridget's Church, Brean, in Somerset, in
addition to being involved in many other Committees.

By the same author

48 Hour Pass – Hong Kong (1995)

The year is 1959, still 38 years away from that 1997 handover, but many thoughts were already being directed to that time. Hong Kong had been quiet since the 'Double Ten' riots of 1956 but now the authorities were aware of a new build-up in tension, with a new Triad – 'The 97', all set to challenge the Golden Lotus Triad who had been on the utmost support to British Rule since the end of the war with Japan.

David Rankin, a Sergeant in a British Army unit based high up on the Chinese border of the New Territories, spends his 48 hour pass in Hong Kong. It is he who rescues Lee Kyung Koh, glamorous leader of the Golden Lotus Triad, from 'The 97', and brings passionate love to her for the first time in her life. This is the Hong Kong of the Chinese as well as the British, of a passionate, but tragic, love affair, and of a Secret Service agent who trained himself over many years in his strict duty of maintaining the staus quo of Hong Kong.

FROM LONDON – WITH LOVE

Walter Rowley OBE

A SQUARE ONE PUBLICATION

First published in 1996 by
Square One Publications,
The Tudor House
Upton upon Severn
Worcestershire WR8 0HT

© 1996 Walter Rowley

A British Library Cataloguing in Data
is available for this title

ISBN 1 899955 14 3

*The right of Walter Rowley to be identified as Author of this
book has been asserted in accordance with the Copyright
Design and Patents Act 1988*

*All rights reserved. No part of this publicaton may be
produced, stored in a retrieval system, or transmitted in
any form or by any means, electronic, mechanical,
photocopying, recording or otherwise, without prior
permission of the publishers.*

*Typeset in Times New Roman 11 on 13 by
Avon Dataset Ltd, Bidford-on-Avon, Warwickshire
Printed by Antony Rowe Ltd, Chippenham, Wiltshire*

To America

Contents

CHAPTER 1

You Never Know

David Lander

I was early into business that never-to-be-forgotten day in November 1955, and had barely settled down to work when the telephone call came.

It was the crisp, cool, but nice voice of Jenny Denton, private secretary to the boss.

"Good morning David," she began; there were not many in the firm who she would call by their first names but Jenny and I are rather good friends, and before I could reply, "come on down, right away please, Mr. G. is waiting to see you." She wasted no time on the telephone that young lady, even with me, though we had amicably wasted time together elsewhere – bless her.

I came on down. I could not think what I had done wrong, nor, come to that, what I had done right, but I came on down quickly. I wasn't really scared of the boss, well not more than anyone else was, he's really pretty human as they all are, but I was a bit puzzled, it was not every day the boss sent for me.

Jenny Denton looked just as crisp, as cool, and as nice as she had sounded, but I couldn't appreciate her for long just then. Mr. G. didn't like to be kept waiting too long at any time, so I was ushered in, swept in, pretty quick.

There have been many times when I'd admired the office of Mr. Michael Henry Govern, with its sumptuous carpet, delightful furniture, lovely pictures, and air of high success, but not this morning, not yet at least. Right at that moment I had eyes only for Mr. G. himself, sat there, behind his beautifully polished desk, looking straight at me as I went in.

He wasted no time – I was expecting that, he never wasted time. Time is money was ever his maxim in business, and, if you want to build up an empire like he has done, don't waste time. There was no greeting of any kind for me, he came right to the point, and it shook me quite a lot.

"How would you like to go to America, David?" he fired out at me.

I saw the grin come over his face, it must have been at the look of amazement which I was certain had spread all over mine, but that grin of his helped. It was a double surprise, first America, and then the David part of it. He had called me that once or twice before, at a business dinner or an office party, or when I had been out to his house, but never before at business like this.

Over the years I had got to know Mr. G. very well. He is a tornado all right, but like most tornados, he doesn't do a lot of damage or harm to anything strong enough to stand up to him. If you are not that strong you are no good to him, you would not last a day. He is strong and fearsome, but with it all tolerant and human. Speed is his love, think fast, act fast, but always think first and give everything due consideration. Listen, think carefully but quickly, then make your decision. I had done that, made my decision and knew what I had to say.

"This is one time sir, when all the considering that needs to be done, has, I am sure, been done – yes sir, I would just love to go."

He liked that I could see, because the grin on his face changed to a smile, and if you think already that I'm a creeper, you're wrong – I would just love to go to America – who wouldn't? – and like I say, I know Mr. G. well. Everything had already been considered as to whether I should go or not – what it was all about didn't matter just at that moment – he had made his decision, and he had expected me to make mine knowing that – to me it isn't creeping, it's just damn good common sense.

"Thought you would David," he said, and I did like the sound of that David – it was a big thing in that Firm, "you'll like America, like it a lot, it's a great country."

"We think," he went on, the new Factory up in Lancashire will be ready right on schedule" – then proudly – "right bang on schedule – the 1st September 1956 – We think you'll make a good deputy to Arthur Lukins when we do start up" – that was news, and right up to my hopes – we'd all reckoned Arthur Lukins was a "cert" for that job, and I'd always hoped I might have a chance of the deputy manager job, and now, was I chuffed – "so we think you ought to have a look at American methods first."

I didn't say anything – you just don't when Mr. G. is speaking unless he asks you to do so or tells you to do so, but I had a lot inside me that was almost bursting out.

"Miss Denton has your complete itinerary," he said."There's one or two visits for you here before you go, and I think you'll have one or two things you want to do yourself – come back and see me just before Christmas – what say?"

I said, "Thank you sir, thank you a lot." But I meant it, meant it real hard, and he damn well knew how hard, and it pleased him, and that was that, and out I came.

I was still dazed when I came out, which amused Jenny.

"You'll get used to it David," she told me – "pleased?"

"Not half," I replied, and I could have a good look at her now, and she did look well, attractive as they make them, she knew what to wear and how to wear it – there was no mistake about that.

"Did Mr. G. tell you the other news – about Lancashire?" she asked.

"He did indeed," I said, "it's terrific – you – you've known for some time, about that and about Lancashire?"

"About a couple of weeks, and I'm happy for you."

"Thank you Jenny," I told her, "that's nice of you."

She took a big file out of her drawer. "Everything you want to know is in here," she told me. "Everything from now till you sail, just after Christmas, and most everything about America. By the time you go, everything will be arranged for you over there, hotels, bank, chaperone, everything."

"Why the chaperone?" I asked.

She smiled, a nice smile at that. "We just can't let a handsome boy like you run loose over there, can we?" and as I grinned – "No, it's just someone to ensure you see everything you should see."

"Everything?" I queried, innocently I thought.

"If you don't see everything with Danny Erikson, I shall be very mistaken," she said – "you remember him, he was over here in July."

I did remember him and said so. Jenny was right, and I had the answer to my query.

"You sail on the Queen Mary, just after Christmas," she said. "You'll have to come and see Mr. G. before you go – we can make a date for that later on."

I was very close to her now – her perfume was lovely, she was jolly nice this Jenny, and I could have put my arms around her and kissed her, but I knew better. It would have crumpled that lovely dark blue frock she was wearing – she was a great one for frocks, even in winter – and she didn't like crumpled frocks, well, not during office hours.

"Fine," I told her, "and perhaps we could make a date for an evening out."

It was her turn to be innocent – "With Mr. G.," she asked, "or with me?"

I lifted her left hand, it was soft and very warm. I turned the hand over and kissed the inside.

"With you, silly," I replied, just as innocently.

"I'd like that," she said, and her eyes were as warm as the inside of her hand – "perhaps, as it's a special occasion, we could have dinner at my place."

Dinner at Jenny's place was a very special occasion.

"I'd like that," I said, and even if my eyes weren't warm, the rest of me certainly was. I looked at her, she was remembering, I think, and I was remembering with her.

"Perhaps it will be my last chance," she went on – "It's even money some American woman will hook you out there, you and – "

"I don't think so," I told her – "but you never know your luck."

That's just it – you never know.

CHAPTER 2

All Aboard

The taxi-driver viewed my large amount of baggage with mock dismay.

"Wouldn't Pickfords move you then?" he asked.

When he began to load up and caught sight of the Queen Mary labels, he warmed up considerably.

"America, eh?" A wide grin sprawling over what was really a cheerful face – "Grand lot of chaps them Yanks – knew a lot of 'em during the war – not nearly enough about now for our liking – good passengers them Yanks – good tippers."

I saw his point. The seven bob I added to his fare at Waterloo, got me into his good books. He was now most cheery.

"Thanks, Guv, you'll do well in the States – have a good time."

The boat train was far from crowded.

"Never is at this time of the year," the only other occupant of the compartment informed me – "we'll find the Mary half empty too."

I liked the man on sight – I'm that way about people, believing, just as the old adage goes, that first impressions are best. He was big, burly, ugly-handsome, if you get what I mean, and friendly – the sort of chap you often meet in the other team's second row – the sort who'd maul you to death all afternoon, then buy you pints at his Club bar all night.

Tony Regan was his name, a couple of years older than me. He was in oil "just a little pipe-line mind you" – this was his second trip to the States, and he obviously knew his way about. We knew a great deal about each other before we reached Southampton.

"Not a bit of good travelling First" – he was most convincing about this – "not in the Queens anyhow. All right in the small Cunarders, but in the Queens First is awfully stodgy – much more fun going cabin."

I hadn't really known that.

"Oh yes," he went on, "a real stuffy lot in the First, private suites and all that. No mixing, no company, you'll have a good time in our class you see."

On the quayside I stood awhile, looking up at the great ship which was to be my home for the next few days, and was to carry me into a new life. She was ablaze with lights and even bigger than I had imagined. She looked tremendously exciting. I was thrilled to bits.

My heavy baggage was whisked away with an assurance it would be in my cabin almost as soon as I was. I followed a young steward, carrying my small bags, along the gangway, aboard, and to my cabin. No fuss, no bother, come aboard sir, and you'll find yourself very welcome. I liked it, liked it a lot.

I liked my cabin also, roomy, comfortable, warm and with two bunks.

"It's all right sir," the young steward told me, pocketing the tip I gave him, "you'll have this one to yourself, so you can spread out as much as you like."

Tony was right, the Mary was half empty, as the young steward quickly confirmed.

"Won't be many travelling this trip sir, we never get a lot at this time of the year. Can't expect many really."

"I suppose not," I agreed.

"Your proper cabin steward will be along soon sir," the young steward said as he went out, leaving me to unpack my small stuff, a task I hadn't finished when my heavy baggage was ushered in by my proper cabin steward.

He was in good form.

"Electric shaver sir? Soon fix that up, you just leave that to me. Now, what about early morning tea? Eight o'clock all right sir? Good – don't want to go killing yourself on this trip you know – take it nice and steady – you won't find many people around much before nine, not these cold mornings, and not tomorrow for sure, we don't cast off until eleven. I'll bring you a bit of fruit with the tea, just to keep the old insides working – now what else is there we can do?"

By next morning Tony and I were quite old friends. He too had a large cabin to himself, and he had settled in as though he owned the ship.

It was cold that morning. There was more than a tingle of icy rain in the wind, whilst the grey clouds overhead were scudding past at surprising speed. Not many of the liner's passengers were on deck with us for the departure from Southampton, many of them had probably seen it all before, but whatever the weather I would not have missed it for anything. I had a sort of tense feeling inside, I still hadn't got used to it at all, but I was enjoying it and loving the excitement.

The vast Cunarder, fussed over by her tugs, came easily away from the landing stage, the space between the ship and the shore increased quickly, the waving figures on the shore, not many of them, became smaller and smaller. The Queen Mary moved steadily down Southampton Water to the sea, off, what was for her, on a normal journey to the new world, and taking me, and many like me, to a new life, new friends and new adventures.

We stood up there for some time, not speaking much, but thinking a lot. In spite of the cold and the wet, I could not bring myself to leave, all this was magic, the ship, the sea and the view, as we passed, quicker now, down the Solent and towards the open sea. My thoughts were confused, there were so many things to think about.

Tony brought me out of them.

"Come on," he said, "let's go and have a couple before lunch," – so down we went, down from the cold and the loneliness of the deck, down into the life, the warmth, the cheerfulness of the bar.

It was surprisingly crowded, gay and very noisy – of course that's one of the delights of a decent bar, the hum of conversation, so that you have to talk loud yourself to make yourself heard, then everyone has to talk louder, and the hum becomes almost a roar – it all adds to the atmosphere.

We pushed through to the bar – that's part of the fun too if you are in the right mood, especially if there are a few nice females to push past, as there were here. I was at once pleased – the draught beer was excellent. Mustn't have too much of this, I told myself, might put on too much weight.

Tony explained the form. He had to talk loud even though we were practically touching each other. I already had my back against a nice much smaller back, as feminine and friendly as any I had ever backed against. I took a quick peek and my eyes met the back's owner. She was dark, trim and nice, and she smiled a lovely little smile at me, so I settled my back just a little more against hers, though not heavily, and she held herself there as though she was enjoying it too. It's great fun, the back game, played properly.

The form, according to Tony, was simple.

"We mustn't get involved too early old son," he was very much the veteran traveller now. "Best to take it easy for the first day or so and see what's what."

I wasn't arguing. I ordered up a couple more beers. The first had gone down fast and well. The back came back to me as I relaxed again. This is the life, I thought, good beer, a lovely back against mine. I could stand this for a long time whilst Tony went on with the form.

"Besides," he said, "you never know what may get on at Cherbourg – some of these French ladies are really oomphs."

I hadn't thought of that, so it was nice to think of it now. I couldn't ever remember having known a French lady, though I've always been told they have lots of oomph – it would be exciting to make sure.

It's amazing what you can think about whilst listening to someone else talking. I was thinking what great fun all this was going to be, and that I must get to know the owner of this back my back was getting so very friendly with, and I was thanking Mr. G. for sending me to America, and thinking of Mr. G. made me think of Jenny, and I wondered how friendly her back could get – funny I had never wondered about that before, and yes Tony, there was time for just one more before lunch, especially as the beer's good and this other back isn't in any hurry to move.

CHAPTER 3

On Another World

Living on the Queen Mary was like living on another world.

If they ever get out into space, and if they ever find that planet Utopia, and if Utopia is half as good as the Queen Mary, then I'll book a ticket on the first passenger rocket no matter what it costs – the Queen Mary was just that good.

"We're sending you cabin class," Mr. G. had told me when I had been in to see him just before Christmas, "but it's pretty decent and you'll enjoy it."

As far as I'm concerned, it was the understatement of any year.

Course, it's a different life, luxury surroundings, practically everything done for you, ease, comfort, good food, plenty to drink, with everybody out to make the best of it all, so how can anyone be other than at his or her best?

Certainly on that first day everything went well as far as we were concerned. Tony did a lot, he was a natural mixer, even more so than the Americans, and down at lunch he soon had our table feeling they had been together for years.

What made it so much better was that the owner of the friendly back was at our table, and, better still, sat next to me. I've thought a lot about that – maybe our backs could be used for more than we use 'em for at present, we don't let them play enough part in our lives. My back knew something at any rate, and the owner of the other back and I laughed a lot about it all when we first met, and often afterwards through the voyage.

She was Lucy Holley. I had time for much more than a quick peek at her now, and she was indeed nice. Dark hair, round features, flawless skin, and an immaculate dresser. Lovely teeth, even and white, she had only the slightest trace of an American accent, and her faint drawl was attractive. She was a perfectionist was Lucy, her make-up was right, her dresses right, and nothing flashy about her, and with it all she was very friendly and completely sincere.

I liked them all at our table, liked them all straight away. Tony did the introductions, simple and effective, the way the Americans like them to be done, Christian name, surname, and a little bit about what you did – none of the mumbling introductions of the typical Englishmen for Tony.

The others, all Americans, quickly responded with the easy spontaneity characteristic of them. There was Tom Holley, Lucy's husband, straight across from me – a pleasant round faced man who was nearing fifty but said he felt more like twenty. Esther Cameron, on my right, fortyish but smart, and carried her age well, wearing horn-rimmed glasses which somehow added to her appearance. She did continuity for a film company and had been on location in Spain making a film I had never heard of. She'd had a week in London and now, to make sure of a rest, was sailing back instead of flying.

Lucy was on my left, then Tony, then Sylvia. This one was Sylvia Lamond, in her early twenties, but mature and quite sure of herself. A dress designer with a big firm in New York, she had been in London, Paris and Rome, and away from the States for over three months. She was from Philadelphia, where her parents still lived. She didn't like flying. I just heard her tell Tony and Tom, and anyhow it was always such jolly good fun travelling cabin class on the Mary.

The way Tony went to town with her convinced me that he had already forgotten his brave thoughts of not getting involved too early, and I grinned as I reflected what the French ladies, including their oomph, might now miss.

I told Lucy why I was grinning.

"Well, they are nice, and have – what you call it – oomph," she told me.

"So have the American girls," I came back.

"They have?" she queried, and I could see the merry twinkle in her eyes, "do you know many?"

"Three," I replied, "you, Esther and Sylvia."

"And we have oomph?" she asked.

"Loads of it, all three of you," I was enthusiastic. "I've never known more oomph than you have."

She laughed – she was pleased, I could see.

"Nobody ever told me that before, sir," she said.

It was an enjoyable lunch with companions like that, and a

vegetable curry, with brussel sprouts and a baked Idaho potato, as my main course. Afterwards, when the ladies had left us, we got to know a lot more about Tom Holley.

He, like Lucy, was from Boston. He prided himself on his appearance and his clothes. Not exactly flashy, but with an impression of wealth. A jeweller, born in the trade and knew it backwards. His father had founded the little shop in Boston in which he had grown up and had inherited. He had been lucky, everything Tom touched turned to gold, or "diamonds", as he himself put it. He had been just twenty-one when his father died, but helped by his mother, who was a very hard worker too, the shop had prospered. It was now a tremendous concern, exactly right and in the right place in Boston.

His mother had passed on a few years ago, and everything came to him, there was no-one else in the family. Until five years ago he had not had time to spend the money he had made, nor had he wanted to, work was all that mattered, it had been his life, his hobby. Then he had met Lucy.

Lucy was much younger than he, but she was great, sure great. He had married her as soon as he could after getting to know her, and now everything was indeed wonderful. But he did not say a great deal about her, come to think of it, neither had she. She was almost a mystery this Lucy. Perhaps, I thought, I'm a good detective.

Dinner that night was magnificent. We were anchored in the roads off Cherbourg by then, and the ship was as steady as a rock. We were to be anchored rather longer than anticipated as, so we had heard, the Paris train was somewhat delayed, and we were waiting for more passengers to come aboard.

It was a nasty night, blowing hard, and we had been warned we would probably get it rough in the Atlantic, but for now it was all serene aboard, though I could think that some of the oomph ladies might be suffering a little coming out to us in tenders. Not that I gave it a deal of thought, there was plenty of oomph sat just alongside me on my left. Lucy and I were getting along famously. I was glad to hear she was a good sailor, and didn't think she would be upset by any weather. Not so Tom however, she reckoned he would suffer if we had bad weather.

In the main lounge, after dinner, we danced. I knew I couldn't ask her for the first dance, though it took Tom a time to ask her, but I asked for the second as soon as the music started. She danced well, as I hoped she would. The floor was fairly crowded and we could not

11

move around much. I held her as close as I dared and we jigged round quite happily.

"Enjoying yourself?" I asked. I was quite close to her as I spoke, and, as she turned her face to reply, our cheeks touched for a brief instant. I liked it, I think she did.

"I sure am," she replied.

I was glad when the orchestra gave us three for this one. Generally, as I told her, I only get three when I'm dancing with a battleship or something. She liked me telling her that. I clapped hard as I could at the end of the third, but those darn musicians wouldn't give me one for an encore.

I'd had the first dance with Esther, so it was my turn for Sylvia when the band started again. This time it was a waltz. It was easy dancing with Sylvia, she was very good. She talked too, not like dancing with Lucy when we had hardly spoken, with Sylvia the conversation flowed. She was very gay, and I learned a lot about her. When we finished our dancing together, I knew Tony had no need to bother about the entente cordiale for oomph. Sylvia had enough and to spare. Tony knew it too, as I gathered from the knowing wink he gave me when we got back to our table.

Later on the Purser came in, and we alternated dancing with bingo. I've played bingo, as housey-housey, a few places and never won anything. I said so.

"Never mind," Lucy said, "there's always a first time."

She was right, and the first time was not long in coming.

The third game was stand up Bingo. This was a new one on me but really quite simple. All the players began standing up. As the numbers were called and you had one on your card, you sat down. The last player standing up, who would, of course, be the last one not having a number on his or her card called out, would be the winner.

This one was fun. Our table started badly, Tom having to sit down first call, and Sylvia the very next. Soon it was Lucy's turn to sit, leaving Esther, Tony and I still standing.

I had a good look round the lounge. It was surprising how many were already out. Everybody cheered when the sitters down sat, this game was causing a lot more excitement than ordinary bingo. The numbers were being called more slowly now, the interval between each call longer, so that everyone could enjoy the fun and the suspense.

We three hung on for quite a few numbers, but then Tony had to sit, amidst roars of laughter from the three sat down. It was about now I thought I'd like to win this game, and somehow I had a feeling I would. After the next number there were only Esther, myself, and three others standing. This was confirmed by the Purser who was doing the calling.

"Only five left," he said into his microphone, which came out loud and clear to us, "two ladies and three men," then, after a long pause, very slowly, "clickety-click, sixty-six."

"Blast," exploded Esther, and there were great roars from our table as she sat down.

Clickety-click had also been unlucky for one of the others, a man at a table right across the lounge, and there were more roars from that direction.

The next number was "on its own number five," which none of us had, and the next "twenty-seven". This brought loud exclamations from a nearby table, and the last lady left in sat down, very disappointed, leaving a man at a table to our left still standing up with me.

"I didn't think," I told the others, and I hoped it sounded fairly casual, "it could be as tense as this."

I badly wanted to win now. I had never felt this way about a game before. I was more than tense, I was damn excited, perspiring freely and hanging on for the next number. Oh lor, I wanted to win all right.

The Purser's voice seemed far off as I heard the next number – "Heinz varieties – fifty-seven."

I gasped with sheer relief. I had not got it. The others gasped with me, they were excited too. As soon as I had realised fifty-seven was not on my card, my eyes turned immediately to that other table. The other man was still standing. Fifty-seven had not put him out either.

"Gosh," I heard myself say, "this is awful," and I felt Lucy's knee give my left leg a nudge as encouragement, but none of the five sat down said anything.

The interval to the next number seemed an age. All I could think of was Lucy saying there must be a first time, and I hoped this was it.

The number came at last – "two eight, twenty-eight."

I gasped again, I knew I had not got that one, I looked left – the other blighter was still standing. It can't be right, I thought, he must have it, but he hadn't. Then I got the awful thought that perhaps I'd missed one and what an ass I would look when they checked. But it was too late for that now, for a while, and the damn lounge had gone

13

so quiet, and I would have loved another cold beer, and why didn't that Purser hurry up.

Then his voice came again, the voice of doom or of success – "one and six, sixteen."

Quick as a flash my eyes were down to my card, and I gasped with relief once more – I had not got it. In that very moment I heard a roar to my left and, looking that way, just caught a glimpse of my opponent sitting down.

Then bedlam broke loose at our table. You would have thought I'd won first prize in the Irish Sweepstake, not just a game of Bingo. They were all mad nearly with excitement, and, by golly, so was I.

The Purser's voice came again.

"Would the gentleman still standing come up to have his card checked please?"

This was it, now, if I'd missed one I would look a fool. But I had no need to worry, it was correct all right. The Purser made a great fuss of checking it, then asked me my name.

"The winner is Mr. David Lander."

The announcement got a big round of applause, and I felt pretty pleased. Back at the table the others showered me with congratulations, and it wasn't till afterwards I wondered why. I hadn't done anything, but just then I accepted their plaudits gladly – after all I'm human – I hope.

I was even more pleased a few minutes later when a steward brought on the prize. It was a bottle of champagne, in the traditional ice bucket, and with the compliments of the Cunard Line. It was Moet and Chandon, and I knew enough about champagne to know it would be good.

So intense had it all been that I had not noticed till then that the Queen Mary was under way again. I could not have said how long she had been moving.

"It'll make dancing a bit more difficult," I said to Tony as we went out for a minute or two.

"A bit," he agreed, "but much more fun."

Dancing again later with Lucy I saw what he meant. I had to hold her much closer, which was nice, and we couldn't move around a lot even though there was more room on the floor, but she didn't seem to mind, and I certainly did not.

I danced the last waltz with Lucy also. Tom didn't seem to want to, but I hung on for a long while until I asked her. Then they were playing "Charmaine", and I couldn't resist that and Lucy. But we didn't waltz much, the Mary was tossing quite a bit now, and we had to hold close together, get used to the motion, and take only short steps. I managed to rub noses with her once or twice, and brush her cheeks now and then with mine, and I think she enjoyed it as much as I did, which was plenty.

The orchestra gave us, "How Deep is the Ocean", as an extra, and we stuck it out, so did Tony and Sylvia, and a few other couples. Once, when the ship gave a big lurch, I held Lucy tighter, cheek to cheek, for just a few seconds – I could have stuck a lot of lurching.

Tony was all for going on to Rose Room, where the orchestra would commence to play in about half an hour, but Esther wasn't for that – she was already beginning to fear the worst, neither was Tom, so Lucy couldn't be either. It had been a great evening, but the Mary was hitting the weather now, and no mistake about it. There would not be many late nighters tonight. I was quite content to say goodnight to Lucy, Esther and Tom, see Tony and Sylvia off to the Rose Room, take a short walk on the deserted covered promenade deck, and call it a night. It was late enough even if we did get an hour back as we went westwards. I was quite pleased with my own steadiness, in spite of the rolling of the ship, as I went to my cabin.

CHAPTER 4

The Great Gale

In spite of my tiredness, sleep was hard to come by. The creakings and groanings inside and adjacent to the cabin grew much worse as I undressed and whilst I cleaned my teeth. By the time I got into my bunk, after having tightened down everything movable I could find, the great liner was really tossing. In my bunk, and with the lights out, it seemed worse still. It was uncomfortable, but thank goodness, I did not feel the slightest bit ill.

As she came out from the comparative shelter of the Channel and into the Atlantic, the Queen Mary met the beginning of a great gale head on. A gale that would lash her, beat at her, do its worst at her, for many hours to come.

I wondered whether to take one of the anti seasick pills Jenny had told me about, but didn't. I don't feel too bad, I told myself, there's no need for it. That helped keep me awake, arguing with myself about the pill. I dozed on and off but was never really asleep, and each time I thought about it the weather seemed worse. I was glad I was taking it so well. I was not a bit sick except when I thought about taking a pill. Perhaps I was a good sailor after all. This did my ego good, and I was more than ever determined to get through without medical aid. Towards morning, during one of my waking periods, I could have sworn now and then I was standing up in my bunk. This is a real bad 'un, I thought, and immediately cursed myself, that had made me think of the pills again.

Promptly at eight Bailey, my cabin steward, was in with tea and fruit.

"How you doin', sir?" he asked. "Not been bad 'ave you?"

I was pleased to report I hadn't.

"Been a bad night," Bailey didn't let up, "likely to get worse too

16

sir, this is just the time for gales. Think you'll be all right sir, or would you like a pill?"

On Bailey's advice I took a couple of pills with my tea.

"Won't do you no harm sir, not that sort, they're good. They'll keep you going. Don't want you stuck in bed all the trip. Bet your life some of 'em will be in this weather."

I was annoyed at first, taking those pills, but felt so much better after them. It's auto-suggestion, I told myself, you won't be sick if you don't want to be, and all the time I knew I was wrong, it's your blessed balance nerves, yes, I know, behind the ears somewhere.

Tony was up on the covered promenade deck. He looked wonderfully fit. Even in the covered promenade the noise of the wind and sea was deafening, whilst the great ship bucked and tossed beneath us.

"You all right?" Tony shouted.

"So far, yes," I roared back. "Didn't sleep much, and I've had a couple of pills, just in case. No need to ask how you are."

"Good thing," came back at me over the elements from Tony, "don't want to be left on my own you know."

The restaurant was almost empty, but we were delighted to find Lucy and Sylvia already at the table, both looking remarkably well.

Lucy told us Tom wasn't coming down, he'd had a bad night and been very sick. She felt awfully sorry for him, but he never had been a good sailor.

Tony and I went through the menu – fruit juice, corn flakes, fried eggs, Wiltshire bacon and mushrooms, rolls and marmalade, washed down with lashings of coffee. Lucy couldn't get over what we ate, though she and Sylvia did pretty well themselves. Our steward Alf, was on his own. His young assistant, Tom, was in a bad way.

"There'll be a lot in a bad way," he told them, "passengers and crew – and the weather'll get worse 'fore it gets better."

Tony knew the answer to that one.

"Never starve yourself if it's rough – plenty of food, plenty of exercise and you'll keep well."

I very much hoped he was right, especially after that breakfast I had just eaten.

The four of us went up to see the weather.

Forward, on the covered promenade deck, we saw the sea in all its majestic glory, in all its strength, in all its might. It was a tremendous sight, one never to be forgotten. The great waves came up like a wall ahead of us. They rose to a colossal height in front, then sank beneath the the great liner as she climbed with great speed to the top of the wall.

We were enthralled with the grandeur of it all. Each wave was a separate thrill as it gained height and solidity before us, and, as we seemed to sweep up on it to the top, to hang poised for a brief second, or was it for eternity, stop each one, till the next wave formed its great mountain of water ahead, and the procedure was repeated.

The rain lashed down on the sea. There in front, on the immediate wave on which we were climbing. A mist of rain, hitting the top of the sea hard and bouncing back to the dark low clouds above.

The noise was a symphony for a million musicians. The whole orchestra of the universe playing crescendo the whole time. It was deafening, but it was beautiful. The swish, the swosh, and the crashing of the waves, was a sound difficult to describe, yet easy, so easy, to distinguish from the roaring of the wind and the lashing of the rain.

We could not speak, could not have heard one another if we had spoken. We just stood there, watching and wondering, thinking our own thoughts. Balancing there, protected by the glass verandah, huddled against each other, with the two girls in between Tony and I.

It was wonderful, yet fearful. How could any ship, even the Queen Mary, live in a sea such as this? Had the Pilgrim fathers encountered such a gale? If they had, however did they reach the New World? A thousand thoughts chased through my brain, a thousand ages of sailors and ships,

Once, as we came to the top of one vast wave, the ship gave a huge shudder as she raced down the next slide. My thoughts came away from sailors and ships, back to my boyhood. I was back through the years to the time when, as a very small boy, I had first been taken on the roller-coaster at the Blackpool pleasure beach. Then I had been afraid as we roared up and down and around at breakneck speed. Here, on this roller-coaster which was the Queen Mary, I was completely unafraid. Here were two of God's wonders, the sea and the wind, in all their strength and power, and I was enjoying the spectacle of it all.

We were reluctant to drag ourselves away. By now the pattern of it all was familiar. The Queen Mary would race to the top of each huge wave, pause there for a second, then race down into the trough of the next, and up on to the top again. It was terrific, and we were held transfixed, fascinated, by the beauty and the wonder of it all.

By lunch time we knew Tom was worse, and Esther was very bad also. Lucy was concerned for Tom, and most thankful the cabin stewardess was still on duty, and was a very capable woman.

There were very few to lunch. The head waiter greeted us as we went in to the restaurant and hoped we were hungry, I was feeling a bit flippant, like I've said, the draught beer was excellent.

"We're being tossed about so much, I would not be surprised to find sandwiches only for lunch," I said to him.

He almost exploded. The look of horror on his face had to be seen to be believed.

"Sandwiches sir," he exclaimed, "on the Queen Mary?" It took him all his time to continue. "Believe me sir, we should serve a full menu on the Queen Mary if atom bombs were dropping all around us."

I am sure he was right.

All that day and the next the great gale raged. The giant Cunarder fought her way valiantly on against the terrific wind and the tremendous seas. She groaned, she creaked, she bucked, she plunged, she rocked and she rolled, but she steadily fought her way westwards, plunging down the troughs of the waves and ploughing up the other side. Jigging, cavorting, then rolling as the wind hit her, she went on and on, whilst life on board for many of her passengers, and for quite a few of her crew, was not worth living. Many died a thousand deaths whilst the Queen Mary tried her strength against all the forces of nature.

What converts to air travel must have been made I could only imagine, and all this time I felt as fit as could be. Plenty of food, exercise, and the pills, kept me going without any trouble, and Lucy, Sylvia and Tony, were equally as fit and untroubled as me.

We had the ship practically to ourselves. A few other passengers appeared in the lounge, restaurant and the bar, but the majority were confined to their cabins and their bunks.

Tom Holley was one of those who had a very bad time. He had been sick until he could be sick no more, but even now could not stop retching. He stuck it well, and we were often in to see him. Tony, always with the well meaning advice to eat something and risk it. Tom dare not, pills had done him no good, he sipped only a very little cold water. He sure was sick and that was that.

He was good with Lucy. "Don't worry honey," he would say when he was able to lie back and talk rationally for a while, "Paddy here can take care of me, you go and enjoy yourself." The stewardess was wonderful, a tough Irish lady Tom had christened Paddy on their first night aboard. She had all her passengers, except Lucy, sick, and yet she managed them all and seemed to devote plenty of time to them all.

"Lucky for me I have you three to look after Lucy," Tom told them, "or she sure would be miserable." Only because she knew the stewardess was so capable did Lucy leave Tom, but she was encouraged also by Paddy herself.

"Sure you're better going out and leaving him, it's me that can take care of him."

Sick as he was, he was her best patient, and gave her really no trouble at all – "not like some of thim others begorrah."

Esther was a bit better on the second day, but couldn't get up. She would stay there on her bunk till the gale abated.

The covered promenade, with its grandstand view of the gale, was the big attraction for all four of us. We never tired of going forward to see the huge seas.

I had told them of how it reminded me of the roller-coaster, and now we called it that.

"Let's go on the roller-coaster," one of us would say, and all four of us would be off, on the cake-walk of the ship's corridors and stairs, hanging on to the handrails, for our front seats on the roller-coaster.

We found time to do many things, and to explore the ship. In the tailor's shop we discovered the Queen Mary tie, one more to add to my large collection. I love ties, can't resist them. We thought Lucy might buy one for Tom, but she did not.

"He's funny that way," she said, "like's to buy his own clothes, so I've never bought him anything like that."

She and Sylvia bought our ties for Tony and I. It was their way of paying us back, so they said, and we both thought it best not to argue. We know it pleased them a lot.

We swam in the swimming pool. This was a great discovery, and, as usual, it was Tony who thought of it.

We had finished tea in the lounge, a very empty lounge with we four, and the two stewards on duty, the only occupants, when he got the idea.

"Let's go and have a swim," he shot out.

I was quick with the reply.

"It's a bit too rough for me outside."

I thought that a huge joke, if a bit too subtle for Lucy and Sylvia to see, but Tony showed what he thought of it.

"Idiot," this quite strongly, "I mean down in the pool of course."

I had never given a thought to this wonderful liner having a swimming pool, but, now I was reminded, I knew she had, so down right-away we went, down the stairs, holding on to the handrails and to each other, experts by now in the art of getting up and down stairs in very rough weather.

We half expected the pool would be closed, but it wasn't, and the steward in charge was glad to see us. He soon fitted Tony and I up with costumes and towels, whilst Sylvia and Lucy, with terrific energy I thought, went all the way back to their cabins for costumes.

Even down here, as far down decks as we could go, the ship was rolling hard with an odd toss and buck thrown in for good measure, and the water swishing from side to side in the pool. It was great fun, and, clambering in, we soon got used to the roll and enjoyed being swept from side to side, as the water went first this way and that. We had to be careful, of course, and we took good care of the two girls, who both looked enchanting in their swimming costumes, doing our eyes, and the eyes of the bath steward, a lot of good.

Tony's romance with Sylvia was blossoming, it was easy to see, but though my friendship with Lucy had blossomed equally, we had become distant, if it can be described that way. We had flirted a lot on our first day of meeting, but since then, it seemed, the shutters were up. I guessed it was because Tom was absent. I don't know a lot about women, no more than the next man, but I reckoned she was the type who could be more gay, even flirtatious, with her husband there, not to show off, not to make him jealous, but in a friendly manner, and could not do so, in case it got serious, without her husband. Lucy sort of confirmed that one evening when we were talking.

"I sure do appreciate you being so kind to me David," she said, "and Tony too," this added hastily. "I like you a lot, and it's been nice being with you this way."

What can you say in answer to that? I did my best – it had been my pleasure to be with her.

"I owe Tom a hell of a lot," she went on, and I could sense this was the explanation for the withdrawal from the flirtation game. "If it hadn't been for him, I sure would not have seen anything like this."

She paused awhile, and I knew enough not to hurry her. Having started, she would tell me what she wanted me to know in her own way in her own time.

"He's twenty-seven years older than me, and he hadn't known a woman until he met me – there was his Mother of course – but no woman in the way I mean" – another pause – "I don't really know why he picked on me, but he did – and he – he's done a lot for me."

She laid a hand on my knee, her hand was very warm and the contact gave me a great thrill. I knew then it was a good thing she had withdrawn from the flirtation game.

"I'll be honest David," she continued, and she was back with her thoughts now, "I married Tom for – well, let's say for security, marriage, protection, money, everything. It was just as though somebody had rubbed a magic lamp for me, but, thank God, it's grown into much more than that."

I wanted to say I was glad, but I didn't say it. Her warm hand was still on my knee, and now and then her thumb gave a little caressing movement, and, looking straight at her, I hoped, in a way, my eyes were not saying what the rest of me was feeling.

"Life hasn't always been milk and honey for me David. I've had to fight hard for a lot of things, and had to fight hard to stop a lot of things happening to me," her voice hardened a little, then softened again, "so I jumped at Tom when the offer came."

Another pause – she may have expected me to say something, but I kept silent.

"I'm so glad I did," her voice was very soft. "We've been happy David, he's a wonderful man. I'm not sure these sort of marriages aren't better than the ones when people are the same age and desperately in love. I haven't known that sort of love from Tom, but he's such a grand man and I wouldn't do anything – anything at all" – I knew the reason for the repeat – "to hurt him – and I know he wouldn't do anything to hurt me – so we get along quite happily and contentedly together – much more so than a lot of folks I know."

I thought the explanation was over now, but I could not think what to say. It was just as well, for there was a little bit more to come.

"I'm honest David," the hand was still there, and the grip had tightened, "there have been times when I've still had to fight, to ensure I don't lose all I have gained – you understand?"

I nodded, I think I understood, but it still wasn't the end.

"The hardest fight is now David – with you, but I'll win it, never fear, because I'm so fond of Tom, I have to win – have to – even though I may regret, when I'm old perhaps, that I never knew a grand passion. I've never known such a thing David – they say every woman should have one" – her eyes were bright and gleaming – "when she will do anything, kill even, for love – I guess someone else must have mine for me."

Her hand came away from my knee – she had finished – told me what she wanted to tell me. She had paid me a great compliment, and I was proud and humble because of it. I thought of Tom, who I had known only for a few hours really, and knew he was the grand chap she had described. As long as he was around she would win all her fights.

I was glad she had told me what she had, but, funnily enough, when I thought about it, much as I liked her, attractive as she was, much as I enjoyed her company, I couldn't think she was the grand passion for me, if men have such things. Come to think of it, Jenny had never been the grand passion for me, though I had been very romantic at times with that young lady. No, I decided men don't have grand passions.

CHAPTER 5

New Year's Eve – and then –

About noon on New Year's Eve the gale began to abate. It was still rough, the Queen Mary was still performing some of her tricks, but the weather improved, and we saw more of the passengers.

Our celebrations were affected because Tom could not appear. He tried hard, but he couldn't make it. He was a sorry sight up there in his bunk, he really had been through it. He was improving now, as the weather improved, but was not well enough to get up. He insisted Lucy be with us, but she was in poor form with him absent.

Esther joined us, determined to see 1956 come in properly. We did our best to make it go well, but we never really managed it.

It was a pity, it could have been a great night. We started with drinks in the Purser's cabin, and should have been a happy party when we got down to dinner, but we were not.

The restaurant was magnificent, transformed into a fairyland of colour, and all the stewards in full regalia. The ship had certainly done us proud. The meal wonderful, could not have been bettered, with the roast stuffed young tom turkey and cranberry sauce a delight. I had my first go at corn on the cob, it was sumptious. I ate a lot but had room for the Christmas pudding.

We should have been having a great time, there was so much to enjoy, with our stewards, Alf and Tom, really looking after us. But it was not to be – Esther was having to fight hard, and Lucy was almost miserable.

We missed her when the New Year came in – she had gone off to be with Tom. I was with Esther when the booming of Big Ben came over the loud speakers – we had got separated from Tony and Sylvia in the crush – and all I could think about was that it must be a recording of Big Ben. I knew it to be long past midnight in London, and that Esther's peck wasn't much to start the New Year with, but cheered up a lot when a healthy and quite nice young person on my left flung herself in my arms, and gave me a real smackeroo, lips, teeth, tongue and all.

"Appy New Year, oui," she said, and I thought hard about all that oomph of the French ladies. Tony was right, we should have been waiting at the top of the gangway at Cherbourg.

Sylvia's kiss, nearly as generous as the oomph lady's helped a lot also, but Lucy wasn't in the kissing mood when she came back. Afterwards I thought I hadn't helped Lucy a lot that night.

We were over twenty-four hours late getting in. It could not be helped. For more than three days the great Cunarder had fought that tremendous gale, and the force of the wind and sea had slowed her down considerably. Even now the sea was still against us, and there was no possibility of making up time.

Bailey let me sleep on till eight the last morning aboard.

"No need for an early wake-up sir," he explained, "we're in the fog and ain't even in the Hudson yet."

He had looked after me well had Bailey.

We were still in thick fog hours later, and there was nothing to see moving very slowly up the Hudson, with the Queen Mary's siren booming at regular intervals, with now and then another siren sounding near at hand or far away. Thank goodness for radar, I thought.

I could not convince our little party that the river was named after an Englishman, one Henry Hudson, an English sea captain who worked for the Dutch, and had first sailed up these waters nearly three hundred and fifty years previously. Esther told me she would have to read it in the reference books before she could believe it, and she sure would make it her business to look it up. I think the others began to believe it after a while.

"Wonder what it looked like in those days?" Sylvia asked of nobody in particular.

Tony beat me to it, it was a chance not to be missed. He was dead serious about it too.

"About the same, I'd say, only I think the Woolworth building was only two floors high then."

It took a long time before I stopped laughing, and the others joined in, which was something,

I wasn't sorry to be getting in, wonderful as it had been, the trip hadn't been what it might have risen to, whilst the last couple of days had been a bit of a strain. Tom and Esther hadn't really got over their bad time, Lucy had seemed right out of it, and only Tony and Sylvia had remained themselves. They had got very close these two, they were a nice couple, suited each other a lot. He'd been a great pal, Tony, always happy and cheerful, whilst I liked Sylvia more with each passing day.

I couldn't think what I had done wrong with Lucy, if I had done anything wrong. We had drifted further and further apart ever since that night when we had been so close. Perhaps you can never tell with women – I certainly can't.

I had flipped over my itinerary that morning before I packed, fondly remembering Jenny as I did so. It was very clear what I had to do. It read –

"Arrival in New York – booked in at the Statler Hotel."

CHAPTER 6

New York

New York was cold, bitter cold, foggy, murky, dirty, and quite un-glamorous. I'd always looked forward to coming here, more than ever since I knew it was on, and now I was here and it didn't impress me one bit.

I had no bother with any of the formalities necessary to get ashore. I had said my goodbyes to the others, somewhat sadly at the end to Lucy. Tony and I promised to keep in touch. I collected my baggage and queued up for a taxi, only it wasn't a taxi anymore, it was a cab.

I hadn't seen a lot of New York from the cab, except that the people were all well muffled up, and I for one couldn't blame them, and that it took us a very long time to get out of the dirty mean-looking area of the city, to somewhere which looked a bit more like the New York I wanted to see.

The Statler was better, brought me out of my depression a lot.

My cab driver, just like the one I'd had in London, was talkative. They must all be the same all over the world. I handed him two one dollar bills, about half a dollar of which was a tip.

"Four dollars," he barked – I thought he had said "one-fifty" – he looked at me – "you English?"

I agreed I was.

"From London?" as he handed my bags to a bell boy.

"Not exactly," I answered, "though I know London very well."

"Nice place London," he said, which was reassuring, then – "I sure guessed you was English when I saw them fancy clothes."

I had to laugh and it pleased him. He didn't know how I really felt. My clothes, my well cut, correct English clothes fancy, after some of the things I had seen the Yanks wearing – still, everybody to his own taste, I suppose.

I got into a better mood at the reception desk when I saw the vision in black who greeted me.

"We have a room for Mr. Lander," she looked up at me and gave me the full searchlight impact of her big eyes.

"We expected you yesterday" –

I shouldn't have said it but I did. I had to get one back to get equal after what that damn cab man had said about my clothes –

"I couldn't come without the Queen Mary," I told her.

"I suppose not," she answered, and hadn't got it.

I told myself not to worry as I followed the boy to the elevators. Bob Hope's gag men would get a thousand dollars for that one – she mustn't like Bob Hope.

My room was nice – bathroom, the lot – no going down the passage for the Americans – what you want is here, where it should be.

The bell boy was business itself.

"Just off the Q.M., sir?" – I'd heard about the way they used initials like this – "sure guess you'll have plenty for the cleaners" – he'd guessed right – "normal service twenty-four hours, express is faster" – I hoped it was, but it didn't always apply back in England – "sure it costs a li'l more express" –

We sorted it all out – normal service would do me – my itinerary said I could have a couple of days in New York if I wanted, just as long as I wired the address in Chicago when I was travelling. I gave the boy a half-dollar coin, just like they do in the films, and I had no idea whether he was pleased or not.

"Coffee shop's open right now sir," he told me before he left, piled high with shirts and other things – "the restaurants will be open at five."

He was my first real bell boy, and I knew he was old enough to be my father.

It was just as I had expected – the room was warm, the cupboards were roomy, telephone, radio, luxury fittings, and there was sure to be a bible in the top drawer of the dresser or whatever they called it.

There certainly was.

I liked this, it was nice, comforting and something familiar. After all, if I looked at it the right way, I was alone in a strange land. I remembered my history – Columbus, on reaching the new world after his long and eventful journey, had knelt down, kissed the ground, and then offered up his prayers.

I'd come about as far as Columbus, probably been rougher than he had known it, though not as eventful. More comfortable – I laughed about that, and laughed more when I thought what Columbus and his crew might have said about Lucy and Sylvia. Now I was here, in my new world, high up in this luxurious hotel, and I was glad to have this bible in my hands. Like Columbus, I said my prayers, but I didn't kiss the floor, there must be nicer things to kiss in America than ground or floors.

I skipped through several of the passages I know well and like. There is strange power in holding a bible, and I thought of so many things, especially what may be in store for me now. Every hotel should have a bible in the top drawer of the dresser.

I lay back on the bed and thought of Lucy. Something had gone wrong, we'd flirted a bit, all in good fun, surely she hadn't been serious that she might lose the battle. Had anything happened with Tom? Surely not that either – it was just that she was a woman, and women are often very strange creatures. Tony was taking Sylvia to her home – they were nice those two, I wondered if it would lead to anything.

Then I did something I never thought I would do on my first afternoon in this great city of New York.

I lay back on the bed and went to sleep.

CHAPTER 7

Laurie Gaydon

A good sleep, a bath and shower, fresh clean clothes, did wonders for me. I felt on top of the world, and as hungry as a hunter.

The woman on the next table was terribly attractive. I was positive I knew her, had met her or seen her somewhere, but could not think where. Had she been a fellow passenger on the Queen Mary? If so, I could only think she must have been one of those I had seen on the first night or early in the voyage, before the gale had really got going, or perhaps she had been a first-class passenger, and I had seen her on one of my visits to the Rose Room, or at the Church Service in the first-class lounge.

It bothered me all through my meal. Through my clam chowder soup, my minute steak with green beans and a baked Idaho potato, and a hearts of lettuce salad with Thousand Islands dressing, through my tutti-frutti ice cream, and now, awaiting my coffee, I was still bothered about her. I was darn sure I knew her from somewhere.

When I had first looked towards her, she half smiled at me as our eyes met. Maybe that was because I was staring so hard at her, maybe not. But several times during my meal my eyes had stolen to the right, to where she sat alone at her table, and she had not avoided my gaze at all, as she would surely have done if she had not known me. We must have met somewhere.

She could only have come in the restaurant a short time before me. We had eaten the courses of our separate meals almost at the same time, whilst her coffee had just been put on the table in front of her. The service had been excellent in this elegant restaurant, elegant even to me just off the Queen Mary. I was glad I had decided to dine here instead of going out to see the town. I was even more glad to find this truly exquisite creature on the next table to me, even if I was so mighty bothered about her.

The three bottles of ice-cold beer I had drunk had made me bold. It was good beer this American beer. I glanced right once more, again our eyes met, I was sure of the smile in those lovely eyes of hers, and, even in the soft light, was sure there was an invitation in that smile. Well, I just had to find out, faint heart never won fair lady, and this lady was the fairest of all.

Just as I rose from the table the waiter brought my coffee, and I very nearly funked going, very nearly put it off until I had drunk my coffee, very nearly, but not quite. If she was surprised at my boldness, she did not show it, nor did she think me rude. As I stood there above her, half apologising and half stating why I was there, she laughed at my fears.

"Do sit down," she invited, "and tell me more."

I sat down – quick – "I'm glad you are not annoyed," I said, and I wasn't speaking so well yet.

"Of course I'm not annoyed," she replied – "why should I be?"

The voice brought something out of what was stored in my memory. It had more than a trace of the Southern American in it, and I was sure I had heard it before.

I was feeling bucked, and relieved. Even in my wildest dreams I could not really have thought she would have been as nice as this about my intrusion. I had to make a little more progress now.

"I'm David Lander," I told her, remembering all I had learned from Tony about introductions to Americans, "I'm English, this is my first time in New York, in America."

"I sure can tell you're English," she answered, and I could not help but notice the perfection of her teeth as she spoke, then –

"I'm Laurie Gaydon, I'm in New York for a short while."

She had not been on the Queen Mary, and she was amused when I told her I was certain I had met her before.

"That sure is an old one for a reserved English gentleman to use," she said, and we laughed together. We were getting on famously.

I had never seen anyone so lovely in all my life. Her hair was chestnut coloured, deep and wavy, obviously very well cared for. Her eyes brown, soft, warm and full of fun. She had a lovely merry mouth. She smiled most of the time. There was an air about her I had never experienced before, an air of warmth I put it. Just to be with her was to be warm and happy.

She wore a black crepe dress, cut fairly high at the neck, and with three-quarter length sleeves. Her only items of jewellery were a single strand gold necklace and a small gold watch, which she wore on her right wrist. Her figure, all I could see of it above the table, looked perfect.

I ordered my coffee brought to my table and asked for a liqueur to go with it. I had to persuade her hard before she would have one. She drank little she said and had never tasted Drambuie, but she enjoyed it when it was brought. I told her how to sip it in very small quantities, to hold it on the tongue for a moment or two, then to swallow it reluctantly. She thought it nice. I told her of my visit to America, and where I was going. She knew Chicago well, in fact her home was not far from there, she often went there. I was surprised, I had thought she was a Southern gal. No, she was from Illinois all right, the Southern drawl was an affectation she had adopted – she was honest. She did a lot of travelling for the company she worked for, and had just flown in from Los Angeles that morning for a two day stay in New York. Yes, she had been in England, but only passing through by plane, and only in London. She was very easy to talk with, I was really delighted.

Later we danced. She was a beautiful dancer, wonderfully light and easy on her feet and followed my movements instantly, anticipated them almost. At first I did not hold her close at all, but as the floor became more crowded, I just had to bring her more tightly into my arms and we danced very closely together.

At eleven p.m. she said, "I sure ought to go," at midnight the same, and at one a.m. "she sure ought", but she still, thank Heavens, stayed on. Earlier she had paid for her meal. I knew better than to offer to pay.

The waiter seemed surprised when she paid in cash, he had brought some kind of bill for her to sign. Her handbag was very expensive looking, and she had a lot of dollars.

When she had first got up to dance, I had seen that the rest of her figure was as perfect as the top part – it's funny how you notice these things so damn fast. She was not tall, but she seemed to fit in to me whilst we were dancing. Half the time I could have sworn it was all a dream – it was that wonderful.

I had three more bottles of beer – I liked this beer a lot, it suited me. She would drink nothing more after the Drambuie. By one-thirty a.m. the restaurant was full and dancing much more difficult on the not very large floor, but so very much nicer as I had to hold her tight all the while. She did not object one bit, nor did she take her face away when our cheeks rubbed. We danced cheek to cheek a lot.

The floor show had come and gone. A young male singer who based his style on that of Frank Sinatra in a competent manner. A young Negress who wiggled and swayed, but had no voice to go with her other attributes, and a line of expensively under-dressed girls whom I had payed no attention to. Why should I when I was with one nicer than all of them put together?

Through it all I was a bit puzzled. When we were dancing we seemed to arouse a lot of interest in the other dancers, and once a photographer made sure he had a picture of us dancing cheek to cheek. Laurie didn't notice it at all; perhaps such was the usual custom of the place.

We left at two-thirty a.m., and by then we had a date for noon the next day. For lunch and for the rest of the day together. I was head over heels in love with her, of that I was certain.

"In a way I'm sorry you're living here," I told her, "otherwise I could have walked you home through the park."

She snuggled up to me as we left the restaurant.

"Just imagine the elevator is the park," she said – "my room is on the seventeenth."

We held hands in the elevator. The boy was much more interested in us than he ought to have been. Surely he'd seen folks hold hands before.

Outside her door she turned to me.

"Thank you David," she told me. "It's been a lovely evening, the nicest I've known for a long time."

I knew what I ought to say in reply but I couldn't say it. I bent my head down towards those full red lips. She moved in to me and she was in my arms. She was all soft and clinging and, as my mouth found hers, she opened her lips just a little for me. The world spun around and my fast beating heart nearly burst out of my chest. Her mouth opened wider and I crushed her closer still to me. I had never kissed like this before.

She moved away from me, backwards so that I had the impression, for a moment, that she was going to draw me into her room with her, but then she came back to me, for a minute, all tongue, mouth and body, and the fur coat she was carrying fell from her grasp to a heap at our feet.

I couldn't speak, I was weak at the knees. I was dazed. My heart was pounding away, my head was spinning – what a kiss, it was atom-packed, and it left me breathless, bewildered and limp. Nothing, ever, had been like this before.

"Bye David," she said, and stood there for a second looking at me, and I wondered if she knew what she had done to me and how I was feeling now. I stood there, I think, long after she had closed the door.

I went down in the elevator instead of going up, then had to go all the way up to my floor again. I was only faintly aware of unlocking my door, of undressing, of brushing my teeth – it was just by habit I managed it.

I sat up in bed with three pillows behind my back. I would not sleep for a while yet, if ever again. Still thinking of her, I took up the movie magazine I had bought down at the stand in the hotel lobby earlier that day. Without thinking I began slowly turning the pages over. Half-way through the magazine a full colour photograph leaped up at me. I stared at it in amazement, gasped and almost fell out of bed. The photograph was of a very, very lovely young woman, with wavy chestnut coloured hair, soft brown eyes, a lovely smiling mouth, perfect white teeth, and a beautiful slim body.

There was no doubt who it was, but the name at the foot of the page was not Laurie Gaydon. It was a very glamorous name indeed.

It was Janice Delane.

Now I knew some of the answers.

CHAPTER 8

The Heat Is On

I was waiting down in the lobby at ten minutes before twelve the next day. I had got over the surprise a little, but I was still a bit trembly. I had almost thought of not meeting her, and you can imagine what an idiot I told myself I was when I thought about that one.

I did not recognise her when she came, just before the hour, though there was something familiar in the walk of the dark haired creature coming towards me. For a second I was frightened to death when she stopped in front of me. Surely it couldn't happen to me twice. I need not have worried – it was Laurie, or Janice, or both, in, as I found out, a black wig.

I had to hand it to her. She was both amused and amusing, and she held my hand as she explained the reason for the wig, so that people should not recognise her and spoil our day, and her hand was warm in mine, and oh so soft, and possessive, and almost straight away we were as good friends as we had been at two-thirty a.m. that morning, and I was so glad to be with her, so proud to have such a companion as this, so wonderful a woman, black wig or not, so very smart in her deep fur coat, so very warm to be with – what were we waiting for? It was our day, hers and mine, a day I would never forget.

Outside it was wonderful. Yesterday's fog had vanished and it was clear, cold, and crisp. It was grand to have such fine weather today after what it had been yesterday, and we walked, hand in hand, slowly, happily, through to Times Square. Already it seemed natural for me to be with the most beautiful woman in the world, black wig, or no black wig, and we took no notice of the passing people, nor they of us. It was my first real look at this fantastic city of giant skyscrapers, and I wasn't anything like as interested as I should have been. Not interested, nor surprised at anything, not even at all the traffic in the city streets, and I was content, because she was with me.

We paused awhile in Times Square. Here it is, she told me, the great white way. Here we were in the area of the theatres, the cinemas, the famous restaurants, and the night clubs, and as Laurie spoke, she made it all real. This was the centre, the pulse, of New York, and indeed of America's entertainment world. This was what they had all struggled for, she told me, struggled hard for, to be part of it all, to belong to it all. Crosby, Jolson, Astaire, Garland, Sinatra, the lot. Broadway or bust, and for everyone who'd made it, hundreds, thousands, had bust. Success and failure belonged here, happiness and misery, triumph and disaster, riches and rags, and she herself had been a part of it, part of all this, where the passing cars, the people, the subways, played it loud and long, the everyday melody of Broadway.

She was right about the rags and the riches. There were many lovely fur-coated ladies – I could not even begin to think of the cost of the fur coat Laurie was wearing – and well-dressed men. There were some mean-looking customers also, some who looked far from exciting. There was much poverty in this city, and even here, in this glamour place, it was so evident. There were many coloured people, from every part of the world – Indians, Africans, Chinese, Japanese, Moors, they were all here, all attracted by the promise of the new world and this great city. What a story New York had to tell, and to think that a British sea captain started it all nearly three hundred and fifty years ago.

We lunched in a Chinese restaurant somewhere, late on when the rush hour had gone, and were almost alone in the peace and quiet, and the warmth of the place. The chow fan was both excellent and inexpensive, and we sat on for a long while over our coffee, with no attempt to rush us or bring us the bill, whilst we held hands, and our knees and thighs touched under the table, and we talked and talked.

Laurie had started her career in Chicago. She had worked all the places girls had to work but it had not worried her. She had never been desperate or without money, her father was quite wealthy. She had come to New York where she had been lucky. She had been the stand-in for the star of the show, and one day the star had been unable to appear. Laurie had played the lead, and from there had gone on, in the way of the story books, until Hollywood had beckoned, and she had been lucky there also, and now she had to wear a black wig in case people recognised her.

I interrupted her –

"Last night – at the Statler – you were not wearing a wig then."

"No, not at the Statler," she agreed, "but that was O.K. – it was to have been a quiet evening on my own."

She smiled at me, gave my hand an extra squeeze, and a little extra pressure on the knees – I loved it.

"A place like the Statler is all right – they look, but they don't crowd – not too much that is."

"I did see a photographer once, while we were dancing – I didn't know the real reason he was there then."

"There's always a photographer David," she laughed now – "Your picture will be in some paper today, or in some magazine – how will you like that?"

I would like it.

It was much colder in the late afternoon, with more than a hint of snow in the air. We took a cab to Fifth Avenue, and wandered through a couple of the big shops. I was too interested in her to be as impressed as I might have been. A whole floor of one store was full of pictures of Julie London and her song, "Cry me a river" – we listened awhile, it was the first time I had heard it, I liked it, so did Laurie.

We had tea together. The tea bags were fun. Laurie had tea with me, although she said she hardly ever drank it.

"You'd better get used to drinking coffee over here," she told me. We'd chosen the darkest corner there was and were holding hands again. Playing that knee game under the table as well, we were getting good at it by now. Suddenly she leaned over to me – it wasn't much of a lean really, we were sitting very close together. She moved her slightly open mouth round my chin and then found my lips. In that second all the electricity they were making in New York flashed up and down my spine.

It was sixish when we got back to the Statler. We discussed plans in the elevator, and as I took her to her room. Inside I discovered it wasn't a room, it was, of course, a suite. Quite beautiful and very comfortable. I had thought my room nice, but this was super. We stood close together in the doorway of her bedroom, looking in.

"I like a big bed," she said, and it was a big bed – "I'm so very restless in bed."

It had got very warm. I wasn't ready with the right answer, She turned half around and lifted herself up to be kissed. I knew the answer to that. My arms made it easier for her. Her lips, her mouth, her tongue, were good, oh so good. My right hand moved from

37

around her, slowly back from her left side to her left breast. It was very nice, even outside the dress she was wearing. Her tongue became very lively. How long we stood that way I didn't know, but it was me who ended it, not her.

"I must go and change," I told her, and I knew I was a coward. "I'll come back for you in an hour."

I could tell she did not want me to go, but I went, consoling myself with the thought that there are only sixty minutes in an hour. It would take me that long to get my breath back – and my nerve back – gosh it was warm.

My laundry was waiting for me. I liked the way it was returned, everything neatly folded and packed, with the shirts on hangers. I shaved, bathed and had a shower, deep in thought the while. This was something I had never known before, this woman. So lovely, so warm, so possessive – I was head over heels in love with her, I knew, and there, of course, was such a thing as love at first sight, but this had certainly rushed up on me, and I wasn't sure I knew how to handle it. I dressed carefully, I had to look good for this wonderfully attractive female.

She looked wonderful as she came to the door of her suite, but not in the way I expected. She was not dressed to go out. She was wearing a Cambridge blue house-robe, which fitted her trim figure delightfully, and made my eyes pop. The large white buttons and the white fur at the collar, set off the blue against her perfect colouring. She was wearing mules on her feet, and was much smaller than in her high heels. She looked, and was, a picture. A more beautiful woman I never hope to see.

I gasped when I saw her. I just couldn't help it.

"I thought we needn't go down – we could have room-service," she said, and if she had been the Queen and I, Sir Walter Raleigh, I would not have just laid my cloak in that puddle for her to walk on, I would have laid down myself, I felt that way already.

We had room-service – chicken in a basket, corn on the cob, sweet potatoes, salad, crisp rolls and butter, ice-cold beer, ice cream and coffee. We ate sat down on the deep pile carpet. It was terrific, but what the two waiters must have been thinking I could not even imagine. It was a picnic, the most heavenly picnic I have ever been to, food fit for the Gods, and a Queen to share it with. I was intoxicated with the beer and with her, mostly with her.

Even if I wasn't used to room-service, the waiters were. I wasn't allowed to pay, this would go down to her, in spite of my protests, whilst the waiters got ten dollars each from her when they had cleared up. It was her treat, she insisted, and I really was not as embarrassed as I should have been. It was the most natural thing in the world for her to give me a meal like this, with the two of us sprawling all over the carpet as most people use a lawn on a summer day. She, in the lovely powder blue robe, powder blue she had told me, not my English Cambridge blue, and I, having removed my jacket and tie, in open neck shirt and the trousers of my dark grey flannel suit. The powder blue suited her admirably, was sort of soft for her, and just a little cool, if you get what I mean.

When I came out of the bathroom she was still sat on the carpet, propped up against an easy chair, with her right knee drawn up, and a lot of her left leg free from the robe. I stood there a moment just looking at her, she was watching me, she must have known how I was feeling. I turned all the lights off except one, and moved down to her. All of me was on fire.

She lay her head back a little for me to kiss her, half supporting me as I came for her lips. She moved her right leg back flat, leaving a lot of this one exposed also. Our kiss was gentle, surprisingly so. My lips opened her lips slightly, and I gently let my tongue explore her mouth. This was heavenly, she was so fragile, so warm, her perfume exotic. I was lost and I knew it.

My right hand undid the top button of her robe, then the second, and then the third. Still we held our lips together, our mouths wide open now. My hand took her breast gently, explored all round it, big and firm and luscious, then with my thumb and first finger I caressed the nipple, gently, slowly, beautifully. I brought my mouth from hers to that nipple, and my hand undid more buttons and went on down. She wore nothing, as I had already guessed, under that robe. My lips were doing a good job on that lovely nipple, my hand slowly, easily, found what it was seeking. She eased her body, low down, a little to help me. Her mouth bit my left ear hard, her teeth hanging on for long seconds, and I could feel the passion rushing through us, from her mouth to my ear, down to my lips through to her breast, down to my fingers and back through to her, mad, strong, heart-beating, passion, oozing through us both and around and around and around. Then she spoke, or whispered, hot and hoarse and low –

"I have a big bed – remember?"

Many ages later the loud ringing of the telephone half wakened me. I felt Laurie stir alongside me, then heard her speaking. I was warm, drowsy and content, the bed soft and luxurious, the exotic perfume of her all over me.

She woke me properly when the fruit juice and the coffee she had ordered came. I half sat up to drink first my orange juice, then a hot strong coffee. She sat on the bed watching me. She looked wonderful, fresh as a daisy.

"What time is it?" I asked.

"Eight-thirty about," she answered, and she laughed merrily, reading my thoughts, then – "you going somewhere?"

I grinned – "Not just yet" – I was rubbing my chin, it was a bit bristly, but not too bad – "I could do with a shave I think."

She leaned forward and rubbed my chin with the inside of her hand, I kissed it as she moved it across my lips. I went to pull her to me but she stood up. I need not have worried, even if I did. She took the tray from the bed and put it on a table at the other end of the room. She came back and took off the robe, standing there for a moment or two, looking down at me.

She was really beautiful, perfect, in every detail. Strong firm breasts, cherry-topped, long slim trunk. Lovely to look at in every way. Somehow, instantly, all that electricity had got back into me, and I was on fire again. So was she.

Afterwards she lay on top of me, looking down at me with her big warm brown eyes. I held my arms round her, gripping her shoulders, pulling her down often to kiss her, and when I was not kissing her lips, eating the cherries.

"You're good for me, David, so very good," she said, and I was pleased, mighty pleased, then suddenly the electricity came on again, and the passion ebbed and flowed, ebbed and flowed, for us both. I held her tight, above me, through it all, and if I was good for her, that was all that mattered, then, at any rate.

CHAPTER 9

We'll Meet Again

The efficiency of the Baltimore and Ohio railroad pleased me. At the reception office in the city I collected my tickets – a roomette had been reserved for me, and I rode down to the depot – the depot mark you, not the station – in the company bus together with a few other travellers. My baggage was taken from me by the redcaps, what a wonderful name for porters, and what I required for the train was waiting in my roomette when I reached it.

How faithful to Hollywood it all was, and how nice to be shown to my roomette by a negro porter. No scrambling for a seat on the Capitol Limited. No pushing, no confusion, as I had often known at home, even when travelling first class. It was great stuff, the noise of the great diesel engines, the clanging bells, just as I had wanted and expected it to be. All I longed for now was to hear the familiar, "all aboard".

Waiting in the reception office I had seen the roomettes described as de-luxe. They were all of that. Beautifully appointed and very roomy, in reality a small private apartment with a pull-out bed, complete toilet facilities and a tap for a continual supply of drinking water. The roomette was heated and air-conditioned. For America, for Americans, it would just have to be.

I heard the "all aboard", the movies were right then, exactly right, and at once the diesel pulled away smoothly and soon we were moving fast. The number of level crossings surprised me at first, but lessened as we left the city and raced out into the country. It was cold outside and the land looked sterile. It was not ploughed for the winter as in England, and I guessed that once the crops were finished, the land was left for the hard, bitter winter, until the spring, when the ploughs would be out in force.

I thought of her all the time. No matter what I did, she was seldom

41

out of my thoughts. She would be winging her way to Europe now, to Spain she had told me, and a big new super which would give her the leading role, as yet untitled – "they often are like that" – and which would keep her away a long time – "too long David, now", she had told me with her lips, and her eyes, her body, her arms, everything, had echoed it.

I had not gone to the airport. She was Janice Delane again, and no wig. Besides why should we say goodbye at the airport when we could do so in the privacy of a suite at the Statler, much, much better, and take far longer over the saying.

"I will come to Chicago when I can David" – this lying wrapped up in my arms. "We will go to High Point – my home – you will love it up there, meet my father – you sure will like him. I'm a bad letter writer, but I'll write – you just take good care of yourself, and wait for me."

For a time we ran alongside the road, the many vehicles, the large trailers, were moving fast, but nothing like as fast as the Capitol Limited. At some stretches of the track we were doing a hundred miles an hour and more without losing anything of the smoothness of the running. I stared out for a long time, not always aware what I was looking at. Time passed by.

In the late afternoon we drew into Washington.

"'Bout fifteen minutes sah," the porter informed me.

I moved out on to the platform to stretch my legs. It was getting dusk and it was cold, there were few people about, so I walked briskly up and down for ten minutes or so and was glad of the exercise, glad afterwards to get back into the warmth and comfort of my roomette.

Laurie came back to me as the train moved off again – she was everywhere in my thoughts, her aroma, her presence, around me still. She would be with me, I knew, for a long time to come, if not for always. With her I had grown up, become a man. With her I had got out of the kindergarten school of love and had graduated. She was so very different to all the other girls, women, I had known. Vital, possessive, demanding, warm. Yes, warm, and then she was heat itself, burning, searing, heat, terrific in her passion, overwhelming in her womanly power. Now I could never be the same again for another woman. I had not known this sort of love existed. Until she came back to me, would never know again. This is the reason I thought that Lucy Holley has never had the grand passion. Perhaps there is one for every woman, but Laurie has them for all women.

Man is a funny animal. Whenever a man eyes a woman up and

down he has only one thought in mind. If he hasn't he isn't really a man, or is so old it doesn't matter. I once read that the difference between seduction and rape is salesmanship, and it rings pretty true. In all forms of life, man, beast, bird, insect, the male is the hunter, and what he's after, mostly, is worth hunting for.

Remembering the girls I'd known, truthfully I remembered the achievements I'd made. How else does a man remember a woman? Most of these I remembered were recalcitrant – I suppose most women are – but go about love making the right way, a little progress at a time, and it all comes true at the finish, that's human nature. However stubborn they are, most girls have their eagerness too, otherwise, and this is certain, there would be no need for the world to go round at all.

I heard once of a man who got his woman by doing absolutely nothing about it, or her. He must have nearly driven her mad, wondering what she had wrong with herself. Whatever they say, they like you to do the chasing, the initial moves have to be the perogative of the male, otherwise, however well brought up they are, they'll soon be convinced you cannot really be a man. Even when they're slapping you for what you shouldn't be doing – perhaps – they're liking it. This man did nothing, time after time. They met, they went out, they drank, they ate, they danced even, he took her home, then nothing. The time came when she could stand it no longer and she threw herself at him. He was a man, had been all the time, and, of course, caught what she threw. That's one way.

With Laurie I had done the chasing. I had gone over to her table that first night, and I had introduced myself. I knew that, but I also knew that I damn sure would not have had the nerve to do it if I had not been positive the invitation was there. We had made rapid progress, but then perhaps there were many such cases. Perhaps I had caught her on the rebound from something else. I must have read that one in a novel, it didn't ring true with Laurie. What was true about her was that she was easily the most lovely, most wonderful, woman I had known, or ever would know, and I longed passionately, for the time when I could be with her again.

Hunger was catching up on me now, and tiredness. Dinner was indicated, then bed. We would be in Chicago at eight in the morning, which would mean an early call.

By now I had been in America long enough not to be surprised at anything anymore, and I should have been prepared for the restaurant

43

car. Perhaps I was thinking of the railways at home, I had certainly not expected such magnificence as I found. The menu too was excellent. There was a fixed dinner or a la carte. I chose the dinner, and had fresh fruit cup, then a Capitol Limited oyster pie with candies, sweet potatoes, southern string beans and the salad bowl. The pie was delicious, and the salad as fresh, as crisp, as any I'd ever had. I finished up with a large ice cream, refusing the cheese, I was so full, then had coffee.

I sat on a bit over the coffee whilst the train rushed on headlong through the night. The car steward was happy about the compliments I paid him and his staff, and interested in my opinion of the railways of the two countries.

"You'll be in for breakfast sir?" he asked. "The porter will call you in good time for a meal before we get in to Chicago."

The roomette was comfortable, the bed very much so. There was every reason, remembering how tired I was, that I should sleep well, but I did not. I dozed on and off, but was awake a lot, heard the familiar hoot of the engine now and then, and knew when we had stopped. It wasn't the meal that kept me awake – it was Laurie, or my thoughts and my dreams of her.

I suppose no man could have such wondrous beauty in his arms one night and not think of her the next. I was wishing hard now I could put the clock back twenty-four hours. How many men have wished just that? How many women also? But it can't be done, which is just another way of saying, make the best of everything whilst you can.

She hadn't told me a lot about herself. Something of how she had made her start in the theatre as a young girl, and how she had got into films, but not really a lot. I didn't even know how old she was. I tried to reckon up, thinking of some of her films, and settled for twenty-six. She had been married, I think, though she had spoke nothing on this subject and wore no wedding ring. Her family home was not far from Chicago, and I prayed she would come whilst I was to be there, but the sort of epics she was now making are not made in a day, and I fancied she would be away a long time.

Was she thinking of me, I wondered? Maybe she was laughing about it all now, wherever she was, and that took my ego down a lot for a time. Then I cheered up, no woman could be as she had been to me and laugh about it. I hoped that was true.

I slept towards morning, so that six o'clock came before I wanted it, but I was awake as soon as the porter banged on the door. There

44

were only two others in the restaurant car for breakfast. Americans, so the steward told me, were not big breakfast eaters. A coloured waiter brought me a cup of coffee just as I sat down, the little label on the handle of the cup said, "this one's on the house". I liked that, it was a good gimmick. I ate a big breakfast, corn flakes, two eggs and several slices of bacon, rolls, butter and more coffee. Even if I wasn't sleeping well, Laurie hadn't put me off my food.

Though I didn't hurry, I was back in my roomette with half an hour still to go before we reached Chicago. It was coming light now and we passed several big farms. Ranches, I would have to call them now. These all looked neat and tidy, some of them giving ample evidence of wealth.

We were approaching the outskirts of a city, crossing over many level crossings with great queues of cars held waiting. The houses were not as I was used to seeing at home, brick and in neat rows. Here there were more wooden bungalows than anything else, dotted hither and thither all over the place. There were no gardens as I knew them. Everything looked barren and without life. It must be very cold here, and it looked as if nature went to sleep for the entire winter.

The porter stuck his head in through the door.

"Five more minutes sah."

I was looking forward to it. Chicago, Illinois. I had read a great deal about this vast city of the mid-West. I knew my film history, knew it had been the haunt of Al Capone and other infamous gentlemen. What a city it must have been if the movies had portrayed it correctly. A hot-bed of vice, with gangsters running the city, and the law, for a long time, incapable of dealing with them.

We were slowing down now. From my first sight of it, through the windows of the roomette, it looked a very busy city indeed. I put on my top-coat and gloves, had to take my gloves off again when the porter looked in. I tipped him a dollar and was assured the baggage would be handed over to the redcaps. The train came easily to a stop, and I followed a few other passengers out. This is it, and heavens, it was cold.

The freezing blast of an early January morning hit me hard after the warmth of that train. The frost fairly leapt at my ears and they were soon a-tingle. There was no red carpet anywhere. I hoped the wire I had sent yesterday, in accordance with my itinerary instructions, had reached where it should have done. Not that anybody would be fool enough to wait out here in the open for me in this cold – walk up the train you tuttle, there'll be someone waiting for you all right.

45

CHAPTER 10

Danny

I remembered Danny Erikson as soon as I saw him. His greeting was most friendly, even if the hand which took mine gave me one hell of a grip.

"Hi David, glad you could make it," he said, just as though I had come around the corner, or from the next room, and I could not, just then, think how far I had come.

Daniel P. Erikson looked around forty years of age – I afterwards found out he was forty-seven. He looked and was tough. He was just five feet eight inches in height, big and powerful looking across the chest and the shoulders, and with long arms. Nobody could have accused him of being an Adonis. He was clean shaven, square jawed, had a pair of merry blue eyes, and owned a leathery tan which gave evidence of years of living in wide open spaces. Too often people say a man looks typically American, but here was a man who did look like that, just as much now as on the day when I had first met him last year back home, at one of Mr. G.'s lunches, when he had come dressed in a light panama suit, flattish straw hat, a loud tie, sun glasses and a camera. I grinned now at the memory of it, after I had got over the way he had gripped my hand, and told him what Jenny had said about me seeing everything.

"You don't say," he told me or asked me, "you sure don't say. She's quite a girl that one."

"She sends her love," I told him. She had said really I was to give her kind regards, but I thought it sounded better the way I put it.

"She did?" this time he did ask, "last year she seemed sorta frightened of me."

I sorta thought he could be right, though I was aware, when she got to know him, she liked him a lot.

"Mr. G. sent his very best wishes," I went on.

46

"He did?" this was just an acknowledgement – "that's nice, real nice – he wrote us – told us what he'd like for you to see – you're on the way up boy, on the way, and that's good."

That did me a lot of good.

With Danny to guide I soon rescued my baggage from the redcaps, all I had fitted in Danny's large Buick easily, and I remembered which side the passenger seat was.

Danny sat looking at me, he was making up his mind about something.

"I have a nice apartment, and a spare room," he said, "it's nice, I think, and you'd like it, you're welcome to it if you want it. Otherwise you're booked in a good hotel round the block from me – what d'ya say?"

I had to think fast. It was very good of him, and he was genuine about it – a week and I would have said yes, but I was here for a long while and I didn't want, couldn't, intrude on him that long. The hotel was my choice.

He tried hard not to show it but I think he was relieved.

"O.K. let's go," he said – we went.

I took it all in, the roads – boulevards of course, seemingly millions of cars, whizzing past on all sides, all the colours of the rainbow, and the city's great skyscrapers. Danny made the drive a sightseeing tour. He knew his Chicago, knew its past and its present. For over thirty miles the city stretches along the shores of Lake Michigan. There were lovely beaches here, miles and miles of them, deserted now, but crowded in the summer months, he told me, with the inhabitants of Chicago itself and many thousands of vacationers. In America you took a vacation not a holiday. I was learning the language fast. Not far back from the beaches were the fabulous hotels, the fine blocks of apartments, towering skyscrapers, looking across the boulevards and the beaches to the open lake.

"This is the Gold Coast," Danny said – "got its name from all the rich folk that lived along here. Way back, if you didn't live on the coast here, you were a nobody – it sure must have been a place."

We came down the Michigan boulevard, fast, with Danny still talking about the city. I just could not get over the amount of traffic. I said so.

He nodded, keeping his eyes straight ahead, he was a good driver, the sort that gives you all the confidence you want.

"We sure have the finest system of roads in the whole of the States

– they have to be good. Folk have to go a long way to work, they want to get there quick, and get home quick, that's for sure. We gotta keep things moving fast, but I've seen some of them a hell of a mess at times, when there's been a pile-up or somethin'."

I thought I would be scared to drive along here – I hadn't got used to it all yet.

Danny laughed – "You'd get used to it O.K. – you sure enough have to – all you need is guts and go in this city – I reckon you'd make it all right."

We came off Route 41 into Hyde Park boulevard.

"That's the Science Museum," Danny told me, nodding left, "go see it sometime."

I caught a glimpse of a large white domed building, the Museum of Science and Industry.

They were very friendly at the hotel, the girl at reception, the elevator girl and Elmer. Elmer was the captain of the bell boys, and, like most of the bell boys I'd come across yet, old enough to be my father at least. But he was a gem to me, right from the start, a little man with a wizened impish face, and a heart of gold.

"If you want anything done in this hotel, just send for me," he told me as he showed me my room.

It was a nice room, a single and not too large, but large enough, well appointed, with the usual bathroom, big cupboards and a box-room – it would do me.

"This here's a quiet corner," Elmer said, "you'll want your own radio – O.K.?"

I caught on – yes I wanted a radio, Elmer could do all the necessary for me. I gave him a dollar as I went down again with Danny. I left him at the door of the hotel.

"You're on vacation for today," he grinned. "Do what you have to do, write your mail – tomorrow you start work. Don't eat much, I'll pick you up half after six, we'll go have a steak somewhere."

CHAPTER 11

Chicago – First Night

We didn't go far for our steaks.

"We'll try the Blue Room for tonight," Danny said when we met, and I walked with him in to the hotel restaurant.

It was enchanting, the decor simple, attractive, and, without doubt, expensive. Quietly and beautifully lit. It was not large and perhaps only in a way the entrance to the large restaurant behind. A small bar, horse-shoe in shape, with room for about twelve stools, took up half the space. A few alcoves with tables, the other half.

We sat up at the bar drinking, beer for me and scotch on the rocks for Danny, for an hour, and by that time I was so hungry I could have eaten a horse, not that I had to. Danny was often in here, and he and the bartender Al, were good friends.

My steak was the biggest I'd ever seen, lapping over the plate. It was done just right for me. With it I had celery hearts, a baked Idaho potato – I was getting real fond of baked potatoes smothered, as they always were, with about half a pound of butter, and, in the American manner, on a side plate, a cole slaw salad with thousand island dressing. It was great, just great.

By the time we had finished eating, and had coffee, I knew a lot about Danny. Knew sufficient not to argue when he paid the check, tonight this was on him. There would be other nights for me. The time went by fast.

Danny looked at his watch.

"Let's go take in the Casanova Club," he said, "it should be warming up there a bit now."

As we left he told Al where we were going.

"You gonna teach David to throw dice?" Al asked with a wide grin – I liked the David part, it meant a lot I thought.

"Sure enough am," Danny replied, he was all smiles also.

"Keep the chain tight then," Al was laughing now.

I didn't get it.

The Casanova Club was nothing to look at from the outside, apart from its startling neon sign which announced the name of the club to the night. Inside it was better, warm and cheery. The lights were not bright, but I could make out a large circular bar, well patronised, quite a lot of tables and a few quiet booths. Danny was well known in here also, he was recognised by the two men and the girl behind the bar.

"Hi Danny," the girl hailed, "how ya bin?" She was attractive, even if her voice wasn't, young, deft at her job, and I noticed that the smart white trimmed jacket with CC on the breast pocket swelled out a lot at the right places. I noticed also that Danny included her and the two men in the drinks. As my eyes got used to the light I saw how well appointed the place was, the furniture, the pictures – mostly of undressed ladies, the trimmings, had cost a lot of money.

I soon found out the reason for the large electric organ in the centre of the bar space. It had intrigued me. Now I saw a striking brunette duck under the bar counter and sit on the stool, heard one of the two barmen announce her over a microphone –

"Our star attraction – Miss Lily Lee."

A spotlight picked her out, the organ lifted out of the bar to well above the counters, blaring out what was obviously her signature tune. I saw her lips phrase the word "Hi", though I couldn't hear it, to Danny as she went up. Danny was well known here.

She was a good turn and popular. I liked her playing and singing immensely, especially so when she sang "Deep Purple", with the light showing her up in the colour of the song. She was easy to look at. She wore a cream costume, cut low in front and very high, in the Chinese fashion, at the side. She showed a lot of leg as her feet moved quickly on the pedals, well worth showing too.

"She's attractive," I confirmed to Danny, well knowing he already knew it.

"Yeah – she sure is," he came back, "maybe she'll come over for a drink later."

Her turn finished, she ducked under the counter and came round the bar to us. She stood on the side of Danny away from me.

"Come round Lil," Danny said – "meet David Lander."

She came round. "Hi David," she said.

I moved up a stool to make room for her between us.

"Pleased to meet you," I put on all my charm. "I liked your act, especially 'Deep Purple'."

"Thanks," she replied, "it's a nice number, I like doing it, and they never get tired of it. You're English?" she asked, "from London?" I told her I was, and went on to tell her a lot about England, she was a good listener – "she sure would like to go there one day".

"It's a great country," Danny agreed, "they sure showed me a time." Somebody must have done a good job back home showing Danny a time, it was obvious he had enjoyed his stay in England.

We sat around, talking, drinking, until Lily went back to the organ. "I gotta earn my money," she said, as she went, "see you."

She seemed to be a very good sort.

"Time to throw some dice," Danny said, getting up from his stool, and I thought back to what Al had said about keeping the chain tight.

The dice tables were small and green topped, each with a bright light shining down upon it. There was a figure behind the one we made for.

"Hi Soph," Danny greeted the figure, "meet David."

"Hi David," the figure said, a nice voice, and I began to get her in focus. She was small, dark, well built, with bright red lips. She wore a black dress, a dress which exposed a great deal of her chest.

Danny explained the game. It was easy. You took five dice from Sophie and rolled them five times. Sophie laid you odds against any number you chose coming up at least a certain number of times. I chose three, and she offered me twelve to one against it coming up eleven times or more. That was the usual bet. I took her on to a dollar. That wasn't the usual bet I found out. Most people backed in fives and tens Danny had five dollars on me. I thought it a good gamble, agreeing with Danny it was easy. Surely I could throw eleven threes out of a total of a possible twenty-five. It was as well I didn't stop to work it out, it was a damn poor gamble indeed.

I rolled the dice slowly across the green top, and saw I had thrown two threes, a good start. At the very same moment my heart gave a leap and my eyes almost came out of my head. I could not possibly help it. Sophie had leaned forward a little to write my score down on a small pad on the side of the table. As she did so, my eyes were attracted as if by magic to the low cut front of her dress, and within, down her body. She was not wearing a bra, and I caught a fascinating glimpse of a full breast, all of it, and beyond. I gulped and gasped, it had definitely not been expected. I collected the dice and paused. The

51

view had disappeared, for the moment at least. Only for the moment, because she would be sure to lean forward again to write down my next score, then the scenery would be on show again. That must be it, a part of the game. The scenery was worth a dollar, or five or ten, and if you won, it was a bonus.

I didn't throw for a second. I looked across at Danny. He was grinning hard.

"You'll need more than two," he said.

I swallowed all the saliva that had come into my mouth, and grinned hard back at him.

"There can't possibly be more than two," I told him, but I wasn't referring to the dice. Sophie grinned also.

I threw again. There was only one three this time, but much more scenery. Both breasts and a long way down the white skin of her body. Phew, this was quite a game, I was getting very warm. It was a good job it was warm inside here or Sophie would catch her death of cold for sure. Now I had an idea what the chain was about. I'd seen a lot more for one three than I had when I'd thrown two. Perhaps the scenery was controlled by your score. The more you scored each time the less you saw, and vice versa.

"If you wanta win you gotta concentrate on the game." Danny was bucking me now.

"Have a heart Danny," I pleaded, "this is the first time I've thrown dice."

It was a great joke to Danny, he'd seen it all before obviously.

I threw four threes next throw. It was a marvellous piece of luck, and it made Danny whistle. There was not quite so much scenery this time, but I did not think that was done purposely, the dress held a little high as she leaned forward. But there was some, and the four threes. That was seven so far, and I wanted four more with two throws to go. I had to throw four threes out of ten. Four out of ten for twelve dollars for myself and sixty dollars for Danny, and two more looks at the scenery.

My fourth throw brought three threes. This was easy. The view was good too. I was excited now and thought I couldn't miss. Surely I could throw one more three out of five dice. I looked at Danny, he was still grinning. Then at Sophie, she was grinning too. She had not spoken all this time, but now she said –

"This is your last throw."

I knew it and I took my time. It might bring me twelve dollars and it might not, but it had been a good gamble. I'd seen a lot and learned what Al meant about having to keep me on a chain. I didn't know about that, but if all the girls were as attractive as Sophie, no wonder the dice games flourished.

I rolled the dice, I saw at once I had got two more threes. I had won my bet. But, even with twelve dollars at stake, my eyes did not give all their time to the dice. Sophie played the game to the last. There was no need for her to write the score down this time, I had thrown twelve threes and she knew it. It must be that the customer was always right, and the number had to be written down. That meant the scenery was on view again. It was something, at any rate, for the losers.

I took my thirteen dollars from Sophie, my own dollar stake and the twelve I'd won. I gave her three back.

"Buy something for yourself," I told her. She was very pleased.

We hung around a while. Danny won a game on fives, and I finished up winning twenty-five dollars, and he well over a hundred. It was a good game – dice.

He dropped me long after midnight.

"Twenty after seven in the morning," he said with his goodnights. "The vacation's over."

Well, it had been a wonderful vacation, and that, as I was learning to say, was for sure.

I dreamed of Laurie that night. She was the girl at the dice table, and I never got past the first throw. But I was as fresh as could be next morning, and ready when Danny came for me at twenty after seven.

Now to work.

CHAPTER 12

The Right Guy

Danny Erikson

It sure was good to see this boy fit in with us so well.

I hadn't really recalled him when his boss had written to make the arrangements, but I had insisted on a good mixer being sent – no snobs, no starch – just an ordinary hombre who would fit in with us ordinary folk. They couldn't have made a better choice.

When you get to be forty-seven, whether you've come up the hard way as I have, or not, you know a lot about people. I sure get to know a lot of limeys in my travels, most of them good, but some duds. I sure didn't want any duds in my outfit. I had insisted that to Mr. Govern. If he sent a good guy, he could stay as long as he liked. If he sent what I call a dud, he would go back pretty damn quick.

We all soon got to realising David could stay with us forever.

He didn't know it all, didn't tell us what it was all about, and that pleased us. He was willing to learn, wanting to learn, knew he was gonna be as lucky as we knew he was gonna be, and he became one of us quick.

You sure had to appreciate his manners. He was more than happy I had met him when he first arrived, and he said so. It means a lot. It costs nothing to be pleasant, but there are a hell of a lot of folks who don't seem to know about that. But this boy did, he was the same with us all, with me and right the way down the whole outfit. The lower down he went the better he was. They all liked him, especially the women. It did your heart good to see him standing in line at the lunch counter, and hear the way those gals behind chatted with him, and how well they looked after him. It did a lot of the staff good, and some of them began to copy him, and that was real good.

The first day in my office you'd a thought he was a new boy starting.

"Do I call you Danny now, or Mr. Erikson?"

"You try callin me Mr. Erikson," I said, "an' I'll send you back home a darn sight faster than you came."

"Right Danny," he replied, "thank you."

We shook him that first day – opened his eyes real wide. Norm Lester, my deputy, showed him round, all the way round, so that he could get the overall picture before we put him through the different departments. He looked a bit hot at lunch break and didn't say much. That night we had a conference in my office, Norm and me, with David looking on. I asked Norm, as I always did, what he thought the count for the day would be.

He whistled loud when Norm shot me the figures, he just could not believe it.

"That's fantastic," he said.

It might have been to him but it wasn't good enough for me. This surprised him even more when I told Norm production would have to be stepped up.

"We gotta get up to seven million, or we're sunk." I meant it.

"Seven million tins," he exclaimed, and his look was a picture. Good job he was there or I could have gotten a lot more angry about it.

"Seven million cans," I corrected him, "you're in America now remember."

He got used to the can business in time, like he got used to every-thing American – elevators, cabs, automobiles, boulevards – like he got used to us.

We didn't crowd him, not too much anyhow. We made him work hard, hard as we worked, and I'll say this for him, he enjoyed that. We encouraged him to see all he could see. Norm worked him through every department in logistical order, and took him or sent him out on a lot of visits. All the companies who used our products took him over for a day or so, sometimes more, and he made a good impression with them all. There wasn't one place where he wouldn't have been more than welcome again, and, in addition to all the usual thanks he said, he never failed to write a letter of thanks next day, in his own handwriting too. It sure tickled me. Tickled my secretary, Poppy, also.

"If you could only learn to write," she very politely informed me one morning, "it sure would mean me only doing fifteen hours work a day."

I've got used to Poppy now. She's grown up with me, and the

55

outfit. I reckon she's a little too old to put over my knee and smack her bottom, but she wasn't always that old as we can both remember.

Poppy liked him a lot. When she had done something for him, he always brought her flowers. I've been around a long time with a lot of women and I always thought flowers was kid's stuff, but not any more I don't. Not after seeing what them flowers did to Poppy. If I'd known about them long ago – ah well, that's another story.

We didn't crowd him after work, or at weekends, his time was his own. But he got in the habit of coming out a lot, either with me, or with Norm and Cynthia, or with all of us, and we enjoyed it. He and me hit it off well. After he got used to our beer he could match me on drink for drink with my scotch, and hold it well. He ate our sort of meals, light breakfast, quick salad lunch, and all he could for dinner. Eating steak, eating anything at night with him was a joy. He enjoyed his chow all right, steaks, Mexican, Chinese, the lot, and he ate ice-cream better than anyone I know.

He and me ate a lot in the Blue Room. It was just round the corner from my place, and he had only to come down in the elevator. It was a sure sign that he was one of us the way Al took to him so fast. I've known Al at the Blue Room bar a long, long while. He knew the good and the bad in Chicago, and he only liked the good, and he sure liked David.

With his coming, we got very much into the habit of going out in a foursome – Norm, Cynthia, David and me. It did a lot of good as far as I was concerned. Norm had been my deputy for five years, we'd been around a bit together now and then. I'd been around to supper with them, I'd taken them out, but we weren't as close as we should have been, and weren't as close as we got going out with David. I got to know what a great gal Cynthia was, how grand Norm was, and I'm glad.

We went about a lot – Don the Beachcomber, Chez Paree, the Kungsholm, the big steak houses, but our favourite place was always the Blue Room, except when Cynthia put on a dinner for us. At the Blue Room bar the four of us would sit up on stools for hours, drinking and yarning away, with Al joining in when he could.

It was at the Blue Room one Saturday night that David got high for the first and only time. He wasn't the only one. I got stinko too, so did Norm, and Al, and, I guess, if we hadn't had Cynthia around, we'd all of got put inside.

We sat on at the bar that night a long time before eating. Al didn't come on duty until nine o'clock that night. We were just going to eat when he came in, and we stayed on again a while when he came. He'd been racing and he'd sure as sure had a day. He'd backed all but the first winner on the card, and had been doubling up at that. We came back, after we had eaten, to hear all about it, and by that time we'd drunk plenty – a lot before we ate and champagne while we ate – and that was how it started.

Al insisted we have drinks with him to celebrate; we should have known better, should have gone on home whilst we were safe, but we didn't. David said a liqueur was what we should have, so we had one – a Drambuie. One would have been O.K., but we didn't stick, no sir, we didn't, we gave a damn big twist.

It was just as well there weren't many in the bar or Al couldn't have told his story half so good. On Saturday nights it gets kinda quiet towards midnight when the boys and girls drift out to the dancing joints along the Gold Coast.

Al had picked one out in the first race which hadn't been in the first three then he had met a guy who had given him one for the second. That one won and Al won a few bucks. This guy had given him one for the third and that won. Al won a few more bucks. Then this guy had given him one for the next race. It worried Al, he was sure he couldn't get three on the trot and he almost decided not to back it, but he did, and it won, and he won more bucks.

It was uncanny, marvellous and unbelievable, all at the same time. Then this guy had given him one for the fifth, and Al thought for a long time before he backed it. After all a guy couldn't possibly pick four in a row, and he had nearly missed backing it, only just got on as the tote closed, and it had won all right, and he won more bucks.

I liked the story, it sounded feasible and Al told it well. I was liking the Drambuie also, even if it was sure coming up fast.

Al had thought of leaving the course then. He was six hundred bucks up then, which would do him a while. This was the time to go home, while he was winning, he'd be a darn foolish so-and-so to lose any on the last race. But he hadn't gone home, he had stayed for that last race, and the guy had given him one for a real bet.

"Back it Al," he had said, "the luck's running for us boy, and it can't lose."

The trouble now was that this guy had given him the one he fancied himself, and again he nearly did not back it. It had been murder for him before that last race, and high as I was getting, I could believe him. The guy couldn't give five successive winners, no guy could, Al had thought. Don't back it, back anything else but not that one. Go on home, don't have a bet, just stay and watch, but don't bet that one, it just sure won't win. But he had backed it sure enough. Follow someone in form had always been for him, back when you're lucky, not when you're chasing, he had been saying that all the years he had been racing, and now was his chance. He had backed it and it had won, won by a block, easing up, and it had been like taking candy off a kid. He had been right there again in the paying out line, like he'd been for the other four races.

Al told it well, he was a good showman, and it improved, I guess, with the telling. He had looked for the guy after the racing, and couldn't find him in the crush. But he'd see him one day all right, and thank him, that was for sure. He was lucky not to be interrupted much in the telling. Only by a small party along the bar who wanted more drinks, and when he re-charged the Drambuie.

It was as well Cynthia was allergic to any kind of liqueurs. She got us home that night. I sure don't remember any of it. I remember the fresh air outside, it was sorta like running from Hiroshima after the first bomb and getting to Nakasagi in time for the second. The way I felt next morning nobody should ever feel, but I was home O.K. She'd got me home, taken off my jacket and my shoes, loosened my tie and my collar.

She took David home next, so I learned later. Left Norm unconscious in the car, and took him up in the elevator and into his room. Then she undressed him and put him to bed, went down and got Norm home.

I was sure mad about that undressing part.

"You and who else?" I asked her.

"Just me," she said, quite cool.

"Right the way?"

"Right down to his birthday clothes, then I tucked him in all nice and comfy, and made sure at the desk they would look after him next day."

"You're just an old so-and-so," I stormed. "You sure didn't do that for me."

"You're a grown man," she retorted, still cool.

No wonder I've always hated the sight of Drambuie since then. But I loved her for it just the same, especially when I knew Norm had got to know about it.

CHAPTER 13

Norm and Cynthia

It was Norm and Cynthia who did more than anyone for him. They took him right under their wing. Their home was open house for him, and he never tired of telling me how much he appreciated them.

Norm had been my deputy for over five years, and I knew I was on a winner when I picked him. Six foot and big with it, dark, handsome, and always cheerful. Born in Canada, he'd left a good job when the Second World War started and flown for the British, collecting two medals for gallantry somewhere along the line, about which he never talked, though he still loved flying as much as Cynthia hated it.

She was English, but she'd lived in Canada and America so long it was hard to realise she was anything other than American. She had dark hair which she kept dressed severely, but attractively, a pair of greyish coloured eyes which refused to look on the black side, and only saw and wanted to see, the pleasant things in life, and a little tilt to her nose, which she said she had got because she was very fond of rabbits as a child.

We sure had fun about that tilted nose when we got to know her well. It was not true, Norm assured us, that she had a little white tail also, like the rabbits. She always took it in good part, she was so much in love with Norm. She was slim and graceful, and once she had accepted me I used her a lot for the business, entertaining, something we hadn't done a great deal of in the past.

Those two, David and Cynthia, sure altered my way of living a lot. Over the years, except for when I was on tour the year before, I'd given all my life to business. In my way I'd enjoyed it, and I was sure proud of the corporation I had built up. But these two, and the family life of Norm and Cynthia showed me what I had missed. Now I knew for certain why my two marriages had failed. The first one, in the

59

struggling days, had started well. Ellen put up with me in a manner no other person could have done. But as the business prospered we drifted apart, and I couldn't blame her at all when she found what she was looking for elsewhere. Ellen did not want a lot, just a family and a home. I didn't supply the family and the home was no good to be lonely in. She's happy now, I guess, married to a book publisher in Kansas City, and we exchange cards at birthdays and Christmas.

I knew a lot more about life when I caught up with Joan, and I had a lot more money to go with that knowledge. We sure didn't last long together. She wanted too much of my time and couldn't think why I should have to spend more time making cans then making her happy. The cruel twist of it is that its the cans that pay the alimony to keep her now, happy, I hope.

Now I got to thinking a lot about what had gone wrong. Seeing Norm and Cynthia so content had me sort of hankering for a happy marriage myself, and with David I always knew how much I needed a son, two sons, or three. Not in the puppy stage for sure, but grown up, old as David. I would have liked that, we sure could have had a time.

Poppy knew how I felt. She's been with me so long and knows me inside out. She encouraged me every way she knew to keep up the foursomes. She loved David, and best of it was she took to Cynthia so well, didn't get a bit upset at the way Norm and I brought Cynthia in to activities which go with big business.

Poppy was wise. She's never married because of an invalid mother, but she reads a lot of books and goes to all the movies.

"We sure better marry him to an American girl," she said knowingly to me one day, "then we'll have him for always."

I knew exactly what she meant, and it worried me a lot. David had been with us for many weeks, the bitter cold of winter was going from the land, the new spring rushing in on us, and all this time he had never shown the slightest interest in a woman.

Don't get me wrong. We'd been around a lot together, I'd taken him to the places where the smartest women are to be seen, and he'd looked at them, yeah he looked, but that was all. He was great with Cynthia, adored her, but only in the real best way. I know because I felt the same as that for Cynthia myself. We went round to the Casanova Club often, he liked the set-up there. I was glad, I liked to go a lot, especially as I owned the joint, not that he knew that, nor did many others for that matter.

I'd gone out of my way to push him at Lily Lee, but he hadn't seemed the least bit interested, not interested in the way you know I mean, and I sure couldn't think why. She was a great girl Lily, for me they didn't come much nicer. She was keen on her name in lights somewhere big, they all are, but she wanted her name in lights properly, not the wasy way some girls manage it by doing what the managers and the producers tell them all the time, instead of when they're just working. Not that she wasn't a woman, she sure was, with all the good things a woman needs, and she was nice mannered and a happy sort. She was just David's size and age, she got very stuck on him, would have given a lot to him, made many of his winter nights a lot warmer without pressing him to marry her and make her honest or anything story-book like that. Yet he never stirred for her.

They sat a long time at the bar together many nights, between her flights on the organ, and whilst I won my own money from Sophie. They would talk about a lot of things, and she would sing "Deep Purple" for him specially, and "Arrivederci Roma", which he liked, and "Stardust", and "Some of these Days", and anything he asked her to sing, but when I was ready to go home so was he, he never wanted to take Lily home. It was kind of funny to me.

We gave her a big party when she left for a long engagement at the Latin Quarter in New York. She was on her way up as she wanted. It was a great party, I'll say that. She kissed him hard when she said goodbye – "come up and see me when you're in New York," she told him.

He said he would, but I'm darn sure he forgot all about it straight-away.

We talked about it in my office after lunch one day. Norm, Cynthia and me. Not for any other reason than that we were so fond of him.

"Could be he's carrying a torch," was Cynthia's opinion.

"Could be," Norm agreed, "but he never says."

"Does he have to say?" she asked.

"Not necessarily" – Norm was thinking this out – "but he's talked about things at home, the company he works for, and I reckon, if there was a girl back home, that sort of girl, he'd have said so."

"That's probably right," Cynthia was thinking also, "He would have told me – I think."

"Why you?" Norm was grinning.

"I'm his sister, his mother" – Cynthia was smiling – "everything, he would tell me."

Norm kept on grinning. I was out of this.

"Everything?"

"Well – sort of everything," she said, "you're not jealous, are you?"

"No – I'm not jealous," he wasn't.

"I was afraid you wouldn't be," she told him, and he smacked her one on the bottom, which she liked a lot, and I guessed it was nice, smacking her on that trim bottom of hers.

CHAPTER 14

We Learn A Little

But long afterwards I remembered how wrong she had been about David telling her.

We took him to a girlie-show, it was part of his education anyhow. He liked it. We had eaten that night in the Sirloin room of the Stock Yard Inn. Norm, David and me had steaks as big as an acre, with french fried potatoes, mushrooms, grilled tomatoes and asparagus tips, a colossal meal. Cynthia settled for prime ribs of beef. It was too early to go home – for us, and we talked about the Casanova Club. It was Norm who suggested a burlesque. David was all for it, he hadn't seen one ever.

It was a new place, one I hadn't seen before, so I was interested. I reckon you just can't help being that way if you are in any kind of business. There weren't any original ideas, but it was well set out, quiet and clean, whilst the waiters and the bar boys wore good clean white jackets. For a honky-tonk it had a bit of class.

I thought David was surprised Cynthia had been keen about it, he was even more surprised to find other women in the joint. I told him with strip joints you'll find women as keen as men. Maybe it's to keep tags on the boy-friend, or it could be they like to see what it is the other gals have got. Whatever it is plenty women like strips. Norm told him he even thought Cynthia enjoyed it more than he did, but I was sure he was only pulling a fast one with that.

I've got to hand it to David, he liked our beer. We would talk about it often. It was lighter, he'd say, sharper, crisper, than English beer. More like a lager for him, but he liked it and could drink it well, always ice-cold. No matter how cold it was outside, and it sure was cold that winter in Chi, it had to be ice-cold his beer. Norm and me were content with water, as long as there was some good scotch whisky in it. Cynthia generally drank John Collins. Two or three of those always livened up the sparkle in those big grey eyes of hers under the mother-of-pearl rimmed glasses she usually wore at nights the four of us were out together.

It was the old procedure. Each girl would appear from out of the curtains at the far end as she was introduced by a loud-mouth barker, walk along the top of the bar, pausing now and then to do a few gymnastics, then disappear back through the curtains. The first one on was hefty and had finished being a girl twenty years or more before, the next one was better, Miss Yvonne the loud-mouth man had called her, and she was better at the gymnastics as well. The third one kept up the improvement, younger, more supple, more slim, but still really nothing to shout about.

We were all watching David, I think, but not letting him notice. He had laughed at the first one, and had not been impressed with the next two. Like us all though, he sat up for the fourth. With this one even I hadn't time to watch David any more. Nor, I guess, had Norm, and I sure don't think even Cynthia did.

Loud-mouth gave her the build up. Miss Pamela, this was the something they'd come to see from all over the world, this was the star of the Chicago night. We hadn't given the build-up a lot of attention, but we gave plenty to Miss Pamela.

She made a slow and slinky entrance through the curtains. She was tall, all of six feet in the high heels she was wearing. She was a beautiful bronze colour all over, except for the colour in her face, the red of her lips, her hair, and the three very small pieces of white silk she was wearing. Her jet black hair hung down behind her in a long bob, and as she gyrated, it bobbed up and down like a pony's tail. She was young, not out of her teens I'd guess, she had a wonderful figure, and she was a beautiful mover. Her face was an expressionless oval with her mouth a full red gash in the middle almost, her eyelashes as long as I'd ever seen. She had eastern blood in her all right, but I could not reckon what nationality she'd be.

The gymnastics were much the same as the other three had performed, but because it was she and not the others, it was all poetry and not at all suggestive. She wasn't on show as long as the others had been. This was the liqueur, not the cocktails or the wine, and as she disappeared through the curtains, she got applause from even this hardened audience.

"Well, whaddya know?" Norm said.

"I suppose they all have to start somewhere, but I didn't know they had them as nice as that." It was praise indeed from Cynthia.

"How would you like that with your coffee and doughnuts?" I asked David.

He grinned and took a large swipe at his beer. I don't think he'd heard that one before.

"All right," he replied, "but I've seen better."

"You have, where?" Cynthia was very interested, so were Norm and me.

"In New York."

"I thought you hadn't been to the honky-tonk before," Norm said.

"Nor have I," he was a bit huffed, "I met her at the Statler."

"Nicer than that filly?" I came in. I'd started thinking hard about the bronze girl, she was really something. We hadn't exactly replaced Lily Lee at the Casanova, and it was going through my head that we could fit the bronze in – some way. She'd have to have a bit more silk for sure, I don't run that sort of place. But if she could only sing, or play an electric organ, or something. With the rest of what she had, I'd have to build a bigger place, and that was for sure.

"Much nicer than that, much nicer." He was very certain.

"I'd sure like to meet her," I told him, and Norm said, "me likewise." If ever I meant anything, I meant that.

"I hope you will," he replied, and would say no more, and we were so astonished we didn't crowd him about it as hard as we might have done, but we were intrigued, very much so, me and Norm and Cynthia. Cynthia wanted to say a lot, I was sure, but she held it back, and couldn't have been so certain then of being sister, mother and everything to him. It passed over but I had a feeling he wanted to say a bit more and didn't know how to go about it. Anyhow, mysterious as it was, we gathered now he was carrying a torch, and the flame had been lit in New York. Yessir, we were intrigued.

Almost as much as ice-cold beer, David liked hi-fi. Like me he heard it for the first time at Norm's place, and like me, like Norm and Cynthia, he got so that he could listen to it for hours. Once you had heard hi-fi, he said, you never wanted to listen to ordinary sound recording again, and I went with him all the way on that. We had a lot of fun with hi-fi. Norm was a wizard and not content with just records. He had a tape machine and when a particular piece caught his fancy, he would record it on tape, then play the tape, when he had finished it off O.K., back through the hi-fi set. With tremendous patience he would record a complete programme of music from radio

65

or TV on a tape, play that back on to another tape cutting out any talk or commercials, then play that on to a third tape, putting in his own remarks as continuity where the intervals occurred, or just cutting out the intervals.

He had some great tapes. We liked all kinds of music, though Norm and Cynthia were much more for the operas than David and me, but our favourite choice was always something of Mantovani. We never tired of hearing this beautiful orchestra, it was magic. Even for a guy like me who sure can't play one note of music, this had everything, melody, depth, meaning, whilst the Mantovani strings were thrilling. All four of us would sit there, not talking, just listening and thinking our separate thoughts, whilst the music played on and on.

CHAPTER 15

We Learn A Lot

I sure enough reckon the Creator knew what He was about when He made the spring-time. It never fails to come around just when it's most needed, after the long dreary haul of the winter. It's the greatest tonic, no bottles, no pills, just fresh air, warmth and a new feeling of life. All for free.

I guess it's always been the same in Chicago, but this year I was getting out and around a lot more with David, and with Norm and Cynthia, and I saw it as if for the first time. The days lengthened and grew warmer, the winter blacks and greys gave place to the greens of spring. The lake – the ice all gone – began to come back to looking blue. You could see it all around, in the streets, where the gals came out from under their wraps and their furs to become frilly and feminine again, in the parks, the gardens, in the shops, everywhere. Winter had gone, spring was here, and the heat of the summer a coming up fast.

We were at Norm's, making plans for a short vacation, either to motor up to the Niagara Falls or to fly down to Florida. I was feeling light-headed, was all for both, David should see them both anyhow whilst he was over here, and Norm and Cynthia weren't arguing. It was just a matter of time fixing.

It was Norm who started it all off. He had got up to bring more drinks, beer, John Collins, and ice-water for our scotch. He flipped a newspaper over on the table, stood up there behind us, then he said it.

"Well, that sure is nice – Nympho's home again."

I was far away in Florida, with the sun, the sea, the sand and the gals, especially the gals, brown as brown all over, but his remarks stirred something.

"The gossip writers will be happy," Norm went on, "they sure must have missed her."

"Missed who Norm?" David asked, more out of politeness than anything else, after all Norm was our host and he was talking. I looked up at David then.

"The Delane woman," Norm answered, "she's back home again."

I saw David suddenly go white, as if he was ill, then slowly come back red again. Cynthia saw it, she was concerned.

"What is it David, are you feeling ill?"

He ignored her, which was very odd.

"Who is the Delane woman?" he asked Norm.

"Janice Delane, the film-star. Nympho they call her along the Gold Coast – local girl makes good, or bad."

"Why nympho?" I couldn't describe the way he looked now, but I could see how tense he was.

"Simple," Norm was flippant, more interested in the newspaper than in David – "Nympho, short for nymphomaniac, that's Delane, eats up all the boys."

Cynthia knew it first, that must be what they call womanly intuition.

"Stop it Norm" – I had never heard her speak that way to him before. She turned back to David.

"You know her David?"

He didn't reply, he just looked at her. He didn't have to, even I knew the answer to that one. I didn't know the answer to the next one, but Cynthia did, even before she asked it.

"She's the one you met in New York, at the Statler?"

He took a long time to reply, it was awful quiet. Norm looked doped, I guess I looked the same, there was nothing he or me could do or say. This was between David and Cynthia.

Quietly, slowly it came.

"She's the one."

"Oh David," Cynthia said, sharp and almost shocked. She went over and knelt beside him, close. She was his sister, his mother, everything, now.

"We didn't know – Norm wouldn't have said that – I'm sorry David."

He was recovering, her sympathetic understanding had helped him a lot. He leaned over and nuzzled his face in her hair. She took his hands in hers, holding them tight. They were playing it hard, and I just wasn't all the way with them, yet. Nor was Norm. After a while

68

David looked up and smiled at us, it was wet in his eyes. But his voice was normal.

"It's quite a story, want to hear it?"

Cynthia was still in the lead. Norm and me were only a couple of extras – we would have fluffed our lines, if we'd had any.

"Do you feel you want to tell us David?"

"I think you ought to know, it will help."

"O.K. then," she said, standing up, "but I want to powder my nose first."

I thought her eyes were wet too.

I don't think he held any of it back. From any other person, any other place, any other time, I sure would not have believed it, but this was all true. He looked more at Cynthia than at us, but he was speaking to Norm and me as well as to her all right. He told it simply, without any fuss, and when he had finished he lay back a bit in his chair.

"Now you know," he said.

I guess there are a lot of things we could have said. Instantly many of the stories I'd heard about Janice Delane were flooding back to me, and I was chewing them over all the time David was speaking. All America knew her well, there'd been a million stories written about her, and a million photographs of her in all the magazines and newspapers. She was big news whatever she did, and the stories went that she did plenty. Most of all the big magazines carried her picture on the front cover every other month, and a lot more pictures of her inside. She photographed well, darn well – they said they couldn't take a bad picture of her, whilst cheesecake with her was a lot of cheese and a lot of cake.

Her films were money spinners, they were just that certain to make millions of bucks, not only in the States, but in England, on the continent and everywhere they showed. She was a sizzler and they knew how to exploit her, her looks and her figure, to the full. All her movies showed plenty of her plenty of the time.

She was something of a local girl, from what I knew of her, the family home was still somewhere round about. She'd made her start here in the City, and she had gone ahead fast. When she was in the States she went to lots of places, generally at night, with most of all the eligible men, and sometimes with men who were not so eligible. She did the same sort of thing abroad, gave much of her time to all the eligibles, and didn't seem to worry about nationality. Now I come to think about it, there had been a lot of pictures recently of her with an Italian Count, or a Prince, or something like that.

Up and down the city, in the bars, the taverns, the clubs and the hotels, you heard a hell of a lot of stories about her. I'm old enough to know that anybody in the public eye, certainly anyone as attractive as Delane, will come in for stories.

They are told about all the big shots, male or female, and such stories improve with the telling. They start pretty easy, and each new teller adds a little bit on, spice or dirt, but just a little bit to make it that much better. As I say, there had been a lot about Delane, and hard as they had been improved upon, there could be no doubt of the old saying – there's no smoke without fire. There was also no doubt this woman had the fire, you could see it in every line of her, and it was pretty true there had been a hell of a lot of smoke.

I hadn't ever seen her, in the flesh that is, but good judges have always reckoned that her flesh was as nice as the Creator ever made for anyone, and I am willing to believe that. I'd heard the name nympho given to her many times, in Chicago many people called her just what Norm had, Nympho Delane, and I'd always judged her, in the way men do judge, to be quite a woman. Now through David, she'd come a whole lot more close.

Yessir, I could have said a lot of things to him just then, but I didn't. These things have to be given time, and I kept out for a while, so did Norm. Cowards that we are, we left it to Cynthia, we could not have done better. It was hard to realise why he had told us all he had, but there was one thing I knew, he was not boasting about it. It was just something that had happened to him, something that had affected him greatly, and it must have been a sort of relief for him to tell it, especially to a woman such as Cynthia.

She handled him very carefully, and very encouragingly as well. He responded to her quite easily, without any worry and with a whole lot of conviction.

"She must be a very attractive woman, David."

I was sure Cynthia knew as much about Janice Delane as Norm and me knew. She went a lot of places where they had talked about her, and she missed nothing. Delane had the same story attraction for women as she had for men, and for my money, they talked about her just as much, more probably, in the women's clubs and in the powder-your-nose rooms.

"She is – very." He smiled and I smiled with him, a little. I sort of had the idea why he was smiling.

"Did she write?"

"No – never – she said she would, she also said she was a bad writer. Perhaps she never had the time."

He smiled again, realising, I think, what he had just said in that last sentence, and maybe knowing the reason she might never have had time.

"Do you think she'll come and see you now that she's back in the States?"

He got just a tiny way bitter at that one I thought. I could have been wrong but I could have been right.

"You tell me," he said, "you're a woman."

Cynthia held on well and kept going.

"I am" – she paused – "but I'm not that sort of woman." I know why she had paused, reasoning whether she should say that or not, but, if he felt it he didn't show it. "Though I do my best, I hope, for my lord and master here" – this was a nice little tit-bit for the man she loved – another pause – she nodded to herself and to him – "Yes, I think she'll come, I sure would if it was me."

"I damn sure wouldn't let you," Norm said, but he was laughing and we all knew how he meant it. I was glad the tension was easing a little.

She bowed to Norm – what a wife, I thought. I wondered if Ellen or Joan might have been like her, had I given them the chance. I'd thought a lot about my marriages since I realised what a gem Cynthia was.

"Thank you, darling – but Janice Delane has nobody to stop her coming. I'm prepared to bet you a new dress she'll come."

"I wouldn't bet against that," I said, more that I thought I'd better say something than for any other reason.

"Just you don't, Danny," she turned the big grey eyes on me – "just you don't, you'll lose."

She had handled it all very cleverly, smoothed over what could have been an awkward time, and I had to hand it to her. Our close friendship between us hadn't been affected in the slightest, and I felt David was pleased he'd got this off his chest. We knew now what had been worrying him, though we hadn't really known he had been worried. We knew why he wasn't interested in women, other than Delane that is, and I could see why Lily Lee hadn't affected him, nice as she was, and hard as she had tried. If they get to the sun first in space, they probably won't bother about the moon – not those that reach the sun anyhow. We knew also that he was carrying one hell of a torch – for the brightest, warmest flame in the film world. A flame which, if what they said was true, was all heat.

Taking him home that night he talked some more.

"Do you think I was wrong, Danny, telling all that?"

"I sure don't," I told him. "I'm responsible for you, so are Norm and Cynthia, I guess, so it's best we know – we won't say—"

"I'm not worried about it that way," he interrupted.

"Maybe not," I said, "but you know how we feel about you."

"I do indeed, and I'm grateful," and I had no doubt he was – "I'm glad I got it out, I think, I've been bursting to say something for a long time now –"

"You know much about her?" I asked.

"Well, I've read everything there is to read, I know she's been married three times, but that doesn't make her – "

He stopped short. I knew what he wanted to say, yet didn't want to say it about her.

"It sure does not," I assured him. "My first wife Ellen married again, and a woman further from that sort of thing would be hard to find." I was sure that was right about Ellen.

"No, three marriages don't make a woman a nymph." The nymph part was brutal, but I said it purposely, it didn't seem to worry him.

"You really think she'll come and see me, Danny?"

"You remember what you told Cynthia when she asked you that?" I said, and we both laughed, and I damn near hit the side walk a real plonker. We settled again and I hope he realised it was the laughing, that caused it, nor the whisky I'd drunk at Norm's. "Yeah, she'll probably come at that – like I said, I wouldn't bet against Cynthia. Why don't you write and invite her?"

I was not sure whether I meant that as a joke or not, but he took it seriously.

"Oh no," he said, "if she wants to come, she'll come."

CHAPTER 16

An Invitation From Al

He didn't want to go in when we got to the hotel, so I parked the auto and we went into the Blue Room bar. Al was glad to see us, and we propped ourselves up on the stools in front of him.

We talked about this and that for a while, then I pitched it in, hard and fast, straight at Al.

"Delane's home again I see."

I think David knew why I had pitched this way, I hope he did anyhow. He looked down into his beer while Al took strike.

"Yeah – I saw her picture in the news, them Counts in Europe sure will be feeling cold at nights."

"You know her, Al?"

"Sure, who doesn't?"

"She sure is a honey," I was encouraging him, and wondering when David would up and blast me one.

"Sure is," Al agreed, "and always plenty of bees around her, she likes the bees, the more the merrier."

David was finding out Norm hadn't invented anything about the way Chicago talked of Janice Delane. I wondered if I'd gone far enough, and whether to change the subject. I didn't.

"So they say," I said.

"So they say," Al agreed enthusiastically, he didn't seem to realise David wasn't in on the conversation – "so Taps Miller says for one–"

David looked up then and came in, quite calm.

"Taps Miller, who's he?"

"Taps" – Al thought everyone knew the gent. "Taps Miller keeps the Continental down in the lights, used to be the best dance director in the business–"

"He knew her – really?" David asked.

"He knew her," Al was emphatic. "Knew them all Taps, he sure

did. Taught her how to hoof – couldn't teach her anything else though
– she knew all the rest when she was a kid – "
I came back in then.
"Like to go down to Taps' place one night, David?"
He thought awhile.
"Yes, I think so, I think I would."
"Come down with me," Al invited. "My next night off – say,
I'd sure like to take you two down to the lights, we'll go see the
town. The Continental isn't bad, not bad at all. I'd like to see Taps
again."
We accepted, of course, a night out with Al would be fun anyway,
though maybe not for David if he heard a lot from Taps.
As we drank our last drinks, I let Al in the picture just a little.
"David knows Delane," I told him.
"You don't say?" It was something to see the look spread all over
his face – "You don't say?"
I did say, but Al ignored me from then on. He rubbed his chin,
opened his mouth wide, looked at David, rubbed his chin again, then
grinned.
"She sure is a nice piece of pie."
It wasn't what he wanted to say, we knew it, and he knew we knew
it. We laughed. I was glad David was taking it so well, glad he hadn't
thought fit to blast me one when I'd started it all. I know the world I
was thinking, and it's better this way.
"Lovely," David agreed, just that.
Al's face was terrific. He was bursting to ask all the questions, but
dare not.
"I seen a lot of her movies," he said, "that last one – with Gable –
was a wow – boy she sure sizzles – I sure would love to see her, for
real."
"You said you knew her?" I queried.
"You know how it is," he gave me a look which was much different
to the way he was regarding David. "She's from Chicago, and you
talk about them, just like you know them. I sure would like to see
her in here."
"You may do just that," I said, as we left.
His face lit up – "you don't say," he came out with it again, and
his eyes followed us to the door, not me really, just David. Whatever
they said about Delane didn't matter, David knew her and Al knew
David.

"See you David," he bawled as we went out. He'd forgotten about me.

Back in my place I poured myself a large shot of Dimple Haig, and looked up all the new magazines I had round the place. There were plenty of pictures of Delane – in Rome, in Paris, in London, on location in Spain somewhere, always with a man, in Rome, Paris and London, always with the same man – an Italian Count, like I had thought. He was a handsome chap, swarthy, and a bit elderly. No, she wasn't getting married or anything like that one article said – they were just good friends.

Delane was a magnificent looking woman all right. Shapely as they came, upright, bubbling over with life in all the pictures, happy, gay – she didn't look as if she was carrying any torches for anyone, but there was plenty of flame about her – when she was dressed she looked marvellous, when she was undressed she looked even better. I wondered if she would come and see David, somehow, after looking at these pictures, I didn't think she would.

I looked up the meaning of the word, nymphomaniac. It didn't tell me anything I didn't already know.

I poured out another stiff Dimple.

CHAPTER 17

'Taps' Miller Talks Delane

Al insisted the night was on him at the Continental, even when I said I thought Norm and Cynthia should come along.

"Look Danny," he said, "you four been great buddies of mine, I sure appreciate your company a lot, it will be my pleasure, let's say it's a date."

Al has loads of dough, and, as far as I knew, no wife nor family. I remembered how much money he makes on the gee-gees. It wouldn't hurt him one bit to let him have the night, and it would do him a lot of good.

Yeah, I said, it was a date.

We met in his bar. He was always a meticulous dresser, and tonight he looked real smart. It was strange to see him on the wrong side of his bar. He was just raring to go, and for that matter so were we, David especially. Since that first night he'd told us about Delane we'd talked a lot about her, seen more pictures of her, and he didn't seem to be worried. Far as we knew she was in Hollywood, that's what all the gossip and pictures about her seemed to indicate.

I thought we might eat at one of the big hotels down town, but Al had it all fixed. We were eating at the Continental. He'd been in touch with Taps Miller, the eats were laid on and Taps was looking forward to meeting us. Taps didn't know the real reason for our coming, I'd made sure that Al knew nothing more than that David had met Delane. We were not to go too early, Taps didn't want us to see the Continental looking empty, so we sat on at the bar for an hour or so. Al enjoyed meeting those of his own customers who were in the place, it was the first time he had ever spent any part of his night off in his own bar.

The Continental was nicer than I'd expected it to be. Quiet, softly lit, and very smart indeed, one of the nicest of these sort of joints I'd been in down in the lights. We all liked what we saw, and I couldn't think why I had never heard about it before. Sure there are a lot of such places down there, and naturally I spend a lot of time in my own joint, but the Continental had class, and was worth shouting about. There had been a huge pile of dough spent on it, and, as the night wore on, we could see it was paying big dividends. I was thinking I ought to buy myself a place down here. The Casanova was O.K., it was making good money, but it was uptown, not really in the lights, and we really didn't cater for the type of patrons the Continental attracted.

Taps was just the sort of guy you'd expect from the sort of place he owned. Quiet, soft-spoken and very smart. The suit he was wearing cost a pile of dough too. I ought to know from what I spend on mine. I had a feeling I had met him before some place, but you meet so many guys out and around, and I couldn't be sure. He gave us a swell greeting, our reception could not have been better had Delane herself been with us. Taps and Al were good friends, and friends of Al were friends of Taps. I could see we were in for a good night. I wasn't wrong.

We got the best table of course. He had a little bit of a floor show – a few girls so that the male customers would enjoy themselves – "the older males," he said, grinning at me – a better than average five-piece band, and a young singer who was sure to get into the big time – a male –

"For the older females?" I asked.

"Sure," he said, "just that, he packs them in this Eddy, you wait and see–"

The dance floor was small.

"Big enough," Taps told us. "Those that wanna dance like the close stuff, gives them a thrill, and the dough's made from the tables, it sure is, so tables is priority."

Al had chosen the meal with tremendous care and good taste – I could not have bettered it myself. Honeydew melon, then smoked scotch salmon and capers. The main course was roast tom turkey and cranberry sauce, braised cloved American ham, green peas, asparagus, and corn on the cob, with a Continental cole slaw salad. For dessert we had fresh strawberries and cream, and even with that, and after all he had eaten, David had to have ice-cream. Al hadn't gone for any wines, he'd played safe and let us drink our own drinks. With our coffee he thought we ought to have a liqueur, but I told him I'd beat him to death if he mentioned the word Drambuie. I have one hell of a memory. We didn't take liqueurs any more.

By the time we'd got through all that the Continental was full, and we saw Taps point about the older females. Those that were here, and there were more than a few, were loaded with jewellery. I'll say this for the American female, she doesn't mind carrying extra weight, especially if it's gold, silver, diamonds and rubies, and the older they are the more they like to carry. It could be that they have more carrying space. The girls were nice, well-dressed and could really dance. I'll say this for Taps, everything had to be top class. Eddy Lambert was good, not my type of singer, but good, and he sure did wow them, especially the old gals. I've grown up with Crosby, Martin and Sinatra, and I stay with them, but Taps could be right about this Eddy boy.

The night wore on and Taps hadn't had a lot of time for us. We weren't worrying, running this place was a big job, and we were happy anyway. All of us danced in turn with Cynthia – how she put up with us I sure do not know, but she seemed happy, even when I had her out on the floor. The five-piece were hot stuff. Five happy-go-lucky coloured boys who really made your feet tap, though once or twice I wondered if my ear drums would stand up to them. We were pretty content, and I was doing a whole lot of thinking as well as watching and listening.

I blamed it most on Cynthia – in a manner of speaking. For a long time now I had been thinking about the lonely old age I was heading for. A bit off yet for sure, but, if I didn't do something about it, it would be lonely. The way Cynthia and Norm acted, I could see what I had missed. At forty-seven I wasn't too old to get hitched again, provided I could find the right mate, and this one would have to be right. If I did I knew what I was going to do – I'd hand over the top spot in my business to Norm. He'd run it well for me, and it would continue to bring in the dollars. Not that I needed any more really, I'd enough and to spare now. I was even thinking I'd ask David to stay on as deputy to Norm, though that sounded a bit disloyal to those folks in England who'd sent him. I sure liked the boy and knew how well he would do with Norm. David had learned the business fast once he had gotten over his initial amazement, like us all now, he talked in terms of millions of cans.

I'd keep the Casanova, that was doing me no harm, but I'd buy a place down here in the lights, something like this place of Taps'.

There was plenty room for another place like this, so I wouldn't be doing any bad turn to Taps. The more I mused about it, the better it shaped up, all there in my brain, like the way the can business is. I'd put Al in to run my place, that is if he would take it and I was pretty sure he would. He could run it O.K., he had the go and the savvy, and to help, I was thinking Taps would most likely take him in the Continental for a time, whilst my place was being set up. There it was, and there was nothing I didn't like about the plans at all, except that there was just one hell of a problem to start it all off. I had to find me a new wife, one as good as Cynthia, who would put up with me, and train me like a proper husband. That was all.

Taps was free at last.

"Come on in the office," he invited, "you seen all there is to see out here. Let's go somewhere quiet and we can talk a little."

We were barely out of the table before the captain was showing another party to it. Business was good and the floor show was due to come round again. Last away from the table, I saw that the new party included a couple of female aircraft-carriers, and on their flight-decks they were showing plenty of the sort of trinkets women like to fly.

I sure bet Taps was proud of his office. Like the rest of his joint, it was smart and furnished in the best of taste. The pictures on the wall told a lot of his story before he began to take it up. He had them all – the old groaner himself, Sinatra, Powell, Gable, Garland, Astaire, Grable – my number one gal over many a year, Davies, Dietrich, Ellington, Cooper, the Dorseys, Armstrong, Horne, Martin, Charisse, Groucho Marx, the lot, and in one corner, just as big as any of the others, and looking out of this world in full colour, and in the complete glory of her ripe womanhood, Janice Delane. All of them were signed, many of them with high affection, to Taps. I warmed to this slim, debonair man, who was obviously in the high regard of so many great people.

He talked – he could talk – quietly, softly, no bluster, no boasts, honest and sincere, and we were with the stars, with those people whose pictures were there all around us. He knew them all, had always known them all, and they were all great, he told us. All of them.

We sat relaxed, comfortable, in this very comfortable office of Taps', whilst he spoke of many of them, intimately, how they looked to him, and how a lot of them got started to the great white way and to international fame. Fred Astaire, the greatest tapper of them all –

you should know Taps, I thought – Eleanor Powell, Cyd Charisse, both lovely, long-legged, nimble of foot and wonderful rhythm girls, Judy Garland, terrific, intense, a great hoofer, and – Janice Delane.

He had got around to her without me nosing in to help him. I was thinking how I might make use of her picture to start him off, but I didn't need it because her own natural ability, her super sense of rhythm of her feet, were something he would always be able to talk about in the same breath with Astaire, Powell, Charisse, Garland. She was just that good.

We had all in our own way, I reckoned, hoped he would be able to tell us a whole lot about her, not just the dirt, but what sort of woman she was for real. We listened hard, and I wondered what the others were thinking, especially David. Al wasn't in on it with us, but he listened just as hard – you sure had to when there was a guy who could reminisce like Taps could, and the subject was a gal like Delane.

Taps had taught her to hoof. She was very young, perhaps not sixteen, when he had first seen her in a chorus row, and she'd been all glamour then, so that the rest of the gals looked as if they were in the shade all the time while all the lights hung on her. She sure was beautiful, he said, like a young she-leopard, feline, sleek, graceful. She was watchful and ambitious, she knew darn well where she wanted to go, and she was sure going to get there. He had only to show her a step once, however intricate, and she had it. That was the wonder of her, her timing and the fact that her feet could do nothing wrong. How she would work, she was never tired, never wanted to stop dancing, stop learning. She couldn't miss being a hit, there was nobody in her class and she had rocketed upwards, the most beautiful shooting star he had ever seen.

Somehow I enjoyed it all a lot. We'd heard nothing but dirt about the girl around Chicago for a long time. She was every gossip writer's idea of a female Casanova, with a string of conquests longer than him, and she had covered more territory than even he had. All the stories about her couldn't be true or she'd never have had the time to get out of bed, never have made all the films she had been making. Yeah, I enjoyed it, but I had to know what Taps thought about her as a woman, I knew the others wanted to know, so I gave him a prod.

"You hear a lot of stories about Delane up and down the lights, Taps, what was she really like – you know – as a woman?"

He knew what I was getting at, but could not have known why, other than that it was morbid curiosity. I thought for a while he wasn't going to answer that one, wasn't going to say any more about her, but he was only thinking. He made sure we were all O.K. for drinks and took his time, perhaps he was getting it all clear, the memories he had of her.

"Like you say, Danny," – it was coming slow – "there are a lot of stories about Delane – I've heard more than a few – but for me she was the greatest – "

I sure would have liked to see what my face looked like. I could see David, and Norm and Cynthia, and, if my face was like theirs, I must have looked darn surprised. There had been no mistaking the way Taps had called her the greatest. I really didn't know what I had expected, what any of us had expected, but it hadn't been that, not even for David with the way he had known her. I was wondering what Taps saw in our faces, but he gave no sign of anything unusual, he went on talking –

"In addition to everything else that girl has, she sure has the biggest heart in the world, that's the trouble with her – she just gives and gives. When she was with me, learnin' to hoof," he grinned a bit, back in his memories – "learnin' – she taught me more about hoofing than I ever thought I knew – when she was dancing she gave everything to it, all of her would come down in to her feet, and she would just give – that's the way she does everything I guess – "

Cynthia interrupted him. It was the first time she had said anything in a long while.

"Every woman does," she was quite hot about it – "for the right man."

He looked at her, the wisdom of ages in his look, and I remembered then we hadn't any idea of a wife, or a woman, in his life. Perhaps he was like me – without.

"Yeah," he said, "yeah, but Delane can't find the right man – she's tried a lot for sure – some of them all nice and legal, but she hasn't found mister right, and that's the trouble. Don't get me wrong though – she doesn't give to everything or to everyone, there are some things she hates, but at sixteen she couldn't pick out the mean from the good – but she learned as she grew older –"

He paused, none of us spoke this time.

"Sixteen" – he was remembering way back – "she sure was a flame – hot pants, the other gals called her right from the start – they could have been so right – like I say when her heart was in it, she gave her all – her heart was in dancing, so she gave. There wasn't one of the boys who didn't go for her, not a one. Sure she was lucky, always had dough, dressed well, didn't have to count her dollars like the others. Then she met the Lamp guy – Johnny Lamp, as I recall – a slim, mean little jerk, but he sure could hoof it, quick as the devil and snappy as hell. She went for him, it must have been the dancing – and fast as you could say jack rabbit, we had a wedding in the show. It sure was a time – her daddy came on down, played up hell – but he couldn't stop it, nobody could stop her when her mind was made up. So there she was, sweet sixteen and married for keeps."

He paused again and looked at us, he knew he wasn't boring any of us – we were waiting for him to come back to the telling. He sure could tell a good story, and this was for true.

"For keeps did I say?" he grinned. "Yeah, it lasted four weeks, then they were fighting harder than Joe Louis ever fought – she was far too good for him, he was a tramp – pity the way he could hoof – so one day she up and left him, left him, left us, left the show, and the next thing we knew she was in New York, doing a small spot in a Gus Risman musical."

He took another pause, and we waited again. He was having to think a bit, all this had been a few years ago.

"Sure Johnny Lamp was a tramp, that was the only time I ever knew Delane make a mistake, after Johnny she learned, and, like I say, from then on, she would pick the mean from the good. The stories began to start when she left Johnny – he just hadn't been able to keep up with her bedtime exercises, he told the boys and girls, and one or two of the bright boys began to make up dirty poems about it – I forget most of them, but they were all about the lamp that hadn't enough juice for the bulb. I didn't believe most of it – Delane was class and Johnny wasn't good enough for her, that's the way I saw it. Sure I couldn't reckon what she had seen in him in the first place, but what the hell – what do a lot of women see in a lot of men?"

We didn't begin to try to answer that, he didn't want one, it was just his way of telling the story.

"Maybe you know what happens next. In less than a year she was playing lead for Gus, and getting some good notices. I was in New York for a time, and saw her now and then, and I heard the stories. She and Gus were going to get hitched – I couldn't catch on, Gus was older than me then, and I could give her thirty years. He sure must have been going nuts in his old age, anyhow, so the stories went, it wasn't essential for him, he was getting all the comforts from her then – they never did get hitched, after about a year, when she'd gone as far as she wanted to go with him, she upped and left the show, the urge was on her to go West and Hollywood was waiting there for her – I got all this, first hand, from Dolly Day. Dolly Day and me been old friends for a long time, and it was Dolly that Delane had ousted from the lead in Gus's show. Dolly was fairly honest – said Delane was younger, nicer, newer, than she was, and free with everything for a price. The price? Dolly out – Delane in. Dolly was bitter, maybe you couldn't blame her, she'd been living with Gus a long time. It was Dolly who started the real dirt about the way Delane was with men, and the dirt got dirtier when Gus went and died that same year Delane had left. Could be he died of sorrow, but a lot said he died a satisfactory death. By then Delane was on her way in Hollywood.

He replenished the drinks – it was amazing how quiet we were sitting.

"She did herself well in Hollywood – you sure must know a lot of it. She married a camera-man named Richards, and he got her in the movies. That lasted a year, and by then she was in, and, I guess, Richards was out. She progresses, does Delane, and the next hitch-up was Arthur P. Parker, the director, you sure must know all about him, and in between Richards and Arthur P., she had a romance with a guy whose name I just forget, who was a script writer. He was a good one – oh yeah, Sammy Sollack, that was him. The gossips said he couldn't write hard enough for her, but she was hot on him for a time. Funnily enough he faded out, and hasn't written a lot since, yeah – maybe the gossips were O.K. about it – maybe he ran out of writing. Well, she left the Parker man like you know she did, and since then she's been the rounds. Sure, she's front page news, and what she does the press boys make a lot of, and knowing her, I reckon she puts on a lot of show for them. The studios help, they encourage her a lot. Her own company pay the best publicity boy there is, and they don't pay dollars out for peanuts. Not that it's all wind and no water – oh no, I sure didn't say that. Remember what the press said when the Dennison boy ran home to Mamma and Pappa three months after she married him four years ago – keeping up with Delane is like keeping up with the Jones's – impossible. Well, O.K. so she's got a lot of sex she doesn't want to keep – it fills the movie places."

He stopped there, and at once David came in –

83

"I've read that she's only been married three times – there's no mention of a man named Lamp."

Taps looked hard at David, he was a wise old guy, this Taps, he knew his world, and I think he was thinking what I thought he was – about David.

"Sure – that's what the books say – me, I'm not a great reader – but they're wrong, take it from me. I was there when she got hitched up with Johnny and it was legal, that's for sure. But I don't reckon even she counted that one, perhaps she was just exploring what getting hitched was like."

"Yet you say she's the greatest?" This one was from Cynthia, and it was a good one at that.

He drew back a little, but not too much.

"Yeah," he said, "she is so, in a sort of way. Me, I'm not the judge of what should be what – anything she does with herself and her spare nights is her business. We got a guy comes in here most every night, drinks better than a bottle of whisky everytime he's in, and he's one of the nicest guys I ever seen, do anything for anybody. It could be like that for Delane, like this guy and his thirst. Get this folks, it's one hell of a tough world Delane wanted in, she wanted in and she wanted to get the best out of it, and she's given a lot away to get it, but that's her nature, and you just can't alter nature. She just gives and gives – she's not a great one for dough – I'm only one of the boys who knows how much she's given to things and to people she's fond of – that's how I see it. When you see a gee-gee streaking along and winning a lot of races, you look back and blame the breeding – a lot of that goes with Delane – I met her daddy and he knows. He doesn't altogether blame his little girl. She's made some guys happy" – I could not help looking at David, though I tried not to – "if ever there is a beautiful woman, it's Delane. Then some of it's publicity – you know how it goes. Her company, like the money her pictures bring in, like I said. One thing I know, she never fails to come in and see me when she's in Chi – she was in last year, that's why I reckon I'm right, Delane's never found what she's been looking for all these years, maybe she never will, maybe there isn't such a man."

He stood up – he'd talked a long while, it was time to go take a look round his place, there were many others he could spend time with. We were on our way too – we'd had a good night, learned a lot even if we had not got to know it all. We sure would go back and see Taps again – he and Al had done us proud.

There was just one more thing he said as we gave our thanks. We were waiting for Cynthia, she had gone to the powder room, just five men together. Taps looked hard at David.

"You met Delane?" he was certain of the answer, I knew, but he asked just the same.

"I met her," David told him simply.

Taps smiled –

"You sure are a lucky boy," he said.

We all smiled then, even David, but I didn't reckon he knew whether he was or he wasn't.

CHAPTER 18

Big News

We had a sort of light day the next day. I took David down to the Chicago stock yards. I'd told him a lot about the yards and he'd been down once before, not long after his arrival in Chicago, when it had been cold and raw, and snow underfoot. We'd always said we'd take him again. Norm was away, and I fancied a day out of the office – funny I wasn't anything like as keen on my office now as I had been only a few months before, but Poppy was always there, and, like she always says, she can manage, and that all I do is just sign what she puts up for me.

We had a quiet day, watching some of the auctions. David said the first time he had been there he had been amazed at the number of cattle, hogs and sheep that were bought and sold, but he was used to our sort of figures now, and nineteen thousand head meant as little to him now as it did to me, except that it was a hell of a lot of work for the big meat factories, which were a part of the vast area of the yards, and except that all this was part of the reason for the millions of cans we were turning out every day.

We looked in at the office for a while and I signed what Poppy said I had to sign, whilst she asked David how the day had been, and if he had taken a good lunch, and was the smell too much for him, and all that sort of thing, and he gave her all the nice replies he could, kissing her hand when we left, so that she was stood there staring after him, like they always show you in the good movies. Poppy was sweet on him for sure.

We drove back through Harlem, a district I knew fascinated him, with its mile upon mile of miserable looking dwellings, and its hundreds upon hundreds of little black boys and girls playing in every street. I dropped him off, and he said he would have an early night. Like me he was tired after our night at the Continental. I had hardly got in my own place when the telephone rang. It was David.

"Drive me down to Midway later on, will you, Danny?" he asked. "I have to meet a lady."

I knew exactly who the lady would be.

CHAPTER 19

She's On Her Way

David Lander

Elmer handed me the cablegram with my room key. I didn't open it straightaway, just rode up in the elevator with it in my hand, wondering, and knowing, who it was from, looking hard at the outside of the envelope. There wasn't a lot in it to read when I did open it, but there was lots to think about.

"Midway – ten tonight – Flight 387 – love – Laurie."

Well, it wasn't a lot, all that was needed probably, and the "love" part was pleasing. She was coming as Laurie Gaydon, not Delane, and remembering what she'd told me in New York, that was pleasing also. One thing puzzled me, there was nothing about accommodation – if she had booked in at one of the big hotels down on the Coast, she would have said so, after all, another dollar or two wouldn't break this girl. So, even in that short cable, handed in just after two o'clock that afternoon in New York, there were three things I could be very happy about. The love she had sent, the fact that she was coming incognito, and – I hoped I was reasoning this correctly – I was to arrange her accommodation, which meant she wanted to be near me.

I was still thinking about that, feeling very vain, whilst I spoke to Danny on the telephone. He didn't seem at all surprised, if he was he kept it to himself.

"I'll bring over a waggon and you can drive out to Midway."

That wasn't what I wanted – I didn't want to go on my own, I wasn't really sure I knew the way out to the airport, I could find it all right, but I would rather he drove me out, and I wanted him to be with me. I told him so.

"No, no, no," he said into my right ear – "I'll drive you out there O.K., leave you, then you get a cab back – you sure don't want me around."

"You come with me Danny."

"Is that how you want it to be?"

"Yes."

"O.K. then, if that's the way you want it."

We made all the arrangements – we'd had a bigger lunch than was normal for us, guests of one of the big concerns in the stock yard, and it was too early for us to eat yet. He'd come for me at eight, we would have a drink in the Blue Room bar, perhaps something to eat, then he would come out with me to Midway.

"Thank you, Danny," I said into the telephone.

"My pleasure," he told me back, "I sure am looking forward to seeing the lady."

I went down to reception, and was happy to find a male clerk had just come on duty. He was discussing the ball games with Elmer.

I did what I had come down to do, hoping I had been as casual, as man-of-the-world about it as I had wanted to be, and that I hadn't gone too red in the face. Yes, the hotel had a nice suite, lucky it was vacant just now in their busy season, three floors down from me, they were sure it would suit my friend.

"Is this to go down on your room account?" the clerk asked.

I knew I went red, very red, then.

"No, no, not to me" – how fast it came out, I wasn't really all that much of a man-of-the-world, "her name is Miss Laurie Gaydon." I was so precise.

The clerk wrote down Miss Laurie Gaydon.

"Yes sir, we'll be happy to have the lady stay with us," he told me, without a trace of what he might have been thinking.

Elmer took me up again in the elevator – the elevator girl was off duty awhile. He regarded me with a new kind of look, or maybe that was my imagination.

"Is she English?" he asked, it wasn't a bit pertinent, just a friendly question from a friend.

"No, she's American," I told him, "I met her in New York, she's coming on a few days holiday – vacation."

"That's nice," he said.

I put the fan on in my room. It had got very warm since I had opened that cable. I would have to take Danny's advice and have air-conditioning in the room. I took my jacket off, and my shoes, and lay back on the bed. It's my favourite position for thinking, and I had a lot of thinking to do now, before I had my bath, my shower, had a shave, and got ready to meet Danny.

There was no doubt I had got well settled in to the American way of life, and I had been very happy here in Chicago. Happy in my work, happy with Danny, with Norm and Cynthia, and with them got very much into a steady routine which was most comfortable; now this cable from New York had thrown me right out of my stride. Yes, I had thought about her a great deal, couldn't remember a day when something hadn't reminded me of her, and now she was coming, as I never had thought she would. I was already terribly thrilled, terribly excited, about it, the very thought of meeting her in just a few hours time had me all warm and sentimental, but somewhere, deep inside me, I was scared too, and with it all I was very confused. I wasn't sure I had wanted to be jolted out of this comfortable manner of living which I liked so much, or was I? I just didn't know.

In the last few months I had got so used to being with Danny, and with Norm and Cynthia, we were so good together and they were so good to me. I had got used to the noise and the bustle, the speed of living, to living in a hotel, to the elevators, to subways, to boulevards, to automobiles, all shapes, all sizes and all colours, to eating in coffee shops, in steak houses. I'd got used to everything, to drug stores, to drive-in movies, to clubs, taverns and joints. Got used to it and loved it, it was all so exciting. But I had never got used to the thought of that lovely woman I had met in New York, and the more she was in my thoughts, the more confused I had got about her.

For a long time, when I had first come to Chicago, I had looked on it all as a dream, a vivid, exciting, delightful, wonderful dream, a frightening dream in a way, but just a dream, something which had been part of me and then gone by, just like a dream. As the weeks went by, I had been getting over it a lot, knowing well that I would never see her again, when suddenly, all the talk of her had brought it all back to me. Perhaps, until that night at Norm's, when I had first heard her called that nickname, I had remembered it all happily, a terrific sensational, romantic adventure with the most beautiful woman in all the world. Then, when I'd heard the stories, I had realised there was a lot that was strange about it, and probably about her. How I felt about it was questionable, sometimes I was even trying to console myself for the adventure. That first night, when we had kissed outside her suite, she had drawn back a little, and I had thought then she wanted me to go in with her, but I had been frightened to follow the invitation, if it was an invitation.

Surely, I had told myself, women don't give you that sort of lead within a few hours of a first meeting. But the more I thought about it, the more I knew it had been such an invitation, and if I hadn't been so scared – often I tried to convince myself I had been too surprised, not too scared – I would have known what a real woman was like, that night, instead of having to wait until the next night.

Was she a real woman, was she tender and romantic, and had I done something to her which no man had ever done to her before, or was she, well was she a nymphomaniac? I had to be very vain to think I had all the glamour that she had fallen for me just like that – they don't even do that in the movies, well only in the Continental movies. When I weighed her up against all the girls I had known, she was a whole lot different to them. But then, in all fairness, she was a whole lot more lovely than any I had ever seen before, much more beautiful, much more warm, much more vital. Perhaps all American women were like Laurie, and I had a false impression of women because most English girls were so very cold. Then, come to think of it, surely there were English nymphomaniacs, must have been, otherwise they would not have phrased a word for them. I could have seen how Lily Lee compared to Laurie, she was nice and I had liked her a lot. I might have got a better idea of American women if I had been warmer with Lily. The trouble was, and I knew this damn well, I wasn't interested in any other women, thinking of Laurie had kept me away from them – any other woman would have seemed ice compared to the heat of that wonderful, beautiful, incomparable, female.

I hadn't thought for one moment she would come to Chicago. I hadn't been surprised even when she had never written – don't kid yourself Lander, for her it had happened and forgotten, for me it had happened also, and would never be forgotten. I had read all the magazines about her, there were always a lot of magazines at Danny's, or at Cynthia's, and I bought a lot myself. Any mention of Delane meant I was a customer, and there was always a lot about her. There had been a lot of photographs of her in Europe, and I had to admit there had been a lot of time when she hadn't been on location, or whatever they call it making films, when she had been round the cities, and the play-places.

I often wondered whether I had been wrong in telling the others about the meeting in New York, whether I had been unfair to her. In a way I was very glad to have told them, and yet, other ways, I was sorry. I hadn't told them it all, but they knew she and I had been lovers for a night, if that is how it could be described, but it had been something sacred, for me at any rate, and I often thought I should have kept the secret. In all truth, I hadn't told them in any sense of bravado, it was just that it had been boiling up inside me and I had wanted to tell them, these people who were my good friends. They had taken it well, in the spirit I had told them, and afterwards, I never heard Norm say a word about her, or against her. Danny did, often, but he meant well, meant to get over to me that it had just been, well, what it had been, and I wasn't to let it upset me or affect me, and I was sure he had done all he had done in the best possible way.

Cynthia had been much more concerned about me, though I don't think she let either Norm or Danny know how much. She had been shocked, of that I was certain, when she had first heard it all from me, but had got over it fast. I could see why she was shocked, to a woman like Cynthia it must be that way, but she and Laurie had a lot in common, and I had reasoned, from the way she and Norm often spoke, and from what she said to me, that she was a sort of nymphomaniac too, but only for her own husband. That was probably it, most women are nympho for the person they love, and now and then someone like Laurie comes along, and then she is all nympho. I really didn't know, and it was affecting me, and had affected me, there was no doubt. It had been an experience I would never forget, and it looked now as if it was to start all over again. Now I thought about it, male that I am, and celibate as I'd been, and a good thing too.

We had a few drinks at Al's bar, and didn't eat. I wasn't hungry, and Danny said he wasn't either. I was too excited to think of eating.

We told Al we were going out to Midway to meet a friend of mine. His eyes lit up, and he must have badly wanted to ask who, but he didn't. We left fairly early and drove out nice and steady. It was hot and sultry and boiling up for a storm. We hardly spoke, Danny concentrating on driving, whilst I was thinking a lot and listening to the radio, hearing Nelson Riddle's wonderful orchestra playing my new favourite melody – "Lisbon Antiqua", and Teresa Brewer telling me to "Believe in love", which could well have been an omen, and put me right in a romantic frame of mind, but then an up and coming gentleman named Elvis Presley sang something hot, which may well have been very romantic for all the girls, but for me wasn't that way. I was in the mood for the beautiful orchestrations of Nelson Riddle, and the lovely Mantovani melodies, and very much in the mood for the supreme creature who must be getting very near to Chicago and to me now, and, wonder of wonders, no longer afraid.

Midway was always busy, Danny told me. The busiest airport in the world, with an average of a thousand planes taking off and landing each day. We were early and stood awhile out in the open, hearing the roar of the powerful engines above us –

"I sure bet there's a dozen and more stacked up there now, waitin' to come in," Danny said, and up there, somewhere, was the angel who was coming down to me.

It was a fascinating sight to see these great planes coming in to land, with their landing lights on full in front of them, like giant fireflies coming in from the dark of the night sky, and now and then, we would hear an even greater roar of engines or scream of jets, from the far end of the runway, and racing across in full view one would take off, lifting slowly, noisily, bound for who knows where.

Danny was puzzled when we got inside the main building.

"No photographers – Delane must be slipping."

It was only then I realised I hadn't told him she was coming in as Laurie Gaydon, wasn't wanting any reception committee obviously, except me. I explained it all, he was still puzzled.

"They'll recognise her," he told me, "she's so darn well known, everyone knows her picture."

I bet him they wouldn't.

"Name it," he said.

"A night out at the Continental."

"Who – you and me?" he asked.

I was confident – "No – all of us – you, me, Laurie, Norm, Cynthia – if it can be arranged."

"You sure as sure have yourself a bet," he came back at once, "it would be even a pleasure to lose that one" –

"I'm glad you think so," I was certain I wouldn't lose.

93

CHAPTER 20

Janice Delane

Almost on ten o'clock the announcement came over – Flight 387 from New York was coming in. My heart beat much faster, I was tense, excited, wanting so much to see her, and still not scared. It had been so long since that night in New York, had she changed about – no, she couldn't have done or she would not be up there in the sky overhead now. Lord, how pent up I was. I think Danny was excited also. I was glad he was with me now.

She looked absolutely wonderful, as I knew she would – startling, devastating, beautiful, the most fascinating woman in all the world. She had a lovely tan – Spain must be all it's cracked up to be, I thought. She was a vision in a smart, un-crumpled white suit, slim short skirt, so that her bare tanned legs, disappearing into brown high-heeled shoes, made her look attractively long-legged. The black wig didn't spoil the effect one bit. She made straight for me when she saw me, her brown eyes sparkling.

"Hi David," she greeted, and flung her arms around me, kissing me softly, strongly, wetly, a long kiss, bringing her body right in with it, so that all the manhood within me was churning up hard, and I wasn't at all sure where we were, and not the least bit worried it was all so public.

I remembered where I was and what I was doing here, remembered too who was with me.

"Danny," I said, as if he didn't already know, "this is Laurie – Laurie Gaydon." He looked a picture, a big grinning picture. "Laurie – meet Danny Erikson."

"Hi Danny – nice to meet you." She didn't seem surprised I had someone with me. For a moment she gave him all the warmth of those big brown eyes, and all the fascination of her vivid personality – I think it rocked him a lot.

"Hi," he answered, "it's my pleasure."

We got her and her baggage in the Buick. Her bags were very smart, all marked with the initials L.G. She sat in the front seat between us, showing a lot of lovely tanned knees – I hoped it wouldn't put Danny off his driving – I knew he'd seen a lot of knees before, though I was sure he had never met anyone like the woman who owned these knees and was now sat close to him, but he drove well, like he always did, in spite of that.

It was as though Laurie and I had never been apart, it was exactly the same as it had been in New York, we were completely together. She was warm, gay, talkative, cuddling up to me, happy, and in great spirits. I was very glad Danny had come along, I needed my left arm to put around this lovely wench, and my hand would have been wasted holding a steering wheel.

I was right about the accommodation, she wasn't booked in anywhere – had left that to me and was pleased at the arrangements I had made.

"That sure is fine David, I want to be near you while I'm here."

I wanted to ask her so many things, but I didn't, not even how long she would be staying in Chicago. I just sat tight alongside her, content to be with her, while she talked and told us how glad she was to be back in Chicago, and how much she missed it when she was away. Danny and I hardly spoke, we listened and hung on to every word.

Elmer met us at the door. I hadn't ever remembered him on duty this late before, but there he was, all smiles and efficiency. I had been right about the interest he had shown when I'd booked the suite, and I was pretty certain he had stayed on duty especially to see the lady who was visiting me – he couldn't even wait for the next day, but perhaps I was wrong, perhaps he did do late duty. Anyhow, whatever it was, he liked what he saw now. He sure was happy to greet Miss Laurie Gaydon, so was the clerk at reception. I had the feeling I had gone up a great deal in their estimation – it does a lot of good, that sort of feeling.

Laurie played up well.

"Anyone would think I was a movie star or something," she told the two of them, "the way you folks are spoiling me."

Danny and I looked at each other and grinned. She certainly was a great girl, and she had knocked two more mere males for a loop – three, I corrected myself, looking at Danny again.

95

She didn't go up to her room just then. She was just a little bit hungry, and was very glad we hadn't eaten, and she would come in and eat with us now. She didn't often eat on a plane – in spite of all the travelling she did, she didn't fly well and rarely ate, now she would like something, after she had been to the powder room. Elmer could take her bags up to her suite.

"Yes Mam, Miss Gaydon," Elmer said, he was happy to do just that.

She liked the Blue Room bar, it was cosy, intimate, she liked that type of place. We sat up to the bar on stools as we always did, only this time we had Laurie in the middle, and if it had been nice before, now it was doubly so, and more and more than that. Al was all smiles.

"This is Al," I told Laurie. "Al, this is Laurie Gaydon."

"Hi, Al," she said, "you have a heavenly place."

He was very pleased – he was thinking hard, I could see that.

"Hi, Laurie," he answered, and then, "an angel like you sure is welcome."

It was her turn to be pleased – she was, so was I. It was exactly what I was thinking about her.

Al served our drinks – scotch-on-the-rocks for Danny, of course, beer for me, and Dubonnet for Laurie. He looked hard at her, I was sure he knew who she was. He smiled when she took the glass. Yes, he knew now. He played it well too.

"Someone I seen reminds me a whole heap of you, Laurie," he told her thoughtfully, "someone I seen in the movies – Janice Delane."

She kept looking at him, taking a little sip of the liquid, she was smiling, a lovely smile.

"She's a honey that Delane," he went on, "she sure is – you ought to go on the movies, Laurie, you sure would be a wow."

I wasn't sure whether I was annoyed or not, but she wasn't at all worried, she kept on smiling.

"Thanks, Al, that's nice – I might try the movies one day."

Danny took up the game –

"Yeah, Al, – now you come to mention it – Delane is kinda like Laurie – not so nice though, and she isn't dark haired like Laurie–"

I took a big gulp of my beer, I didn't know what to say, Laurie did.

"But you won't tell anyone else boys, will you?"

"Cross my heart," Danny said.

"Me too," Al came in.

I wondered what she would say to me, but it didn't seem to have upset her – perhaps she thought they had just recognised her in the normal way.

We did not go into the restaurant – we ate in one of the small alcoves – it was nice. We had prawn cocktails to start with, then prime rib steaks served in butter sauce, rissole potatoes, spinach, and a Blue Room salad. The rib steaks were massive, and I was the only one to manage a dessert afterwards, fruit salad with ice cream, Laurie and Danny settled for coffee.

"Where you put it all," Danny said to me, "sure is a mystery."

He had done well himself, so had Laurie, considering she had only been a little bit hungry. She agreed with me.

"Yes, I eat well, not when I'm travelling though – I enjoy it and it never seems to put any weight on me – my vitals haven't varied for ten years now."

I told her Danny knew who she was, I had been weighing that one up for some time, and that he knew we had met in New York.

"I'm aware he knew me," she said, she turned to Danny – "I sure could see it in your eyes, your whole expression, when we first met – I was right?"

"You sure were right," he was in complete agreement – "it wasn't till we reached Midway that David told me we were meeting you – I reckoned we had gone down to meet Janice Delane."

"You were disappointed?" she asked, and smiled.

"Now, how do you answer that," he said – "no sirree, I'm not disappointed, but I'm in one hell of a spot – I know you but I've only seen Janice Delane's pictures – no, I sure am not disappointed."

"Danny lost a bet with me tonight," I said, "owes us a night out."

"How come?" she asked.

"I was sure enough they'd recognise you on the plane, at the airport, even though you were travelling as Laurie Gaydon," he told her. "I was wrong."

"It's the wig," Laurie said, "it throws them all out of line, though some of them look hard at me, more especially the women, and one or two have even said how like Delane I look, even David did not recognise me the first time in the wig in New York."

"It is the wig," Danny agreed, "but knowing you now – I would recognise you again – "

"Sure you would," she said, "but not many people do – some of the press boys know me for sure in the wig, but they're good guys – well, most of them are good guys – and they hold it for exclusive."

"It is hard, being in the public eye like this," I suggested.

"Oh no, David, it isn't so," she said at once, "I like it – I'm used to it now, but I still like it, but for peace and quiet I just have to wear the wig, or – excuse the modesty gentlemen – I'd be followed everywhere – you have no idea what some of the folks will do."

"Well, I lost my bet tonight," Danny said, "and now I put on the party at the the Continental."

"If you'll come Laurie," I put in quickly.

"You know the Continental – and Taps?" she was surprised.

"We do," I assured her, and I could tell some explaining was necessary – "Al and Taps are old friends, and one night, down there, Taps asked us in to his office where we saw your photograph – it's lovely Laurie – he told us a little bit about you."

She thought a moment. "Nice I hope. Taps knew me when I was just a kid, and when I didn't know a lot about the world. He taught me a lot, how to dance – he's a great man, Taps, they don't come a lot nicer in the business."

"We like him," I told her, "especially when he told us you were the greatest" – I saw her eyes light up – "he's very fond of you Laurie."

"Dear Taps," she said, "I'm fond of him." Then to Danny – "so you have a party at Taps' – will you ask me?" I thought that just a little strange, I had already asked her, but Danny was happy.

"It's in your honour," he beamed at her.

"Well Danny, that's real nice – I'll look forward to it – it will be nice to see Taps again, when will it be?"

"Name the day lady," Danny was really in his element now.

"I'll fix it with David," she said, and it stopped the little jealous feeling which was creeping up on me.

"You do that," said the happy Danny, "it will be my pleasure."

He was a great guy Danny, and I was annoyed at myself for being jealous of him – steady down Lander, I thought, there's no reason for that. We told Al about the party as we were leaving – I saw the look come in his eyes. Laurie must have seen it also.

"You know Taps well, Al?" she asked him.

"I sure do – Laurie," he answered, and I thought for one horrid moment he was going to call her Janice.

"Will you come with us?" Then, to Danny, "It's O.K., isn't it Danny?"

"Sure is O.K. Laurie, anything you say," Danny said.

Al looked at them both, he was beaming, for two pins he would have jumped over the bar and hugged them both – it was a pity I hadn't two pins.

"Will I come – will I? you just try and keep me away. Gee thanks, Laurie, thanks, Danny – it'll be great just great."

Laurie, and Danny, had made his night in a big way, he was still voicing his thanks, ignoring his other customers, as we left.

I went up in the elevator with Laurie. Danny had left us to roll some dice at the Casanova – he said he had enjoyed the night a great deal. He was a great guy. We saw him to the Buick – gosh it had got hot in the streets, from afar I thought I heard the rumbling of thunder.

"Thanks Danny – you've been great," I said.

"I enjoyed it" – the way he was beaming at Laurie, there could be no doubt of that – "listen David, you just take that vacation we been talking about while Laurie's here."

I nearly asked what vacation, we had been planning a week-end somewhere, it was true, but this was different, then I saw what he meant, but he wouldn't let me thank him then.

"Call me tomorrow with the plans," he said. "That's if I'm included."

"You are – I'll call you," I shouted as he roared off. I looked down at Laurie, I was holding her close, hugged to me with my left arm – "that's all right Laurie?" I asked her – the red rear lights of the Buick were way down the boulevard by now.

"You say, darling," she said, "it's O.K. by me."

"Give me thirty minutes, darling," she whispered in the elevator, "then come on down."

The thirty minutes took thirty hours to go by. I got my electric razor out and ran it over my face – it was warm in the bathroom and I thought I ought to have a shower, but I didn't have one – I was afraid I might go one second over that thirty minutes. I looked at my watch a dozen times. Outside I could hear the thunder now, and through the window I could see vivid flashes of lightning, the storm was coming up fast. I had never known time go by as slowly as this. It had been just after ten when we had met her at Midway. She'd been in Chicago three hours and I had only kissed her once. That kiss was still with me, tingling on my lips, but I wanted more, much more.

Laurie was in a powder blue robe – not the one she had worn in New York, this was of lighter material and had no buttons up the front. I closed and locked the door behind me – I took her in my arms – she was on fire, so was I.

I knew just what she was wearing under that robe – a beautiful smooth satin skin, a lot of it burnt bronze by the sun. She pressed herself against me, and I could feel the full length of her all the way down. She couldn't say anything – I was keeping her lips, her mouth, her tongue, too busy. When she did speak I hardly recognised her voice, it was hoarse, agonized.

"Oh David, it's been so long – "

A long time – it had been an eternity, an eternity of aching heart, inactive body, but now she was here, we were together again – now I could be a man once more.

Across the room I saw the open door of her bedroom: I picked her up in my arms, still kissing her, she was so light, so easy, to carry.

I put her down, gently, between the twin beds. With her back to me, she unzipped the robe and let it fall to her feet. My hands reached round her and took full possession of her breasts as I kissed her lovely bronze shoulders. Then slowly, very gently, I turned her round in my arms – she was all bronze, as far as I could see down, except for the two big red cherries I remembered so well. In supreme ecstasy I kissed her again, a long lingering kiss, then went down on one knee, bringing my lips slowly from hers, down her chin, her throat, her chest, to the large exquisite cherry on her left breast. I could feel the tremendous surging within her. She brought her mouth down to my left ear –

"Come home, Daddy," she said, "your house is on fire."

Outside the storm had really started. Inside, my storm which had been boiling up longer than the one outside, had started too, so had Laurie. Just like the forces out-side, which had been let loose and would flash and thunder again and again, so we two inside were let loose, and the forces of nature, which were fusing us, were as power-ful, as wonderful, as natural, as the forces outside – forces which were lighting up the whole city of Chicago.

CHAPTER 21

The Delane Movies

We talked, now and then, far into the morning. Talked about many things what I had been doing, what she had been doing, about her plans for the future.

She was so pleased I was happy here in Chicago. When she had lived here she had always been happy. It was a great city, her city, the city she had sort of grown up in. Here, in Chicago, she had started her career, she loved it, always had and always would, more than any other city in the world.

"More than New York?" I asked.

"Much, much more, for sure."

"I like New York," I told her, "like it a lot."

"You do, David?" she was surprised, "you were only there a short time you said."

"Two whole days," I agreed, "but I liked it, that's where I met you."

She was so pleased. I felt the pleasure of that remark all over her body.

"That's sweet," she said, and she climbed up a little in my arms to give me her open mouth.

We didn't talk for quite some time after that.

She was interested in Danny – he seemed a good guy. I tried to tell her just how good. I told her of Norm and Cynthia – she was so glad they had looked after me and was looking forward to meeting them, especially Cynthia – she must be a real hen turkey the way I spoke about her. Sure she didn't mind them being in on Danny's party down at the Continental, all my friends were her friends. She liked having folks around at parties – she loved a crowd, just so long as it wouldn't be crowded afterwards – she had come to see me remember.

It was my turn to kiss her for that.

Sure she had come to see her father as well. She hadn't seen him for a year now. perhaps she didn't come to see him often enough. She would telephone him and arrange to take me to see him. We would spend a couple of days up there, in the big house in Apple River Canyon, a wonderful place really in lovely country, about a hundred, one hundred and fifty miles away. I would be sure to like it there, and I would be sure to like her father too. It was such a lovely place – High Point they had named it. Like everyone else who knew it, I would be sure to wonder why she didn't stay up there all the time, it was that beautiful.

That gave me the chance to ask the question which had been on the tip of my tongue ever since I had met her at Midway.

How long was she staying?

"Seven days, darling, a whole week."

She was enthusiastic to have so long a vacation, but to me it was a very short time.

"Five days down here with you, David, and two up at High Point, with you and my father. He'll be longing to see me – I'm so cruel to him – I just don't ever write" – that was something I already knew – "just think of it, seven whole days, darling, with you."

I still knew that seven days would go by so fast.

I loved the way she told me about her films, we had such fun.

The movie she had just made would be a sensation – she hoped I would be able to go to the big opening night with her, but I hadn't much time to think about the cheering crowds, all wondering who the man was Janice Delane had with her, and the T.V. men, the reporters, the camera men, and the searchlights of that wonderful night, nice as it was to think of.

The movie was so true to life, they had decided on the title – The Searing Heat. It was about the Spain of two hundred years ago, or a hundred years one or the other. She was a Spanish Princess, a woman of very great beauty – that was true to life anyway – she was proud, fearless, a dominant woman, who ruled the surrounding territory with a rod of iron. Everyone was frightened of her, everyone. One day, in a great storm, a British man-of-war had been wrecked on the coast not far from her castle, and the villagers had rescued one man, a young officer, from the sea, had nursed him back to health, and now he had fallen in love with one of the village maidens – this was so true to life, they always rescue only one man, and it always has to be an officer, officers have all the luck. She laughed when I told her that, and said not always, and when I thought of that and where I was just then, I knew she was right, but she wanted me to be quiet so she could get on with the story, and after we had kissed a while, she went on.

Of course one of her trusted servants had got to hear of this and had brought the news to her. This made her very angry and rightly so. It was her rule that everything thrown up on the coast belonged to her – she had made that rule and she did mean everything – so one day, when all the villagers were out fishing – the men anyhow, she sent this trusted servant and a couple more down to the village to bring back the British officer. They were good servants, they brought him back all right, even though they had to beat up a few women and kids in the doing.

"It sure is a great scene, darling, when the officer sees me for the first time. Sure he hadn't wanted to come, he'd fallen hard for the village girl, who wouldn't, those British officers were at sea for years at a time, they say, but when he sees me, he falls for me at once."

That would be true to life also, no village maiden I had ever seen could have stood a chance with this woman, and even if they had, British officers are not fools, they would have appreciated Laurie just as much as I was appreciating her now. I told her how very true to life that part was, and that pleased her a lot.

When the village men got back from the sea and discovered what had gone on, they were real angry. Princess Donita – that was her name – had gone too far this time, she had gobbled up a lot of the young men in her time, and now, it had to end. To the castle they marched, led by the maiden's brother and goaded on by all the women of the village – all the village women hated the Princess – that would be a great scene also where Laurie and her officer watched the villagers all coming up the mountains to attack the castle. The attack had been beaten back, and a lot of the villagers had been killed, but, in the attack, the British officer had been fatally wounded.

"He dies in my arms, darling" (they always do, I knew that) "he takes a long time to die" (I knew that also) "and afterwards, over his grave, I swear eternal vengeance on that village. It's such a wonderful scene, David, we had to do it so many times before Richard – the Director – would say O.K."

Then she and her men descend on the village that night. The village is taken by surprise, and they burn it to the ground, and she lets her men do what they like with all the village women, except just the one girl, the maiden the officer had been in love with. The Princess has her roped, and she is taken back to the castle to be given to the Princess's half-wit brother – we hadn't heard of him before – a great oaf of a man who has to be kept under lock and key, and who has got rather lonely, hence the village maiden. On the way back to the castle, the procession passes the grave of the dead officer – Henry his name was – and the Princess is stricken with remorse. Suddenly she knows that a British officer would not want any village maiden to be given to a half-wit oaf, even if he is the brother of a Princess, so Donita lets the maiden go, and afterwards becomes a lot more friendly to the villages around.

It seemed wonderful, and I enjoyed every minute of it. It was really romantic, her films were all romantic, and it would be in full colour and on the new wide screens which were just coming in, and she would look glorious, of that I was very certain.

"Course, darling, it takes much longer than I've taken telling you" – and that had taken quite some time with all the interludes we'd been having – "there is one scene where Henry and me go bathing in the mountain lake, you sure must know they didn't have bathing costumes two hundred years ago, so we just bathed in the costumes we had to start with. I guess they'll cut that a bit in England and over here, but in France and Italy and Spain, and places like that, it will be O.K. That's why I'm so tanned, darling, we sure had to do a lot of sun bathing for that scene."

She'd seen the rushes, and thought them wonderful. Spain was wonderful, sure it was cold when they first got there, some of the scenes were in winter, and she hated the cold, hated it here in America even, where at least they did have proper heating, and she hadn't liked Spain. But it was wonderful in the spring-time and in summer, and she'd simply loved it then.

She was so happy that I agreed with her. The Searing Heat was bound to be a great success. It was easy for me to agree, all her films were always a great success, they couldn't miss, and the formula for success was always the same. Plenty of her, plenty of love, passion, frenzy, hate, jealousy, plenty of fighting and killing, plenty of everything the film goers love and pay plenty of money for all over the world. Added to that, of course, I was in the right place and the right mood to appreciate the telling, holding the heroine close in my arms through it all. Even if we couldn't go bathing in the mountain lake in the altogether, we could do a lot of things even more wonderful, and I didn't have to worry about a horde of Spanish villagers coming and killing me, at least I hoped not.

Her next film, the one which she was soon going off to make, would be equally sensational. This was to be a story of Japan at the end of the Second World War, and she played the part of an American nurse – an officer to be sure. One day the American General visited the hospital and saw her. He fell in love with her at sight – again so true to life – arranged that they should meet again, and she eventually fell in love with him. He took her away somewhere, up in the mountains – there always had to be mountains, Spain, Japan, everywhere – to a beautiful little shack he knew about, neglecting his duty, neglecting his military duty at any rate – and something happened down at the Base whilst he was away with her – even American Generals can't be everywhere at once, though it seemed to me he was in the place where the right things were happening – and there was one hell of a row about it, because the Crown Prince was murdered, or something like that – I could imagine the one hell of a row. The General was taken back to the States in disgrace, to be court-martialled, and the nurse hitched a lift on a plane and got to the court just in time to say what a wonderful General he was, and to plead, in her wonderful pleading style, for him. How it was all to end she just didn't know, they hadn't decided on that yet, and they hadn't titled it either, but it would be just great, all filmed on location in Japan, and the entire company were going off just as soon as she joined them the next week.

The Japan story sounded marvellous also, and it was wonderful to think that right at this moment I was her American General – I had only been a second-lieutenant when I had done my National Service in the British Army – and she was my nurse. I liked the sort of uniform my American nurse was wearing, it suited her so, all-over bronze and cherries, and I was certain a lot more American Generals would be court-martialled if they were all like Laurie – the American nurses, I mean.

I was in great form, often chipping in with what I thought was something funny. Sometimes she laughed and then I would laugh too. We had great fun, and sometimes she would get just a tiny bit cross, but only for a second or so, and once, when I said something, she replied – "nuts" – with great scorn.

"Whose nuts?" I asked.

'You sure are," scorn all gone and laughing.

"I sure am, about you," I agreed, holding her tighter now.

"Oh, darling," she said, melting all over me until she was pure liquid love.

Later she was more serious, more serious for quite some time. She just knew The Searing Heat would be good, all those connected with it were so very satisfied and she herself was. The settings, the cast, had been just what she required, and she had given her very best to it – there could be no possible doubt, it would be great. She very badly wanted the new movie, the one about the General and the nurse, to be the best she would ever make, badly wanted that. It could be her last.

This was a great surprise to me. I had read a lot about her and her films, so many articles written by the best film writers, not just the more romantic stuff, but the real story of her, and all, without one exception, had agreed that she was right at the very peak of her career. Never lovelier than now, at her best as an actress, and there was no reason at all why her films should not continue to be money-spinners for many years to come. Now she talked of the next being her last.

"Often, David darling, I get so tired of roaming about the world on my own" – I couldn't be the slightest bit ungallant about that, it was true I had never ever seen a picture of her on her own, always there was an escort, and recently there had been this one particular escort in Europe, but she had told me this with such sincerity, and it must be true.

"I sure have got to the point now where I want to stay put somewhere, and just be content and relaxed." Great actress as she was, she wasn't acting now, absolutely true – perhaps she is going to marry this Italian Count, I thought, and this is her way of telling me, but it couldn't be that, she couldn't tell me a thing like that at this time, and in this situation.

Going up to High Point to see her father always made her feel this way, but this time – "please believe me, David" – it was much more than it had ever been before. She ought to get married – again, perhaps this was the Count, or – no, that was too unbelievable, even though it made me gasp for breath, it could be me – ought to get married again, and settle down at High Point – maybe she would, she was thinking hard about it for sure. She was so confused about it – she had tried marriage before – "You surely know that, darling?" – and they hadn't worked, but she was older now, mature, had the success she had then craved for, and which had so affected the other marriages, though she had to admit she hadn't picked as wisely as she could do now.

"I could still make one film a year, David, and have High Point, and a husband, always to come back to – have a home, and a man." Why all this, was I the man? Was she really then in love with me? Oh no, that couldn't be, surely, even in my wildest dreams it couldn't be me.

"Happiness is something I haven't had a lot of, David – yes, I know what they say, I have this, and I have that, I have money, fame, I have travelled, but honestly, darling, I haven't known a lot of real happiness, sure I know whose fault it is, I sure know that, but even now it isn't too late."

I held her close to me again. We were both warm, warm and moist in our perspiration of love.

"I can't have children, David–"

She must have known the effect that would have on me, and I knew she hadn't said it in case I was worried in any way. She went quiet – I didn't speak. I didn't really know what to say. After a while she went on – "It was when I was married to Arthur, Arthur Parker. Something went wrong inside and they cut all the mother out of me – they do these things to women, David."

I had a vague suspicion they did, but how they did and why they did had never bothered me, nor had I ever known anyone it had happened to, until now. She didn't tell me any more, and I still didn't want to think about it, especially about her.

"I sure do love children – perhaps it's because I can't have them that I love them so much – if I get married again – I shall adopt some – up at High Point I could have lots up there – you'll see when we go there."

Remembering again what I had read of her, this was a new side to her. I had never seen a photograph of her with children.

"I've seen a lot of children all over the world, all sizes, all colours, they're so lovable when they're children, it's only when they grow up that colour and everything is wrong. It would be just fine staying stable with a real man – at High Point, and having lots of kids up there."

For some reason, even though she was here in my arms, and had given me so much of herself, I had the feeling that she wasn't telling me all this to prepare me for marriage and for High Point – it wasn't for me at all – it seemed so very strange.

"I'm growing old, darling, rising thirty-three" – this did surprise me a lot, I had got my arithmetic about her age sadly wrong somewhere, and had the impression she was about twenty-six – "I sure don't want to be old, old and lonely."

Now I could say something, could say exactly the right thing. She certainly wasn't in any way old. I made sure she knew what I thought about that.

"Nonsense, darling," I told her, "absolute nonsense. You're eternally young, you're the most wonderful, beautiful, glamorous young woman in all the world."

"You're sweet, David, so sweet and so very good for me," she said, so softly and so very nicely, and how could I be other than proud and vain and happy, when she spoke this way, this bronzed super lovely woman, the most adorable creature of all time?

She moved her left arm slowly across my chest to my right shoulder, pulling herself up, with my help, on top of me. Her mouth came down on mine. I held her steady above me for a minute while she did what she wanted to do, then my hold on her tightened. Outside the storm had long since passed over, but here, inside, our storm was still with us, had not decreased in its intensity, but was more wonderful, more awe-inspiring, more beautiful, than before.

CHAPTER 22

The Heat Is On Again

She fell asleep before I did, breathing evenly, gently, alongside me. I was happy and content, relaxed and even refreshed by the glory of loving her, and what it had done for me.

I could sense now how deeply I had been affected by her, and the experience with her, in New York. I knew now that I had not really been myself the whole time I had been here in Chicago, knew that right deep down inside me I had become a different person because of her.

All my life I had been easy-going, content, happy and care-free. Life for me had been gay, merry, easy, and with no real worries. Everything had always gone well for me, there was no reason why that cheerful state should not continue for ever. I had a good job, excellent prospects, nothing could go wrong. I'd had some girl friends, of course, all men have them. Adventures also, happy, to me they had always been happy and light affairs into which I had not got too deeply involved, not even with Jenny Denton, with whom I had been more serious than with anyone else. Not too serious, because Jenny was a career girl first, and a woman second. She could be a lovely woman, had been for me, but I was sure she preferred the power she undoubtedly held in her job to the power over one man marriage would bring.

That was how I had regarded life, and the way in which I had regarded love. Then, in New York, I had met Laurie Gaydon, met her in the same way as a lot of men meet a lot of women, expectantly, eagerly, with an air of high adventure, well aware of what a woman was, and what they could do for a man, and do to a man. That she was very lovely, the like of which I had never seen before, meant nothing out of the ordinary. She was a woman and I was a man. It would be the same as it had been before, nicer perhaps, but that was all.

How very wrong I had been. How very little I knew, and what a lot there was to learn, and how quickly I had learned. Laurie had been, without doubt, a terrific surprise to every one of my senses – I could not, at first, say she was a shock to me, because I was with her then, and the thrill of her, the enjoyment of her, drove away all other thoughts, or would not, just then, let them enter into my brain. She was unbelievably beautiful, tremendously warm, had terrific charm, and she was easily the most sexually possessive woman I had ever known – in fact, much more so than I had ever imagined in any woman. That had been the surprise, that I could meet a woman of such wondrous beauty, so very famous, so, well – so out of reach really, and yet, within twenty-four hours of knowing her almost, we were lovers, and she was what she was, a woman of great sexual energy.

As soon as we had parted, I think, the surprise began to develop into something deeper, but not yet to shock. In the weeks that followed I had much time to think about her, and think of my experiences with her. I did a great deal of reading about her, anything, everything, about Janice Delane was of interest to me. Weighing it all up, thinking back to what had happened with her, looking at the many photographs, reading the many stories, of her, I could not but realise that she was a very unusual woman. Either that, or I had led a very, very sheltered life. That was reasonable, reasonable to my way of life. I had looked at many a girl, thank God there are so many who are worth looking at, and always there had been a hope of complete harmony while my thoughts ran riot, if only for a very brief second. That must be so with every man. But, even in my wildest thought riots I had never ever expected to achieve what I had done with Laurie. That, to me, just wasn't the way of a man with a woman. I gave it all a lot of thought, deep within me, and never letting it out to the new friends in this new life of mine. After a while the whole thing eased a lot, and I began to forget her; after all, I would never meet her again.

Yes, I was getting over meeting her, would probably have done so, would probably have shown interest in other women, although with Cynthia always in the party, I did not seem to need women. Then came the shock, that night at Norm's, when we had spoken of her in the way he had. Norm could have had no idea of how deep the wound went in that night. I shouldn't have let him speak that way, I should have got up at once and told him he was wrong, that he was insulting a very fine and lovely woman, but I couldn't do that, just couldn't, couldn't, because, little enough as I knew about the meaning of the word, she had been, well she had been, that way with me. The confusion now was awful and the shock was hard to take.

Danny had rubbed it in, rubbed it in hard and often, every possible opportunity, and I had never even got up and roared at him to stop, never tried even to make him see the good side of her. What a coward I was. Yes, the shock was there inside me, and I did not know how to feel about her. Whether to be glad I had known her, if only for a passing moment, or whether to be very male and think that I could have done with a little more of her time, or whether to be sorry for her. I just did not know.

Of course, not knowing what to do made me worry. Like the shock, the worry was kept inside, and now I had the added worry that I should not have told the others, good friends as they were, what I had told them about her and of our meeting.

It was all so silly really to worry this way. It did no good. Life was still good to me. I had everything a man could want, or almost everything, good friends, work I was happy and interested in, comfortable living, social contacts, and I could have had anything else I wanted. It was certainly not for want of opportunity, nor for the want of Danny wishing it for me.

Danny had long wanted me to have an automobile of my own. Have it on the firm he often told me. Go and get one, or let him get one for me, find myself a girl, have yourself a time. Cynthia too, after I had told them of Laurie, was like Danny, and had given me a few gentle hints that a romantic adventure with some nice young woman would do me much more good than harm. But I hadn't wanted any romance, firstly, because I was so content to go about with the three of them, and secondly, because of the feeling for Laurie deep within me.

Danny had done more than talk about me finding a girl, he had found one for me. I had a fair idea why we went round to the Casanova Club so often, and knew he was pushing me hard at Lily Lee. He was pushing her at me, and it could have been great fun. Lily was very attractive, pleasant and terribly friendly, and I was pretty well certain there could have been a romantic dalliance with her without a lot of rope around my neck. Whatever I had thought and felt about Laurie, I had not failed to see the invitation in Lily's eyes, when we had sat close together many a long hour, talking happily together

111

about so many things, everything we could talk of but romance, and the invitation had been in her voice in many of the songs I had asked her to sing, and she had sung for me. But, I hadn't accepted the invitation, hadn't wanted to, and the reason, of course, was Laurie. I had grown very friendly with Lily, but in much the same way as I was with Cynthia, and, I think, being platonic with Lily had made her more keen on me than she ought to have been.

So hard as I had tried not to show it, hard as I had tried not to acknowledge it, the anxiety of her had been there inside me, had waned a lot, and then had waxed tremendously as I had worried about the stories of her being a nymphomaniac. It had developed into a type of neurosis, and that was a horrible thought, something I didn't know the ins and outs of, and that began to worry me even more.

Now the cause of it all was with me again, and I no longer had any thought of all the worry she had been to me. There was no anxiety, no neurosis, no nothing, only that she was here, beautiful as I had known she was, as warm as I had known her before. Warm – warm wasn't enough – she was heat itself, soft, radiant heat, loving and possessively demanding. There was no doubt about her any more, she was a nymphomaniac with me – a nymphomaniac for certain, or there isn't such a woman, and the loveliest there has ever been, and I was so happy she was lavishing all this loveliness on me.

So I had cast off the worries, the inward thoughts and the inward doubts. I knew her for what she was, and I was gay, happy and content, back to what I had been before I had known her, before that first contact with her in New York. I was happy now to be part of her life, part of her love-life. I would enjoy it and take what I could.

I knew what the trouble had been. When we had first met in New York, I had fallen violently in love with her – that had been the worry, that had been the neurosis. Now she was back with me and I didn't think I was in love with her, but I was in love with what went with her, and, in any case, I had given over worrying, at least that was I thought now.

She stirred a little in her sleep and I hoped, for a moment, she was going to come awake. But she slept on, moving round a little so that her back was cosily against my front. I put my arm around her middle and went peacefully, happily, to sleep.

She woke me out of a deep sleep about ten o'clock. She looked radiant in the powder blue robe, and I knew how lucky I was to have a woman such as she to play games with. I hadn't felt her get out of

bed, she hadn't wanted to wake me then. She'd taken a shower –
Americans always take things – they never have them like we do –
and had been up half an hour.

"I've ordered coffee and fruit juice," she told me, "lots of it."

"Lots of it?"

"Yes, lots, I ordered for two."

She saw the look on my face, it must have been expressive – she
laughed.

"Surely you can come and take coffee with me – there's no harm
in that."

I suppose there wasn't, but then, suddenly, I thought of something
else, and I groaned, out loud and very miserably.

"What is it David?" she asked. I must have looked as horrified as
I felt.

"I hung the 'don't disturb' notice on my door last night, but I
forgot to cancel my early call."

I had an arrangement with the reception desk for an early morning
call at six-thirty a.m. every weekday morning, and could well
imagine how that telephone bell had been ringing that morning.

She caught on fast, and laughed again, a lovely laugh making me
quite certain that it was very amusing to her even if it wasn't that way
to me. Like me, she knew just how the brains trust down at reception
would be wondering, for a while, why I wasn't answering, then,
certain as could be, they would think of the suite three floors down,
and it would be all very plain and most obvious. The women were
on duty in the early morning, and women think of these things, and
really, they couldn't miss. Laurie saw it all so clearly, as I did, and
kept on laughing. She was loving it, the expression on my face must
have been a big help to her.

"You know what?"

"What?" I asked.

"They'll know you are a big boy now."

I had to laugh then, she said it so very nicely, and if she wasn't
worried about it, and she obviously wasn't, why should I worry? As
she said, they would think of me as a real big boy, and I knew I would
go up in their estimation, not down, in a way and that did my ego
good, so I laughed.

I heard someone in the outer room – it was a boy with the coffee
and the fruit juice. She brought the big tray in and put it on the bed.

"You haven't a robe," she said.

113

I hadn't, but I could have put some clothes on and gone into the other room. From what she had said about the robe, I knew I hadn't to do that.

The fruit juice was very refreshing, the coffee good, and hot, and strong.

We drank and talked awhile. It was so good to be with her just like this. Behind our talk the radio was playing just the sort of music I like.

"That's beautiful," I said.

"Sure is," she agreed – "I think it's Jackie Gleason – it is nice – Music for the Love Hours, he calls it."

"That's nice, and appropriate," I told her softly.

She looked at me and smiled. If ever I saw love and passion in a woman's eyes, I saw it now in those warm brown eyes of hers. The music played on – sweet, haunting music, thrilling violins – playing melodies I knew. "Serenade in Blue", and "Our Love", and others just as haunting. I had finished my coffee – no, I didn't want any more – she knew what I wanted now.

She took the tray away, as she came back in the room, she paused at the window.

"It sure will be warm today outside," she said.

She came to the side of the bed – the violins were really haunting now – wonderful, inspiring music – she pulled the sheet down a little way and looked at the top half of me.

"Comfortable?" she asked, and her smile was beautiful, sparkling even in her big brown eyes.

"Nice," I replied, I was so enjoying this heavenly prelude.

She leaned over and kissed me, very gently, at first. Easily, slowly, carefully, I slid down the zip of her robe, down as far as I could, and still kissing me she stepped out of it. My eyes were closed but I knew exactly what she looked like, knew the full glory of all her womanly beauty. My right hand tenderly took her left breast, hanging down, in its palm, then sweetly caressed the cherry in time to the music, slow, heavenly music – music for the love hours. Our lips, our mouths, never lost contact as she came on down to me.

It was very warm indeed – even in this air-conditioned room.

CHAPTER 23

Invitation To A Ball Game

We were eating brunch in the restaurant, scrambled eggs, bacon, toast and coffee, when Elmer came looking for me. His eyes lit up as he saw me, saw us together, I could tell he was thinking what a lucky guy I was, and I bet he knew where I had been all morning. A lady wanted me on the house telephone. I excused myself to Laurie and followed Elmer.

It was Poppy at first, for a few moments. She hoped I was enjoying my vacation. I grinned hugely and wondered what she would have said if I told her just how happy I was, but I couldn't adequately have described it, so didn't upset her. Then Danny came on – he hoped I was O.K.

"Good," he said, when I told him just how O.K. I felt. "I got news. Norm's got some tickets for the ball game tonight, can you make it, you and Laurie?"

We could make it, we hadn't made any plans so far, and we expected to see Danny and the others.

"That's just great," Danny said, "we'll collect you – half after six – O.K.? Now, hold on David – Cynthia's here, she wants to talk with you."

"David," Cynthia had a nice voice, "How are you?"

I could have told Cynthia more easily than I could Poppy, but I would have had to be near Cynthia when I told her, to see how she really took it.

"Wonderful – just wonderful," that was just the way I was.

"We want to see her," Cynthia went on, "don't keep her to yourself too much."

I was a bit puzzled, it didn't fit in.

"You're coming to the baseball tonight?" I asked.

"Of course, David, that's why I called – we'll have supper back at our place afterwards, something cold but nice, if you would like to come."

"That's lovely of you, Cynth," I told her, it was funny the way she let me shorten her name, she wouldn't allow anyone else, not even Danny, to call her that – "certainly we'll come."

"You're sure?"

"We're sure," Cynthia's a great hostess and I was sure Laurie would like her very much – I hoped Cynthia liked Laurie.

"I'm so glad," she said, "I do so want to meet her – so does Norm" – I could bet money on that – "he says hi – 'bye David, we'll see you."

I went back to Laurie, she'd had my meal kept hot. She was pleased to hear we were going to the baseball, she liked the game, and was glad about the arrangements afterwards. She looked forward to meeting Cynthia and Norm.

"I envy Cynthia, I haven't known a real settled marriage – I guess I've missed a great deal."

"I think Cynthia probably envies you a lot more than you envy her," I said, "with your films and your clothes, and your travelling" –

"I'm sure not," she argued, "they're not everything."

I agreed they might not be everything, but they were a lot, even to Cynthia, and to most other women they would seem everything. There must be millions who would change places with Laurie.

"You're right, David, in a way, but you know how I mean it."

I was beginning to know how she meant it, and I certainly had to confirm that Norm and Cynthia were very happily married. We refilled our coffee, we were in no hurry to go anywhere, and it was nice and cool in the restaurant.

Laurie was very thoughtful, and serious.

"The trouble with marriage is that women are getting far too dominant. We have much more freedom nowadays, and, especially here in the States, we have possibly over-developed in that sort of way, if you see what I mean."

I saw what she was meaning, and told her. I was quite content to listen to her. I was with her, very close to her, and that was all that was important just for a while. "I'm sure God made men to dominate women," she went on, "and that was fine. But, we've grown out of that, none of us are happy to play a supporting role, certainly I never have been."

I didn't really agree with that. I knew a few, I thought, who were well content to play support, just as long as they could make their presence felt once in a while, Cynthia for instance, but I didn't say anything, didn't interrupt her train of thoughts and what she was saying.

"Me now, I've always had too much of my own way, too much freedom, I know that for sure. I'm too excitable, too dominating, and it's not good for a woman to be that way. I should have met someone real strong, someone who would have run me, but I never did, nobody ever tried to dominate me, perhaps, if I'd had someone who would beat me now and then, it might have been different."

I didn't think she was acting it, it sounded very sincere. I suppose all women have these sort of phases, and remote thoughts, and to a woman like Laurie who had always, as she said, had things go her way, it probably sounded good, but I could think a lot of women would argue with her for a long time. I thought she was going to ask me if I would beat her, but she didn't, and I was glad. I didn't want to beat her, I just wanted to love her, I was just like all the other men in her life. Perhaps she was right. I didn't know.

CHAPTER 24

The Ball Game

I had long looked forward to my first baseball game. Norm, a great baseball enthusiast, had often talked about the thrills of the game, had told me a lot about the rules, and, of course, now and then I had seen a bit of baseball in films, so I wanted no urging when Danny had told me about Norm having tickets. It was all the more pleasing that Laurie would be along with us.

Norm and Cynthia loved their baseball, and went to as many of the big games as they could. I knew that one of the local teams, the one we were to see that night, was the Chicago White Sox, and I had been aware, over the past two or three weeks, of the rising interest in the series of games they were now playing against the New York Yankees.

I was intrigued by the system whereby the visiting team, in this case, the Yankees, came to play a series of games, not just one, against the home team. Some games would be played in the afternoons, some in the evenings. It was to be, without any doubt, a fiesta of baseball, and I had seen, as the time for the coming of the Yankees approached, how the baseball fever had mounted everywhere. It could be seen in all the newspapers, I could sense it down at the factory where everyone talked and read baseball nowadays. I had sensed it in the restaurant – now baseball was an extra course with the menu. Everyone talked baseball, Norm especially, but Cynthia talked it, so did Danny, and Al, and Elmer, everyone, everywhere.

Norm knew all there was to know about the game, he had told me he knew as much about baseball as he knew about cans, so he knew a lot. He knew the rules, and he knew all the players by name, not only those of the White Sox, but every other team in the American league, and in the National league too. He knew those of today, those of yesteryear, and those who would be the stars of tomorrow. He was the number one baseball enthusiast of all time, and a walking encyclopedia of the game, all rolled into one, and he had made very sure I knew how good a game a ball game could be.

Laurie knew quite a lot about the game, and she had met some of the Yankees, last year somewhere, so it made the evening all the more interesting. We asked Elmer what the form was about the two teams, he was nearly as enthusiastic as Norm.

"You goin' to the ball game t'night then?" he asked, and his eyes lit up when I told him we were.

"You sure are lucky, you two, could be a great ball game t'night."

We gathered that the Yankees were doing very well this season, were above the Sox in the league table. The Sox had improved recently, after a shaky start, and playing against the Yankees always brought out the best in them.

"Yessir," Elmer told us, "the Sox sure should knock them Yankees for a loop t'night, they sure could, and I sure hope they do – you'll see a ball game t'night, and that's for sure."

That afternoon Laurie added a lot to what I already knew about the game. She had got excited and the baseball fever was with her. We spent the afternoon sunbathing on a very crowded beach not far from the hotel. No one recognised her, of course, the black wig and the sun-glasses made sure of that, but the bikini she wore didn't hide a lot of her glorious bronzed body, and I was aware of the admiring looks she got from many of the males. My white body must have looked pretty conspicuous against her, and she was very careful to rub my back, and chest, arms and shoulders, and legs, with oil. She didn't want me to burn, not there on the beach anyhow.

"You prepared for a late night?" Danny asked when he collected us. We were. I saw his eyes light up when he saw Laurie, she looked a picture, black wig, bronzed face and legs, red suit with white trimmings, and red high-heeled shoes, again sort of edged with white, and if you thought that black, bronze, red and white didn't go together, they really did with her.

We drove round for Norm and Cynthia. Cynthia looked good too, in a cream suit and a mauve jacket, which suited her beautifully. We hadn't time for anything but the introductions, but right from the start, as it always is in America, it was Laurie and Norm and Cynthia, just as though they had known each other for years.

Norm was keyed up already. He told us that the Sox would win, he was sure of that. I said, with my thoughts on football back home,

119

that the advantage should be with the home team.

"Sure is," Norm agreed, "but it doesn't always apply. Sure the home team should win, they bat last and they know what they have to do, the coach should be able to dictate the play, but it doesn't always work out, that's for sure."

I learned a little more about the game from that. The away team always took the first innings. Then, as I already knew, when the away team were out, the home team went in to bat, and so on, until nine innings each had been completed. If there was no result then they went on until there was. Sometimes a baseball match went on a long time.

"I sure don't think you'll be bored tonight, David," Norm said, and from the way he looked now, the way even Danny was getting excited, and with two luscious girls like Laurie and Cynthia with us, I just couldn't help thinking he was right. I would not be bored.

It was great. They had me out at Comiskey Park early so that I wouldn't miss any part of it. We were in our seats more than half an hour before the game was due to commence, and already this vast park, the home of the Chicago White Sox, was nearly full. We had good seats, Norm had paid three dollars, fifty cents, for each of them.

"Everyone has a seat," Norm had to shout at me to get above the roar of the crowd, "there's no standing, well – not until someone scores a home run, then the whole darn place stands up."

I was in the centre of the five of us, the place of honour, with Laurie on my right, and Danny next to her, Cynthia on my left with Norm on the outside of her.

"Norm, darling, no fighting," I heard Cynthia tell him.

"Does he fight?" I was very surprised.

"Fight?" though she was right alongside me she had to talk loud, "does he fight?" she gripped my arm in her excitement, "he's terrible at the ball games – sometimes I just don't know why I come with him – you just see."

Norm just grinned at me, and winked.

Danny leaned across Laurie to speak –

"This sure is a hard game, like every other game, they want all the luck they can get, it's all luck and temperament. If they could all do what the crowd tell them to do, it sure wouldn't be a game at all – you just watch this crowd, boy."

I was watching the crowd, it was terrific entertainment. The vendors were all hard at work and all doing a roaring business.

Whatever they were selling, beer, nuts, hot-dogs, ice-creams, cokes, the crowd bought plenty, trade was very good. Danny, Norm and I had a beer as soon as we could get one, it was poured into a cardboard container, with the vendor retaining the bottle. Norm shouted an explanation.

"These don't hurt, bottles do. If they let the crowds have the bottles, there would be murder done at most games, you'll see, David."

We had another beer just before the game commenced. I liked it, even here ice-cold beer, just the way I liked it. We had hot-dogs as well with this beer. Laurie and Cynthia had cokes and hot-dogs. Laurie, like me, was loving it. She'd probably seen a lot of baseball games, but never seen one this way before. She was very happy, talking away, shouting almost, to Danny and I, calling me darling which was wonderful, and leaning over me to shout something to Cynthia and to Norm. She held my hand, then put her arm through mine, we sat as close together as was possible, and when she leaned to talk to Cynthia, she kissed me in full view of the others, and the whole stadium for that matter, and it was all so very, very wonderful.

The floodlights came on, it was magic, a breath-taking sight. The great crowd, banked high all around this vast stadium, the green sward below us, a beautiful lush green in the brilliance of the lights, save for the diamond itself, the track along which the batters would race for dear life once they had struck. It was tremendous, with the crowd, the air full of excitement, and the tension still rising. Below us the players were limbering up, I watched all their gymnastics, their throwing, their catching, missing nothing. I was very excited now, the beer, the crowd, the atmosphere, had got me going. I had been excited at football matches at home, but never like this. It was terrific, it was sensational.

It never let up all night, not one little bit, nor did the crowd. I got a great kick out of the crowd. The Romans at their feasts, no matter who they threw to the lions, no matter who won their chariot races, could not have bettered, nor worsened, this crowd. They roared, they howled, they booed, they hissed, they applauded, screamed, shouted, whistled, moaned, groaned, cursed, stood up, sat down, swayed and cheered. I loved every part of it, would not have wanted to miss one minute of it. The more exciting the play got, the more beer the vendors sold, the more beer they sold, the more the crowd roared, the more the crowd roared, the more exciting it all became, up here in the stands, down there on the field.

I had never seen this kind of rivalry before, it was raw, spiteful, vicious, and with a lot of hate thrown in for good measure. It put every football match I had seen at home, even the most bitter local derby, in the old ladies tea-party class. The fights were legion, and together with the rows and the arguments, were not confined to the field. The crowd grew fighting mad, it all started down there on the field when one batter, who had nearly had his brains bashed out by what seemed from up here a deliberate pitch at his head, made straight for the pitcher. There was no mistaking the menacing attitude, and immediately a free for all lasting several minutes, and involving players, managers, coaches, was on. It spread right through the crowd with amazing speed. Just near us at least three fights had commenced, and I heard Cynthia bawling something at Norm, hanging on to him with all her might. Laurie was hugging me in her excitement, and just to her right, Danny looked to be in a terrific argument with somebody. It was absolutely terrific. The crowd kept on roaring, roared their approval, or disapproval, whichever side they were on, at the players, or at some section of the crowd fighting, then they found they were thirsty and roared for more beer, then roared some more because of the beer.

We were all roaring too, we couldn't help it, we just had to roar, it was a part of the bedlam. All five of us were cheering for the Sox, we were from Chicago, the Sox just had to win, and I was most surprised to see how many supporters the Yankees had here, there were a lot of the enemy near us, some sat alongside Norm on his left, that was why Cynthia was hanging on to him so tight. We three men drank a lot of beer, it was lovely, ice-cold, and added to the excitement. It didn't cool us down, nothing could have done that in the heated atmosphere of that game, but it oiled our throats so that we could shout a lot louder, and so we enjoyed it all the more. Laurie and Cynthia drank cokes, and were very vocal also – those cokes must have been good.

The floodlighting made it so grand. I couldn't think that an afternoon game, played in daylight, could ever be as exciting as this. The lighting was marvellous, it added so much to this great park, to the green of the field, to the packed stands with their rows upon rows of roaring, howling, bawling, excited spectators. The lights blazed up, out of the bowl of the stadium and into the sky above. It was a miracle of electricity that the night could be lit up in this manner.

Yes, it was certainly the floodlighting. The stands, the field, the crowd even, looked far better in the lights than when we had first come in. The players seemed to move faster, the lights giving them added speed in all they did, their arms twirled faster, their legs ran faster, and because of the lights, they were not just playing, they were sparkling.

The game was even; there was no score at the end of two innings, there hadn't looked like being a score. Norm leaned over to bawl at me.

"The pitchers are fresh – right on the line."

I got what he meant, when they began to tire a bit we would see something. There had been some good hits already, but not the hitting I was expecting, waiting for, still it was great, with the fielding great and the throwing amazing.

Micky Mantle scored the first home run, the first of the game, and the first I had ever seen. It was magnificent, a beautiful soaring hit right into the stands at the far end of the ground, a hit that was a "homer" all the way, a hit which brought the great roaring crowd to our feet, everyone of us, and roaring even louder. There was another Yankee on second when Micky hit that one and the Yankees were two up.

We were dismayed, in spite of the pleasure, of that great hit. The Yankees had already won two games out of the three played in the series so far, and must not be allowed to go further ahead. The Sox knew that well, and in the fourth innings, drew level at two–two. The crowd went mad, we five as mad as any of them – this was fantastic, the beer sales went up and up. Norm had said a true ball-game enthusiast drank a beer with every homer, no matter how many beers you had drunk before, you must have one with every homer. We were determined to keep up the custom, we seemed to have a beer vendor to ourselves.

At the end of the ninth innings the two teams were level, six–six. Neither team scored in the tenth innings, and I thought this cannot go on much longer, no humans can stand it, the crowd, the players, any of us. We'd drunk a lot of beers, but I was stone cold sober, drunk with excitement, but sober. Laurie and I had hugged each other, kissed, held hands, roared and shouted, and now and then, she had hugged Danny, and I had hugged Cynthia. Norm had almost been in more fights than Archie Moore had been in all his life.

There was no score again in the eleventh innings, and in the twelfth, Micky Mantle came up again in his turn for the Yankees. Norm groaned.

"If anyone can do it, Micky sure can."

He was dead right. With the second strike Micky hit as true, as long, as important, a homer as he had ever done. Keen as my eyesight was, I didn't realise for the barest second that it was a hit. I thought the umpire had signalled strike two. If Micky's first homer had been a scorcher, then this was a super-scorcher. I came to my feet, roaring, with the rest of the crowd, with Laurie, with Cynthia, with Danny, Norm, with them all, and in the first motion of the rise, I knew that Micky had hit. The roar was tremendous, there would never be any roar to compare with it ever again. The ball, pulled a little, hit right up in the top of the stand to our left, leaving the run home a mere formality.

Everyone went mad. The Yankees supporters went mad because Micky had hit it. The Sox supporters went mad because Micky had hit, but for most of them it was a different kind of mad. For me, much as I wanted the Sox to win, it was a truly wonderful hit and fully deserved to win the game.

"That's it," I heard Norm yelling through the din, "we'll never make it now, never make it."

He was right again. The Sox went into their innings knowing they had to score to keep the game going, with the Yankees perfectly aware that, if they prevented a score, they had won. It was a great battle of tactics the last innings of the Sox, even though I didn't know enough about the game to really appreciate it properly. Norm did, and he knew how it would end.

"We'll never score, never."

For the third time he was right. The Yankees strategy was supreme, and hard as the Sox batters tried, they could not score. When they were out, the Yankees had won, after twelve innings, by seven to six.

I looked at my watch, it was twenty minutes after midnight. I could not believe it, but it was true. Norm summed it all up, it was quieter now and he had no need to shout.

"What a ball game – the best ever."

I could believe him, and as Danny said as we made for the exits, they were not all as exciting as this one. It was perhaps just as well.

Back at Cynthia's we ate cold fresh salmon, which was absolutely sumptuous, with great red flakes of flesh which melted in the mouth, and a huge salad bowl of lettuce, tomatoes, cucumber, raddish, olives, everything, and hot buttered rolls, and afterwards great portions of ice-cream and raspberries, then coffee, and for me, there was a never ending supply of cans of Schlitz beer, and we talked and recaptured the thrills of the game over again.

It was as though Laurie had been with us for years, as though we five had been born together, and grown up together, and it was all so wonderful.

Norm put on the hi-fi, with some of his best tapes, especially Mantovani.

"These are David's special requests," he told Laurie.

I saw the look in her eyes then, and I knew just how she was feeling, and later, back in her suite at the hotel, we didn't even need the music for the love hours; we had our own music, the music of our hands, our mouths, our hearts, and our bodies, and the orchestration of all these was delightful, soft and rythmic, rock and roll, swing and sway, quick and slow, sweet and hot, composing the most beautiful melody which lingered on, and on, and on.

CHAPTER 25

The Heat Is Less

I didn't think Laurie was so gay the next day. Not despondent, but quieter and certainly more thoughtful. I thought it must be to do with her father and the telephone call she had put through to him that morning. I had been out when she had made the call, had been round to a nearby florist where I had sent roses to Cynthia from Laurie and I, and had brought a dozen red roses back for Laurie.

"Thank you, David," she said, "you're so very sweet," and she kissed me, but I didn't consider she had put a lot into it, although she was pleased I had sent the flowers on our behalf to Cynthia.

I tackled her about it.

"Something wrong up at High Point, darling?"

She smiled at me.

"Nothing really, David, other than Daddy always worries about me, and, at these times, I'm worried about him. Oh, there's nothing wrong, but I always feel I ought to spend a lot more time up there – I haven't seen a lot of him in ten years now, and when we speak, and I remember what it's like up there, I always feel I should come home and stay home more. I know he feels that way."

"I don't blame him," I said.

"You're sweet," she said, and she paused for a minute, looking out of the window, out to the lake, out across the top of the Science Museum and the beaches. "You're very sweet, darling – you all are sweet, and that's what makes it worse. I feel now that I ought to stop here, you all are so happy, such good people, you, and Norm and Cynthia, and Danny, and my father up there."

"Why don't you stop?," I asked.

"Why don't I?" this time she asked herself, and then immediately gave the answer. "I just can't stop, not yet anyhow, my option comes up in December, but that's a long way off, and I have to do this picture in Japan, I want to do it, I want it to be good – then I can stop, then I can sort of come home."

She paused again and came over to me. I held her quite naturally in my arms as though we had rehearsed it for twenty years. Her warm brown eyes were not as full of sparkle as I had seen them, she was thinking hard about something. I kissed her, her lips first, then her ears, each one in turn, then her throat, and the melody had started all over again for me, but not for her – she was still thinking hard.

"Will you be here, David?"

It was quite a fast one to bowl at me and took me by surprise. I couldn't be here in December, according to schedule, I was due home in about two months time.

"I could be," I told her.

"That's nice," she said, that was all, and her thoughts, whatever they were, stayed with her.

She had made the arrangements for our visit to High Point. We were to go up on the coming Sunday morning, spend the night up there, coming back on the Monday night in time for her to catch the night plane to New York. Yes, it was a day earlier than she had first planned but it had to be that way, she just had to be in New York on the Tuesday morning. I thought it would be better for us to go up to High Point on the Saturday, coming back Sunday night, then Monday would not be so much of a rush, but I didn't say so, didn't make any protest or suggestions about her plans. She had made them and they had to be. Strangely enough the time wasn't racing by as quickly as I had thought it would do, and there was still a long time to go before Monday, even if there was to be a day less to share with her, and I was certain it wasn't the fact that she was going off one day early that was making her more thoughtful.

We went into the city, round all the big stores, Marshall and Fields, Carson Pirie Scotts, and them all. There were some beautiful things to see in the stores, even if we didn't buy any of them, and it was lovely just to be with her.

Laurie looked gorgeous in a silk shantung suit, with a little box jacket, and a long slender skirt, in the style that became her so much, so that she looked long and slim and luscious, which she was. The suit was in her favourite colour, of course, powder blue, with broad white cuffs to the half length sleeves, and a single large gold button on each cuff. A lot of people looked hard at her, on the streets and in the stores, but I didn't think they guessed who she was. It was just that she looked so beautiful, so cool and so fresh, and she was a woman that every man would turn and look after, not once, but twice, and every woman would turn and look at her also. I told her so.

"You say such sweet things, darling," she was very pleased, and hugged my arm even tighter. Once, in Marshall and Fields, she stood in front of me, very close, to re-arrange the white handkerchief in the breast pocket of my jacket. Her touch was magic, so that I looked straight down at her and whispered –

"You're a sweetheart, Laurie Gaydon."

"You're so nice, David," she whispered back, reaching up a little to kiss me, even here where we were, just brushing my lips with hers for a second, and if anyone noticed, I didn't know, nor did I care, but even so, all day long, she was not her real gay self, and once or twice still thinking and far away from me.

We had a double-decker sandwich in the San Roma Tavern, and I had my usual ice-cold Schlitz beer and she had a vermouth-on-the-rocks. The sandwiches were huge, crisp lettuce and tomato, and spicy green pepper, made of lovely fresh bread. It was nice in the Tavern, cold even in the air-conditioning, quiet, peaceful, as we sat there close together, very close, our knees and thighs touching where they could, with soft music playing from somewhere, audible, but soft, so that it would not interfere with conversation, but still she was quiet.

"Can I not help?" I asked.

"Help?" She was surprised for a second, then she saw what I meant.

"Oh, David," she was very sincere, "I'm such a beast acting this way, aren't I?"

"Well, I wouldn't say you're a beast, but I would like to know what's upsetting you. It isn't me, is it?"

"Of course not, silly, why should it be you? I guess I'm just a little bit out of sorts, I'm sorry, darling, I'll snap out of it."

She was much more herself after that, but it had taken her a long time to snap out of it, whatever it was.

She saw a costume which took her fancy in one of the big dress salons and we were inside for quite a time. She didn't buy it after all, it was not quite her size, even though it was her colour, but she caused a lot of commotion in the salon and had all the assistants nearby goggle-eyed, even in that very smart, very fashionable establishment, with the assistants not one bit out of place. Smart as they were, she outshone them most visibly.

She didn't buy the costume but, after a lot of discussion with me, she did buy some briefs which were very very snazzy.

Tiny little things, two pairs in powder blue, and two pairs in white. She inspected them a while, then turned to me, holding one pair across her front, low down. She was smiling wickedly.

"Do you think these will look nice on me, darling?" she asked.

The smart, goggle-eyed ladies were staring hard at me now. I hoped I wasn't blushing too much.

"Of course, darling, you'll look delightful in them" – I hoped also that my voice sounded as cool, as calm, as I had tried to make it.

"You're so sweet, David," she cooed, then turned to the ladies to have that confirmed.

"Isn't he just sweet?"

They were even more goggle-eyed now, even though they agreed I was sweet. After all, the customer is always right.

So she wanted to play, did she? Right, Laurie, I thought here goes.

"If only you wore pyjamas, darling, I'd buy you some shorties, like those over there."

A lot of pairs of goggle-eyes followed my pointing finger to the shorties.

She was enjoying herself very much now. I'd asked for it, and she wasn't going to let me get away with that.

"Oh, darling, you're so wicked," pause for just the right amount of time to make sure all the goggle-eyes were back on her. "You know you won't let me wear pyjamas," another pause, then she turned to the ladies. "He insists I sleep in the altogether, even in winter" – another pause, she was good this Laurie, or perhaps it was Janice Delane now, with a wig on, the pause was to let them take all that in – "but it's so nice – we're never cold, not even in the winter, are we, darling?"

I thought they all loved it – I certainly did. After she had paid for the briefs, and she had to play this part up by informing the horrified ladies that she had to buy her own nice things, as they could see, just to look nice for "sweet man there" – a supervisor and three other goggle-eyes escorted us to the door, just as if she was royalty, as, of course, she was.

"You'd make a good actor, David," she told me, and we laughed and laughed out in the street. Quite a few people must have thought we were mad.

Back at the hotel I telephoned to Danny. He thought it best not to come for dinner, he'd have a bite on his own out of his ice-box, it had been a late night last night, and he'd been working all day, remember? Besides, tomorrow night was his party at the Continental.

I was just about to hang up when he had the idea.

"Do you think Laurie would like to see around the place, David?"

"I think so, Danny," I said.

"Fine, ask her," he told me, "bring her along in the morning. I'll call Cynthia and have her be there, we can show them around, have lunch in the canteen – I'd sure like that."

I said I thought she would like it also, it would be nice to take her around the factory.

"Fine. I'll send for you – 'bout eleven – that O.K? Fine, David, we'll see you, have a good time tonight."

Laurie liked the idea as I thought she would do. We went and had a couple of drinks in the bar with Al before eating, he was pleased to see us, and we told him all about the baseball –

"I would'a like to have come with you," Al was ignoring his other customers a bit, I thought, "but we're down at Taps' tomorrow, so I can't have two nights off in a week. We'll sure have a ball at Taps' place tomorrow – Danny called to say he'd booked a table – it sure will be great."

I didn't think Al was going to be wrong.

CHAPTER 26

Taps' Place

Laurie was much more herself again next day – Friday – she had got over what it was that had been worrying her, and was sorry she had been out of sorts.

I didn't see a lot of her after we got down to the factory. There was an urgent letter waiting for me from Mr. G., one I just could not ignore. I had sent him some details on a new internal process Norm was experimenting with, and now he wanted a full report. It was very interesting, something on the lines of what they were doing at home, and he wanted the report in much more detail, and by return of post. He had written to Danny to make sure it would be in order. He had left nothing undone that had to be done. Mr. G. never did. There was a nice little note inside from Jenny, sending her love and hoping I was still happy. She reminded me to make sure of the booking with the Cunard company for July, and also that she took size nine in stockings. She'd read somewhere that the bare leg look was coming in fast in the States – seamfree stockings, and she would like some of those if I would care to bring her some, please. She thought they would suit her legs. I thought the same, and I made a mental note to ask Cynthia which were the best make to buy for Jenny. Cynthia wore seamfree stockings, in fact I had often thought she went about bare-legged, but she didn't, not like Laurie who loved to go about that way, she wasn't a lover of stockings, but then she was lucky, loveliest of legs, the beautiful bronze nature had given her in Spain, and a freedom from hairs which she said was unusual in a woman. Her legs were a delight to the touch, smooth, satin skin, long and never to be forgotten.

Cynthia was there when we arrived, and Danny took them off to show them around. They would catch up with Norm somewhere around, he was already out, there was a bit of a hold-up on one of the production lines which had peeved Norm a lot, so he had gone

131

to put it right. Poppy found me a young secretary from out of the big administrative office, a nice girl I had worked with before, Marcia something or other, a tall cheerful blonde, young, healthy and sensible, and a special protege of Poppy's.

Danny had got Mr. G's letter, and there were no difficulties about what I had to do. Norm had left me all the briefs, the report-trials, even copies of the blue-prints, they were very good about it, and all I had to do was sort it out, shorten it so that only the important data was in – Mr. G. didn't like anything irrelevant, and that was that, but it took me until late on in the afternoon, and it was only finished then because Marcia was such a grand worker, and could sense how I was thinking, framing the report.

I snatched a quick lunch with Marcia, and with Poppy, in the cafeteria, and we were almost finished eating when Laurie and Cynthia came in with Danny and Norm. Laurie's coming attracted a bit of attention as it always did everywhere. Even from Marcia who wasn't really in the picture.

"The boss has got himself a bit of class today, who is she?"

Poppy looked at me, but I was smiling. It was as well, she might have been more haughty with her reply otherwise.

"She just happens to be David's girl-friend, that's who," she told Marcia.

"Is that a fact?" Marcia asked me. She was even more interested, and not at all taken aback by the way Poppy had spoken to her. It's something nice about America and Americans, they do like to know a lot about you and about what goes on, yet to me they never seemed to be offensive with it in the way we know it. It was just a very healthy, friendly interest, and no more.

They didn't see us at first and when they did Laurie waved, and, of course, I went over to their table.

She was having a great time and she and Cynthia were asking all sorts of questions, and they had certainly brightened that morning up for many of the employees. She said that after lunch Danny was going to take her and Cynthia down into the city – she really must buy something nice for Danny's party tonight – and did I mind, and should she come back, or would I meet her back at the hotel?

I knew then that I was going to be some time still, so I thought the hotel would be the best place. Norm said he would run me home later on in the afternoon.

Marcia finished the report about four, and I took it in for Norm to scan through it. He thought it good, so that was pleasing. I took Marcia in to Poppy's office, and thanked them both. I wanted to buy Marcia something, she had been a great help.

"No, David, it's been nice working with you," she said.

"For me also," I agreed, and I knew I would buy her something in spite of what she had said – "I could do to take you back to Lancashire with me when I go, I shall want someone like you."

It puzzled her.

"I thought you worked in England," she queried, and she didn't mind my laughing when I told her why.

Poppy was more serious.

"We were hoping you'd stay with us, then Danny'll retire and get married all over again, and we'll have you and Norm run the show, and you can have Marcia for your secretary."

That was a surprise.

"You're kidding, surely?" I asked her.

"I am not," she was adamant. "We talk and that's the way it could be, but he'd have to find himself a wife first, and you'd have to stay."

"That's wonderful, Poppy, but I couldn't do it, I have to go back. Danny has never said anything to me."

"He sure knows about the having to go back part, and won't say it, but he thinks it and says it to me, and we'd all like it."

"I sure would," Marcia chipped in.

"You're so great," I told them, and I meant it, "you and everybody, but it's impossible, I have to go back."

"Hey," Poppy called after me as I was going back to my office to tidy up "what have I done wrong, you haven't kissed me today."

I went back and kissed her, not on the hand this time, but a proper one, on the lips.

"You're a sweetheart, Poppy," I told her.

Marcia was watching from the door.

"I wish I was old Poppy," she said, "so he would kiss me."

The book Poppy threw at her nearly hit me.

Laurie looked simply heavenly when I called for her just before seven. It was in a deep gold colour, the creation she was wearing, and it fitted her so well, I thought they must have melted it around her while she waited. Cut low in front, lower than I had ever seen her wearing before, with the slightly longer than usual skirt, slim but cut up the centre at the back. The trimmings, wrap, bag, shoes and gloves, were in her colour. She looked what she was, a sensation.

"You like it, David?"

"If you'll give me time to get my breath back, I'll tell you how much."

"That's nice," she said, and she was pleased. "Cynthia and Danny helped me to choose it – they thought it was nice too."

I had got my breath back a little.

"Nice," I told her, "it's sensational."

"You're so sweet, David," but I couldn't kiss her or anything just then, it would have crumpled her all up – crumpled the dress anyhow.

Strangely enough it wasn't as good a night as I had expected. Perhaps I had expected too much, perhaps there were too many of us, perhaps I wasn't in such good form as I ought to have been, perhaps some of the others weren't, perhaps the night at the baseball had been so terrific, we were still suffering the reaction from that, but I had known better parties.

It was a good night, a night over which Danny had taken a lot of trouble, as had Taps, and we all enjoyed it, but through it all I thought there was something missing.

The champagne didn't help. It did to start with, and we all got a bit merry, but then I got a bit fed up with it and slowed down on it, so did Cynthia and Norm, but Danny didn't, nor did Al, and most surprisingly, Laurie didn't either. I knew Laurie didn't like a lot of drink – one, yes, or two at the most, but never a lot, and I was surprised how she kept going with Danny and Al. I was sorry I hadn't kept to beer, for me, Schlitz beer was better than champagne, and I could have drunk a lot more of it than I did of the bubbly, but, once I had started on that, I couldn't go on to beer. I had enough sense to know that.

We ate well. Danny hadn't chosen a set menu, just the table and the champagne. I ate a mixed grill which had everything in it but the Chef, the two girls had Chicken Maryland, and Danny, Norm and Al, steaks. There was nothing wrong with the eating part of the night at all.

Taps was so pleased to see us. He kissed Laurie and loved her in the black wig. It was the first time he had ever seen her in it, as a rule, when she came to see him, she was Janice Delane. She was happy to see him, you could see that, she did so much want us to know how great Taps had been for her when she had been just a kid and a nobody, she owed a lot to Taps.

"You have got along without me O.K.," he told her, told us.

"Maybe," she replied, "but I got along a whole heap better because of you," and that was very nice and most humble. What ever else was swell about Laurie, she certainly had no swollen head.

By the time the floor show came on for the first time, we were a noisy party, at least some of us were. It wasn't however, out of place, the Continental was a bit noisy at the best of times, and little wonder, it was crowded and everyone had to talk loud to be heard even, and that's what helps to make any place. The quiet is only for duets, anything above that number generally wants and makes noise, and the Continental was a place to do just that.

The girls were good. I'm sure we were all thinking about Laurie in her younger days, watching the girls, and I'm sure she was thinking that way too.

"They're good, Taps," she shouted at Taps, when they had finished and gone off to loud applause. She was sitting in between Taps and Danny then, and I had been moved up to make room for Taps.

"You should know, honey," he told her loudly, "they have to be good to get by with me."

Eddy Lambert sang well. He was a good turn and very popular with the patrons. Laurie took a big interest in him, and he in her. The older females didn't get a fair share of the Lambert charms that night, he sang mostly for the vision in bronze skin and gold dress who sat there almost on top of him – we had the front table again – especially, "Arriverdeci Roma", which he finished off with, all the rest of us could have been at home, but that's only natural and I couldn't blame him. If I could sing like him, I'd be singing to her, and I consoled myself with the thoughts that there were other things in life besides singing.

Eddy got a great ovation, and Taps brought him over to meet us, which was another chair at the table, and more champagne, but she was enjoying it a lot, and the party was really for her. She was surrounded now by four men, Danny, Taps, Al and Eddy Lambert, but, bless her, she remembered Cynthia and called her in alongside her, leaving Norm and I a little bit out of it, but not over-worried about that, and, even in the din of the Continental, he and I talked shop for a while, of the stuff I had sent off in my report to England that day, and what had gone amiss on the production lines that morning.

Laurie didn't miss a dance. The five-piecer couldn't do enough for her, she kept them going on and on, with Danny, with Norm, with me, and even with Al. Danny went to town with her in a big way, he was going strong and enjoying himself. Al was having his ball all right, and, between them, they were keeping the champagne flowing well. I had to wait until the second dance to dance with her, she had the first one with Danny, and she was in great form then. We couldn't move around much, the tiny floor space was jammed full, and, in any case, her dress didn't permit a lot of movement, but we jigged around as near as we could get to the hard-working musicians whilst she sang all the choruses of the songs they played, and all the time we were dancing, I couldn't ask her how much she was enjoying herself, not that I needed to do so, it was so very obvious how much.

I danced with Cynthia, and while we also couldn't move around very much, we could talk. We held our faces very close together, cheek to cheek, and mouth to ear. It was nice.

"She's a great girl, David," Cynthia told me, "I like her a lot."

"I'm so glad, Cynth," I replied, and gave her an extra big hug which brought us in very close contact, and that was nice too.

"Will you miss her when she goes do you think, now?"

It was a funny thing to ask, and asked in a funny way. Of course I would miss her, who would not? Yet, somehow, perhaps I would not miss her so much, now. It was funny and I didn't answer.

She wanted an answer.

"Will you, David?"

"I think so," I said at last, "I think I will."

Cynthia didn't say any more about Laurie, but what she had said had gone in deep, and I wasn't really positive I would miss her now.

Taps took us into his office before the floor show came on again. I think he timed it deliberately to make sure Eddy Lambert sang something for the other customers this time. We talked a lot more in the peace of his office. He had more champagne waiting, in an ice-bucket, and this time I was ready for some. I hadn't drunk a lot in the last hour or so, neither had Cynthia or Norm, but what we hadn't drunk hadn't gone to waste. Danny was beginning to show his a little, which was odd for him, and so was Al, not badly, but just so you knew they had been drinking. Laurie was just a tiny bit high, but in the great form which women are capable of when they are that way over drinks.

Danny did a lot of talking, and if I hadn't known what Poppy had told me that afternoon, I would have been a great deal more surprised than I was.

He was going to buy a place like this down here in the lights. It wouldn't be in competition in any way with Taps, no sirree, but it would be on the same lines as this place, nice, select, well-furnished and well looked after. He had Al in mind to manage the place for him, and Al was doing some hard thinking about it. He liked the idea did Al, but it was a new venture for him and a big step up from just running a bar. He thought he could do it, especially as Taps was going to take him under his wing here at the Continental for two or three months, whilst Danny's new place was being set up. Then, when it was ready, they would have Laurie come and open it, and they would have a great gala night, which would be just great.

Laurie liked that. Of course, she would come and be happy to do it for Danny and Al. It would have to wait until she got back from this new movie in Japan, but they sure had better not have it opened by anyone else, or she would bring John Wayne along and he would shoot them all. She was going to come and open Danny's new place and they would sure have a great gala opening.

Then they started to think of a name for the place. They thought of all sorts of names, with the favourite being "Laurie's", which, they thought was just right. I butted in then, and told them it should be named, "The Powder Blue", and explained that all the decor should be in her favourite colour. They liked that name also, especially Laurie.

"That's beautiful, David, simply beautiful – I like that," she said and gave me a great big warming smile. It was the first time she had even looked at me in an hour, but I wasn't much bothered, it was her party, and she was enjoying herself.

Taps liked that name also, he thought it would go well, and, come to think of it, he knew of a place that was going, it would cost plenty for sure, but with money spent on it, and some imagination, and run the right way, and with the right sort of build-up publicity-wise, he reckoned Danny couldn't fail to make it pay. Then they decided they might, when Danny's new place was established, go into partnership and run the two places conjointly, each one advertising the other.

They were great planners, and I knew something now without any doubt. If you want to make good plans for anything, real good plans, all you need is a lot of money and some magnums of champagne, and the ideas simply roll in.

Up to then, apart from my idea of naming the new place, Cynthia, Norm and I hadn't really been in the planning, but then Danny let his bombshell fall about he was thinking of making Norm joint

Managing Director of the Company, to take over the running of it whilst he spent a bit more time doing the things he wanted to do, and it was time for him to do. He wanted to travel, use up a bit of the money he'd been accumulating all these years. Sure he would have to find a new deputy for Norm first, he knew that was most important because only he knew how much work Norm did, and it was plenty. Then, when he got all that settled, he might even get married again, it wouldn't be so lonesome travelling then, yeah, he might do that, if he could just find the right woman who would put up with him and make him into a proper husband and look after him, just the way Cynthia did with Norm.

That shook them all, even shook me, and I had some previous warning of it, thanks to Poppy. I know it had made a tremendous impression on Cynthia, and Norm too, of course, but mainly Cynthia. This is what she must have dreamed of for years, still dream of, and now here it was, almost coming true. I knew what she was thinking right away, she couldn't keep it out of her eyes, nor could Norm, and I knew damn well Danny had been hinting that way when he had spoken. If only I could stay on here in Chicago as deputy to Norm, if only that. Then all that would be needed would be a wife for Danny, and perhaps even that might come along soon. That was how they were thinking, Cynthia, Norm and Danny, and I couldn't blame them for it. In fact, I was quite pleased in a way that they thought so highly of me. But it couldn't be, I knew that, and I was going to have to disappoint them as far as I was concerned.

The party had certainly developed, whilst the champagne had unleashed a lot of thoughts that might otherwise never have come to light.

It was four in the morning when we went home, and I was very glad we had come with Norm, he and Cynthia, and I also, were sober, but the host, and Al, and my beautiful bronze golden girl, certainly were not. Laurie kissed Taps and said it would not be long before she was back again to see him, when she came to open Danny's new night-spot. She was slurring her speech a little and gay, very gay. She kissed Danny and Al also, when Norm dropped us at the hotel, big slobbering kisses, and it sure had been the greatest night she ever had. I reckoned Al would remember that kiss and this night for a long time to come, he had been out with, danced with, and kissed, Janice Delane. I saw his face when she kissed him goodnight, he would have swum the Atlantic Ocean for her, or run straight up Everest without a stop, I knew the feeling, exactly. I kissed Cynthia and said my goodnights. We were all to go to Norm's the next evening for supper and hi-fi – all except Al who had to work, durn it.

Laurie held me tight going in. I collected her key and my key from the sleepy clerk behind the desk, and I knew he was wondering what I wanted my own for. I sure couldn't be going to use it, not just yet anyhow, not when I had this very lovely and rather tipsy goddess to see home. But I wasn't worried about what he was thinking, or how envious he was.

Laurie turned on me like a tigress as soon as we got into the suite, mouth, arms and body. I held her with my left arm whilst I locked the door behind me, then I carried her, still kissing her, through into the bedroom leaving wrap, handbag and gloves strewn over the floor of the outer room.

She held me very close against her, she was all heat this tigress, all heat and strength. My mouth remained fixed on hers, whilst my arms went round her so that, after a lot of fumbling, my fingers could undo the little hook at the top of the dress and then, carefully, unzip her. The golden creation slipped down from her and my hands feasted on the long luxurious length of her back.

After a while I held her away from me. I wanted to see what there was to see, just for a moment or two. She was the loveliest sight in the world. All bronze at the top, full firm breasts each with the big cherry atop, then a little pair of powder blue briefs, then glorious bronzed long legs, and her high-heeled powder blue shoes.

She was content, I think, to let me look at her awhile.

"Do I look well, darling, in theesh panties?" she smiled, like me, she was remembering the buying.

"You look – look – gorgeous," I could not recognise my own voice.

She was satisfied with that – I had looked enough. She came back into my arms, kissed me one huge kiss with her mouth wide open, then took her mouth away again.

"Take them off, David darling," it was pure ecstasy in my ears – "thersh a good li'l boy."

I was a good little boy.

I was also a good little boy the next night, Saturday, when she sent me away, after we had come back from Norm's.

It hadn't been a great day. She had woken up with an awful hangover, and had been sick most of the morning. We nearly called off going to Norm's, but she recovered a bit in the afternoon and thought it was best we should go. It should have been a nice evening, but even Cynthia's wonderful dinner and the hi-fi couldn't make it that, only Norm and I doing justice to the roast Long Island duckling, which simply melted in the mouth, the corn-on-the cob, the baked potato, the ice-cream, and all the rest. Danny had been through hell that morning and showed it, he kept very quiet. We three left very early, and I knew Norm and Cynthia were pleased. There were no goodbyes, they would all be at Midway on Monday night.

I took her up to the suite.

"Run along tonight, darling, and let's have ourselves some sleep" – she was very sweet about it. "I'm sorry I've been out of it today, but I guess it's being a woman does it" – a little kiss – "you know how women get at times" – another little kiss – "out of circulation" – a little longer kiss, a smile.

Of course I knew that about women. I knew the reason for her bad day. I ran along, like a good little boy.

CHAPTER 27

So This Is Delane

Danny Erikson

I've been around a lot of places, and I sure have seen a lot of women. Over the last few years I had been going to the places where the real smart women went, and I had seen some living dolls. I employ a hell of a lot of smart women, we pay them well, and they spend plenty on what they wear. We had one girl once, a high-yellow girl, who was out of this world for looks and figure and for what it takes, one who used to give me fast heart beats every time I caught sight of her, until she went into some night club somewhere, and she had been great, and I stopped going into the cafeteria about the time I knew she did, and I cursed, for a time, the night club that now employed her. Yeah, I had seen a lot of women, and most always liked what I saw, and I figured I had seen them all, but I figured wrong, dead wrong.

I just hadn't seen anything till I had seen Delane, and the moment I clapped eyes on her, all golden-brown, long, slim, and a vision in a cream suit which was part of her. I knew just that. I was looking for Delane, and this vision, though she was sure a vision, was a surprise, but what a surprise.

The wig I hadn't expected, David hadn't let me in on it properly, but she was a beauty this woman, a warm vital woman, with a person-ality that fetched right up and hit you plumb in all your senses, and I liked her, liked her a whole heap, on sight. Her voice was right, and the way she called me Danny made me glow warm inside, in a man-ner I had never glowed before.

She was so darn nice, people lapped her up right from the moment they met her. Al, who was her slave from the first time he looked at her, Norm, Cynthia, everyone. Cynthia took to her fast, and that was good enough proof she was a woman's woman, which is really some-thing, and then Poppy liked her too, and that was really the clinch.

I know, driving home from Midway that first night, why she had affected David, sat there between us, giving all her attention to him, I knew how much she would affect him, and I had a good notion how much she would affect any man, how much she could affect me – if she tried. I didn't go down to the Casanova like I told them I would when I left them that night. I went on home and got out the Dimple Haig and sat down to think awhile. The whisky helped my thinking, it generally does, it's darn fine whisky. I was thinking how lucky David was, and how I would have liked to have given myself a week's vacation with this beauty, and I wasn't blaming myself any for being envious of him. Any man would have been equally envious, it's just human nature. I hadn't sort of got used to the Laurie part – Laurie Gaydon – I had got to know her when we had been talking of her, as Janice Delane, and as I drank more whisky I liked it that way. David could keep his Laurie, but I sure would like Delane.

I got out all the magazines again and turned up the pictures of her. She wasn't wearing the black wig in any of the pictures, in some of them she wasn't wearing a lot at all, and I sure liked her as Delane, and I knew one thing – none of these photographers could take pictures, none of them did her proper justice, even though I had only seen her in the wig, not without it, I could imagine just how she looked, and these camera boys were not up to what she really was.

Right from then on I got used to her as Janice Delane – mostly as Delane. I found it real hard to call her Laurie, and hard to call her that way to David, or to Norm and Cynthia even. For me she was Delane, and for me she was everything a woman should be, and all the other women I had seen were way behind her, a long way behind.

Cynthia asked me about her the next morning. She came up to the factory as she often did nowadays, and I liked her coming a lot always, and after she had talked with Norm, and with Poppy, she put her head in through the door in her usual manner to say Hi. We were getting so we talked a lot Cynthia and me, and most all of the time I was thinking what a beautiful aide she would make to that big husband of hers when I passed on the top place to him, to them. I was sure it would be to them, they were so good together, and he wouldn't have been what he was without her, nor she without him.

"What's she like, Danny – Delane?" she asked.

I was glad she had called her Delane, it was sort of the way I wanted it to be. I told her how she had seemed to me, and I was enthusiastic.

142

"She must be a wonder," she said, "must be a wonder – I can't wait to meet her."

She looked hard at me.

"Danny," she was very serious, "you're not going into competition with David–"

That was a buster for me, right on the nose. Cynthia's a sensible woman, she doesn't say things just for a laugh.

"Sure not," I told her, "sure not – she's just that much a woman that's all. No, I'm not in competition with anybody, least of all David – he's my boy, you know that – but she sure is a honey and I sure would like to see her without the wig. No mam, no competition, I'm all for Delane, he can have him his Laurie."

"You keep it that way," she told me, still very serious.

I was pleased about the tickets for the ball game. Norm had surprised me with that one when I had got in first thing that morning. Five tickets – he had reckoned David and Janice Delane might like to come along, he had often promised to take David to the ball games. I nearly gave him a double raise this deputy of mine, he sure thought the right things at the right time, and I liked the Janice Delane part. I held back the raise, he didn't really need it, he was on top money now, and he earned it. He was a great guy, Norm.

Cynthia put the crust on the pie. She was all for the ball game too. I knew how she liked ball games, and she'd told me how she had to keep Norm out of fights. It would be good at this ball game with her and Norm, and David and Delane. Then she came up with the supper idea.

"We'll all go back to supper at our place after the game," she said, "would you like that, Danny?"

I said how much I would like that.

"David will like it," she went on, and I knew how right she was, knew how much the boy thought of her, and how much he loved the eats she served up for us, "and it will be nice to have Janice Delane along, can we call him?"

"Steady gal," I warned her, "don't you think you ought to ask Norm?"

"There are some things I can do on my own," she told me, she was a bit snorty about that one.

I didn't take any notice, I was in high good spirits today, in spite of the fact that I had done a lot to that bottle of Dimple the night before.

143

"And some things you can't do without Norm." I wasn't usually so daring with her.

"Some things," she agreed, and she smiled, "just some things – let's call David."

I told Poppy to get him to the telephone somewhere, and remembered, just in time, to call her Laurie when I made the arrangements to pick them up.

It was a treat to see her when I called for them, and how that red suit went with the golden-brown of her was just nobody's business. I still didn't like the wig, would much have preferred her in her own natural hair, but I could see what the wig was for all right. She wanted to be the other woman, not Janice Delane.

David did well for me putting her to sit next to me, and it made it a great ball game. Yeah, I like a ball game, especially when they are like this one was, and I liked this one more than ever because of the bundle of energy that was alongside of me. Sure I can get excited at ball games, and I got excited at this one. We roared and howled with them all, and once, when one of the Sox boys hit a homer which brought us all on our feet, she hugged me in her excitement, and shouted something which I couldn't catch, and though I knew the excitement wasn't for me, I could see what excitement this woman had under her bonnet, and I could do to be hugged a lot more that way, just so long as Delane was doing the hugging.

I missed her a lot when I didn't see her the next day, but declined to go round when David called me in the evening. I didn't tell him, but I had Norm and Cynthia coming, with Cynthia to rustle us up from my stocks the sort of eats she could put on, and then for us three to talk a little. Then I thought of the idea of him bringing Delane up the next day to look around my can business. I could look forward to that.

The three of us talked a lot over supper, and afterwards, mostly about Delane. I didn't need to prod them at all to talk about her, though I sure would have done if it had been necessary, they were as full of her as I was.

Cynthia weighed her up best, but she had the advantage of being a woman herself and knowing what and how a woman feels. I was happy they both liked her so much.

"I think I had the idea I would be very scared of her at first," Cynthia said, "you know, that she would be so important that she would not take any notice of us."

"She might be that way as Delane," I came in.

"Oh no, Danny," quite sharply from Cynthia, "I don't think so, she's too warm a personality to be that way."

So they had found her warm too, rich and warm I thought her, someone you sure wanted to be with all the time.

I said I would like to see her without the wig.

"Me also," Cynthia said, "I guess she'd be even warmer with her natural colouring."

We didn't say anything about her association with David, nor think now about any of the stories we knew, and which we had discussed so freely when we had talked of her in past weeks, until fairly late on, and then it was Cynthia who brought it up.

"David won't be so concerned about her after this week."

I couldn't quite get that – I had a sort of idea what she meant, but wasn't fully with her. I checked on it with her.

"Well," she replied, "it seems to me that the first time he met her it was something out of the ordinary" –

She saw my face and she saw Norm grinning, I wasn't grinning, but like Norm, I could think she was something out of the ordinary all right, but here we had the advantage over Cynthia, we were both men. She saw how we were figuring it, and it wasn't what she had intended.

"Don't get me wrong you one tracks," she told us, and I nearly reminded her it was a beautiful track usually but I didn't say it. She was being serious, and that was how I wanted her to be, how I wanted her to speak about Delane, that way would help the thoughts I had in my mind a whole heap.

"Let me put it this way," she went on, "so even you two he-men can understand – when he first met her it must have been almost beyond his belief that he could meet her, and – this I presume is correct – sleep with her almost straight off – it wasn't sort of natural with him with women, I won't say it's natural with you, Danny, or with Norm, but I think you would accept that sort of situation a lot better than he did. For him it would be like – well, yes, it would be like a little boy on the park when he goes on the part where it says keep off the grass – he's dead frightened at first, and it must be quite an experience for him. Then, when he knows he hasn't been scolded or spanked for doing it, he does it again, and this time it'll be easier for him, even if he does get wallopped for it, and the next time it will be even more easy, and nothing to be frightened of at all, something

145

that little boys do, always have done, and always will do, and get away with. I often think they put those signs up especially to bring out the character in little boys."

I was beginning to see what she meant, and I was agreeing with her. It made sense. It may even have been that I would be just like that at David's age.

"That's how I think she was to David – in New York" – Cynthia had given a lot more thought to it than I had imagined, and she was determined to get her views firmly over to us both – "He's different in a lot of ways about women to you two for instance – English men are, certainly those as young as David are – they're more chivalrous, they put women on a higher plane than our young men do – look at the way he treats Poppy, and it's quite normal to him – when I got home today there was a dozen roses from him and her waiting for me – lovely, weren't they, Norm? – but it was David who sent them, not Laurie, and he sent them for what I did last evening – for supper after the ball game" –

That went home at once, I hadn't sent her any roses today for last night, nor had I ever. She must have known what I was thinking – women are remorseless

"No, you didn't send any roses, Danny," she smiled so nice in her big grey eyes, "and I know you appreciated it, appreciate me, as much as David does" – she made that sound so nice, it was much better than I deserved – "but it isn't your nature to do that, and yet it comes so natural with him" –

Now I could really see how it all added up, she had done her explaining well. She hadn't finished yet though.

"That's how she was to him at first, and, when he thought about it, and I know how much he did think now, it upset him, it must have been a big shock to him. But she can't shock him any more now, and she won't, whatever she does, he's like the little boy on the grass, the male in him will assert itself, has done already if I'm any judge, and he'll keep on the grass as long as he wants to and won't worry any more about the sign that says 'Keep Off.'"

I sure agreed with her wholeheartedly, she was right, and what she had said was what I had wanted to hear, but it was how she finished it off that really quickened my heart beats.

"Now I've met her, and talked with her, though we haven't talked that way, I know what she's looking for, and she certainly isn't looking for David."

CHAPTER 28

Looking For What?

She must have seen it in our faces again, and she knew she would have to explain that. I think Cynthia was liking this. She was sort of redeeming someone she liked, and to me it made good listening.

"She's looking for something a lot more mature than David," how fine Cynthia was putting it, just the way I wanted it to be – "he's only a passing phase in her life. Yes, she liked him a lot, as I've said he's a lot different to the men she's been used to, he's good-mannered and he's gentle, not at all like the men of the world she's accustomed to being with, But he's not for her, not after this is over anyhow, he wouldn't last long with her, not as long as some of the others did, and I'm happy now that it won't really hurt him, he'll just be thankful for the good things she's giving him."

She was giving all her attention to me now, none to Norm.

"What she wants Delane" – that part was specially for me – "is somebody real strong, a big man she can lean on, depend on, a man who will tell her good and hard if she does wrong, and will make sure she knows what's right and what's wrong, a man with time, and money, to devote to her. I guess all women look for that sort of man, and she sure needs him now. It's my opinion she always has needed him, that's what I think of her."

If I had written that speech out for her she couldn't have said it any better for me, or been nearer what I wanted her to say. Like I say, she's a woman and she knows what other women think, and for me she was right about Delane. Sure I knew how they always put it this way in the movies and in books, but some of them must know what they're writing about, and a lot of them wrote just this way.

"That's how I figure her too," I agreed.

Norm kept out of it, he had no need to come in to this, it wasn't his problem.

"It's the only way to figure her," Cynthia replied, "it stands out throughout her life, and the only thing that's a problem now is if she knows yet what it is she wants, and, if not, how long she has to go before she does know."

That made sense also. I couldn't fault Cynthia on anything she had said. I knew she was a good judge of people, of character, of life, and I sure hoped she was right. Now I had to know something from her, it was sort of frightening for a man like me to ask, but I had to know, and I had to know if she was on my side about it. There are times when you have to take a chance, and I had to take this chance now.

"Do you think she's looking for me?" I asked her.

She wasn't a bit surprised. If she was, she sure didn't show it, but she thought for a time before she would reply. I was sure she knew how very important that reply could be for me.

"It could be Danny," it came out slowly and she was still thinking deep, "it could well be, you have all the things I have spoken of."

She stopped so long then that I thought she had said all she was going to say. Even though it wasn't very much, wasn't what I had wanted, it was something.

"Thank you," I said, and I guess I must have sounded as disappointed as I felt.

"No, Danny, let me finish," she cried out at once, her tone of voice being sufficient rebuke for my lack of patience, but the voice softened again as she went on. "You're big and you're strong, you're mature, you could have the time, and you sure have the money, to devote to her, you have all those things. I want to be specially certain you understand the money side of her, it's important, she has money, she must have a lot, and they say her father has money, so she won't want a man for his money, but the man she wants must have money or she would be keeping him, and that's bad, you know that, a man would lose his self-respect, and when that happens it's curtains, and it would be curtains with her."

She stopped again, and here I think she wanted me to give her some sort of lead, but I didn't, in any case, I couldn't, so, after some time, she went on again.

"That's very very important for Delane, it's a must for her, she must respect the man she's looking for, right from the start and all the time, and I think she could be that way with you Danny. You own a big business and that means a lot to a woman like Delane. You're

148

like her, you started at something and got to the top, and her man has got to be like that."

I was very glad now I had asked David to bring her up to the factory the next day, it looked as though things were going my way, and that was sure enough doing the right things anyhow.

"Yes," Cynthia hadn't quite finished, "you could well be what she's looking for."

"I think she's a good judge if she's looking for you." It was Norm, the first time he had spoken for ages, and though he wasn't a yes-man, I thought then he was just being loyal.

"Would I be good for her?" I asked Cynthia.

She didn't need to think hard on that one.

"Of course, Danny, as I say you have everything she's looking for, oh yes, you'd be good for her."

"What about her, would she be good for me?"

I was sure she expected me to follow up with that one. She must have been, she was ready with the answer.

"That's something only you can answer, Danny, there's so very much to think about, much more than with you for her, much more."

"Say what, Cynthia."

"Oh, that's easy, Danny, you know it all really" – she caught my look – "sure you do, even if you won't admit it."

I wouldn't admit that I knew, she would have to tell me, so I kept quiet and she came back on in.

"You know her whole life, Danny – what she's been, what she is. You know just what's going on with David" – she looked at her watch – "she's probably in bed with him now" –

You cruel bitch, Cynthia, I thought, and was amazed at my own vehemence, and regretted the thought at once, regretted that I could have been bitter like that about Cynthia, who was only telling me what I knew to be the truth, and that for my own good.

"Could you accept all that, Danny? Not just at the start when life is just a bed of roses, but always and for ever? You're a big man, Danny, and you will have to be even bigger to stand up to what they will say, and what they will write, about such a marriage. Oh yes, it will have to be a marriage, make no mistake about that, and you will have to accept her like a fresh young bride, and always think of her like that, and never remember the rest. Will you be able to have David with you, at any time, and not think back to how you met her, and how he met her. Will you, Danny? If you can do all that, all that and more, you have your answer, and only you can supply the answer."

"I think I could," I told her.

"You think," she was vehement now, "thinking's not good enough, Danny, you don't have to think, you've got to know."

"You sure have cleared the air a lot."

"You wanted it cleared," she interrupted me, and I did just that. "You want to know why?"

I did want to know why.

"Because I respect you. I've known you a few years now, but it's only in the last few weeks I've really got to know you, and I respect you, and like you – and I like her, even though I've only known her a few hours. If she can respect you, Danny, the rest will come, that's certain – you're all she would want, you have all she would need, so, if you want her, you'd better do something about it fast."

"But I can't take her away from David," I meant that, I thought.

"You don't have to," she replied, "if you're what she's looking for, she'll come a-running when she's ready, and, if she's what you're looking for, you sure had better be good and ready yourself."

It had cleared the air, and I felt better for it, and I couldn't really say I was sad the next morning when David had his report to do, and I could show her and Cynthia how cans were made. Cynthia knew already so I could do all my talking at her, and I could make it sound good, because I was sure on my own diamond, and I had built all this up with guts and blood and toil and heart-break, had put my all into it, and lost two wives in the doing, and now it could pay me back, and get me a third wife, one I could have for keeps.

So I enjoyed the morning, and enjoyed the afternoon also. I couldn't ever remember going shopping with a lady before, and now I had two, even if I was only trying for one. Yeah, I have bought some things for some ladies before, but never had the pleasure that I got out of choosing that gold gown for Delane, and never found words so easy to come by as I found to say how that little-bitty gold was sure for her, and I never saw anyone so pleased before as when I said it, and I sure would have liked to have bought that for her, but I had savvy enough to know I couldn't, and savvy enough to know this was one gal I didn't have to buy, not with money anyhow.

I enjoyed the night at Taps' like plenty, and even though I don't remember a lot of it after a while, I sure remember dancing with Delane, and how she could jig around to those five little coloured boys playing their tops off, and how she was just my size, and we could look straight at each other, and how, though I can't dance none, I could sure dance with her. I remember also dancing with Cynthia, and I asked her was I doing any harm to David, and she said no – then I asked her why she was doing this for me, and she said she was doing it for David too, and then I said that I thought she liked Delane.

"I sure do," she shouted down at me, "like you all, like you a lot, David, Delane and you, and if it goes the way I want it, it'll be best for all three."

I know I blew my nut about buying a joint like the Continental, and that was for true, not just for show, and I was content just so we put on a good party for Delane, and I was sure she enjoyed it, and I got so doggone tight so I wouldn't notice it when she said goodnight and left me, because I knew darn well she would still be with David, and I didn't want to remember where they would be going.

Next morning, like I knew I would, I felt like Lot's wife, and so damn thirsty, and every time I took a drink of anything my stomach multiplied it by ten and passed it all back, so I wasn't going to be at Cynthia's for supper, and I didn't want any part of it, then I knew I just had to go, because I had to take David and her there, and I wanted to be where she was, even if the pain tore me to shreds whatever she did, and I knew damn well now she was for me like no other woman has ever been before, nor ever will be again, and if she had been looking for something all her life, then I had done what I had done with mine, so that I would be here when she came along.

I dropped her and David at the hotel that night with agony in my heart and a smile on my face, and I promised to be at Midway on Monday night when they came down from up where they were going, and I told them I would go and roll some dice, not wanting them to tell me where they were going, and then I went home, straight home, to my friend – Dimple Haig.

CHAPTER 29

A Whole Heap Of Thinking

There are times when a man has to do a whole heap of thinking with himself. This was one such time for me, I had to do some real serious thinking.

Not that I hadn't been doing just that for a long time now. I sure had. Ever since I first got to know Cynthia real well, and realised what I had been missing all these years in the marriage set-up. Yeah, I had been thinking of another hitch-up for a long time but it had to be a real one, one that would last for ever, or until my forever anyhow.

Then there was the can business. It had grown up on me fast, and I knew I had to do something about it. Last year, when I had been in England, I had done some talking with this Mike Govern man about prospects over there and in Europe, and we had agreed those same prospects were bright, if we went about things the right way. For both of us we had agreed, well, nearly agreed, to widen our scope just when the time was right, and it was coming right now. That was why I had been thinking of Norm running the can factory here in Chicago, which would leave me free to do some travelling which would be nice, and travel in those sort of places I wanted to think about along with new business. Europe was sure going to be the place to get into soon, that was for sure, and if I could get me a merger in England, and then somewhere in France or Italy, or somewhere like that, we could just about have the biggest can empire anyone could think of, and it was nice to think of that.

When I had started thinking thataway, I hadn't thought of hitching-up for a third time, it was Cynthia who brought that feeling on, not with her, of course, but with someone like her, good as her, if there were other women like her, and the two, done properly, would go together, so that I would have me a new big deal to think about and set to order, and I would have me a woman who could set me to order, and so keep it all nicely rolling. It sure is good how, once you start thinking, how everything seems to flow on and it all fits in so nicely. The thinking part was easy, especially with a tot or two of Dimple now and then to keep the old brainbox oiled. Yeah, the thinking part was easy, it was the doing part that was going to be difficult.

Not in the can business – I had that pretty well all figured, and thought it would go all right. But durn difficult in the marriage business, that I couldn't miss seeing, more so when this dame Cynthia had set such a high standard, and I couldn't remember anyone with her all-round standard that I had met up with before, looks, and brains, and personality, and polish, and warmth, and drive, and ambition, the last bit for her man that was clear, ambition for him, not for her, and it was all the better that way. Then, right out of the blue, just like it is in the movies, and right out of the sky down there at Midway, Delane had come along, and the impact she had made on these eyes of mine had messed all my thinking and planning up for a little while, and it was only now I was able to get things in the right places again. Well, only in the last two or three days, since me and Cynthia had talked long together, and I had got to know all over again what the woman angle really was. It had done me good that talk with Cynthia, and since then I had included Delane in all the plans, and I just could not make any plans without her being in on them.

Cynthia hadn't been hoaxing me that was for sure, she had just spoken out what she had in her mind, and she was a very honest woman. She hadn't known then what I had told them later about all the plans for the business, so it could not have been just to fool me, to get me all hitched-up to let Norm have the top spot, it couldn't be like that. Not with Cynthia, ambitious as she was for Norm, she wouldn't do that to me. No, sir, she hadn't been hoaxing.

So I had a lot of thinking to do, and I didn't seem to have gotten anywhere with Delane. Good friends sure, we seemed to be that, but no more, and whichever way I looked at it, there didn't seem to be much I could do about it now, except to include her out of the plans, and to start planning all over again.

But it sure was a pity. She had been so terribly interested in the cans when I had shown her round the other morning, interested in how I had started, and how it had all grown, and knowledgeable, so that it was simple to explain things to her, so that from there, it would be just as simple to getting around to asking her what she thought of things.

It was a pity also because I had liked so much being there when she had chosen that golden gown she had worn for the Continental party. It had been my pleasure to be there, to see Delane in all her glory, and it was a whole lot of glory, strutting around, with a whole lot of admiring women trying to sell her something, and she looking at me, and to Cynthia, to know how she looked in this and in that. It had been great and I had so wanted to buy the gold for her, and I would want to buy anything for her, and I could just give up a lot of other things, including cans, when she was choosing glad-rags for that elegant chassis of hers. It was a new part of the world for me, and a world I could get used to being in quick, just so long as I could have Delane.

I wasn't worried about David either, not one way or the other, not because of how he was being with Delane, and not because, if I could have her, he couldn't. I sure believed Cynthia, he was a passing ship for her, and though he was sailing in a very smooth sea with her just now, he wouldn't be there long, and the great thing was, and this was from Cynthia also, he wouldn't be badly stranded when she took the sea away from him. That was pleasing, for I liked this boy, more perhaps than I could say, and it would have been wrong for me to hurt him, and, if it was a case of that, I would rather do without Delane, much as I wanted her.

When I knew it wasn't going to hurt him I didn't want to be without Delane. I had it plain inside me now, had it for sure, she was for me, and I was hoping hard she thought I was for her if she was looking for what Cynthia said she was. It hadn't worked out, she had been quiet tonight at Norm's, hardly friendly, and I hadn't been much better with her, with any of them, but I badly wanted to know what she and Cynthia had been talking about when Delane had helped with the chores after we had eaten. Cynthia hadn't said what it was so it couldn't have been for me, and now Delane was off again, and I would see her once more only, at Midway and that would be when there was a hell of a lot of people around and a hell of a lot of things to be done, and she would say goodbye, and she would fly off, and that would be it, and I would be back where I had started from, only worse, because this time I would know for sure I had really missed something, missed everything.

So it was all one great pity, and I was feeling sorry for myself and taking the only medicine I knew would help me, and that was bad in a way, because I had been taking too much of that medicine, nice as it was, this past week, thinking about Delane, and I didn't want the medicine, I just wanted Delane.

It was then the telephone rang, loud and clear, and I thought what the hell, who wants to speak with me at this time of the night, then I looked what time of the night it was, and it was only eleven, or just after, and it might be something important, so I had better answer it, it would stop the goddam ringing for one thing.

It was Delane, and I wouldn't believe my own ears when I heard her talking in to them, just wouldn't, and just couldn't, but it was her all right, and she was saying just what I wanted to hear.

"Danny," it was music, the nicest melody I ever did hear, nicer than all those hi-fi tapes of Mantovani David liked so much. Darn it, why could I not just forget David and what he liked?

"Danny, I can't sleep. I want to talk, can I come around and talk with you?"

I said she sure could, and I was recovering from the shock and wasn't thinking even of what she had done with David.

"Fine, Danny," the music whispered into my ear, "come round for me."

I would have come round for her if she had been in Japan, or in China, or in Peru, or anywhere, come just as gladly as I did then, just around the block.

"Give me ten minutes," I told her.

"Ten minutes, Danny," oh, how I loved the music, "I'll be outside waiting."

I showed her round my place. It's a nice feeling to take such a wonderful woman around what can only be described as a batchelor residence and be thinking the things I was thinking. I'd spent a lot of money in improvements and better furniture over the past five or six years, and I thought I had a swell sort of home. So did she.

"It's nice," she said, "nice and peaceful, and homey, like it wants to be lived in."

"It needs a woman," I told her, meaning a woman to own it and live in it, so that you could feel her presence in the place, and smell the scent of her, and know the comfort that a woman gives to a place by just being a part of it.

"It does," she said. I didn't know if she was telling me or asking me.

I had removed the whisky and washed the glass before going to meet her.

"Drink?" I asked her.

"No thank you, I've had too many drinks this last day or two, they can be bad for a girl, I would like some coffee though."

"Fine – I'll go make some."

"Let me make it – just show me where everything is – will you have some?"

"I sure will," I told her, "if you make it."

We went into my little kitchenette where I sort of got in her way – it's only a small place – whilst she made the coffee. Back in the living room I got out a little nest of tables and she poured out.

"Do you mind if I smoke a cigar?" I knew she didn't smoke. She didn't mind, so I lit up, and, in between my thinking and imagining, I was wondering what it was all going to be about.

"You were bad this morning," she looked a real picture sat across there from me, a beautiful smiling picture, in a white costume with large light blue dots, and those golden brown legs of hers, and just a part of the knees with the legs, and I felt happy, more happy than I had felt for some time, and a warm feeling which she gave me whenever she was around.

"I sure was," I agreed, "Real bad."

"Me too, it was a great party. I did thank you last night, didn't I?"

"You did – just as long as you enjoyed it, that's O.K."

We weren't getting anywhere, and I was sure she hadn't come around just to thank me for last night's party. But I was in no hurry, she made good coffee, and I was quite content to sit on with her, and wait, wait for what it was she had come to say.

"You were quiet tonight," she said.

"You also," I countered.

"Oh, I talked a lot – more coffee? I talked a lot to Cynthia."

"You did? Yes, more coffee – that's nice."

She poured another cup for herself and another for me. I couldn't take my eyes off her, and she knew I couldn't.

"Yes, it was nice," she told me, "it was mostly about you."

I sat up with a jerk, nearly spilling the coffee all over my lime-green fitted carpet. The smile came back all over her face, reminding me so much of the sun coming up in the little valley in Nevada where I was born, giving all the world a soft golden glow. Now her smile was giving the same glow here in this room, even in the competition of the electric lighting.

"About me, what about me?"

She drank some coffee.

"About how Cynthia had known you for a long time, and about how she had really only known you for the past three months, and about what you said down at Taps' last night, that part where you thought of getting married again."

"She told you that?" I didn't know whether to be mad or glad, or what.

"She told me that," she went on.

"Is that all she told you?" I somehow knew darn well she wanted me to say that.

"No." She stopped at that, for a moment, and my heart stood still waiting for what she would say next.

"She told me she had told you I was looking for something – and that you thought you might be what it is I'm looking for."

I couldn't say a thing, I had expected something, but I hadn't expected this, not quite like this.

"And she told me she thought I was the woman you wanted to get married to."

"She did?" I was very tense and marvelling at her coolness, and I didn't know if that coolness was a good sign for me, or a bad sign.

"She did," and now I could see all the lovely warmth of those soft brown eyes, and I eased a lot – I thought it was going my way.

"What did you say to that?" I asked her, and hung on to the world which had stopped turning, waiting for her answer.

"I just told her that I would come round here tonight, so that you could tell me that yourself, if you want to tell me."

"What did she say to that?"

"She just said you do that Laurie, and I have done – now do you want to tell me that, Danny?"

"I do, I sure do," and I was overjoyed, things had come just the way I wanted them to, and I blessed Cynthia and I saw how right she had been about everything.

"Then tell me, Danny," she said, quietly and simply, "because that's what I've come to hear."

CHAPTER 30

Delane Is For Me

So I told her as best I could, and it was a poor best really, sat across from her the way I was doing, trying with all the power I had to shape the words and the sentences into what they should be for her, and suddenly the one thing that would make it so much easier for me came into my thoughts, and I said what I had wanted to say to her for a long time, and everything I said afterwards became so much easier.

"Take the wig off – for me – please."

"Why?" she asked, and I saw the puzzled look come into the brown eyes.

"Because I got to know you as Janice Delane, I went to the airport to meet Janice Delane – remember?" She did remember. "I don't know you as Laurie Gaydon, for me you're Delane, stop being Laurie, take off the wig, be Janice Delane."

I wasn't sure how she was going to take that, and was happy she took it the way I wanted. I was happier still when the wavy chestnut hair of the colour pictures of her came into full view, and I could see Janice Delane now, not Laurie Gaydon.

She came over to me and knelt beside my chair. "Is that how you want me?"

I put my hand under her chin and lifted her face so that I could kiss her, and when I kissed her I was glad I was kissing Delane, and not Laurie Gaydon and she returned the kiss with a tenderness which was overwhelming in its sweetness, not rough, not tough, not passionate, just a first kiss which was all a first kiss should be. Like my first kiss should have been, when I was fifteen or sixteen about, but wasn't because I wanted to kiss like a man then and do the things it was manly to do, and now I was a man I just wanted to kiss like a boy, with nothing manly about it, just kiss with lips and heart, and this was exactly it, so that I was a boy again, with a boy's dreams and hopes and fears, a boy again but a boy with a man's knowledge, which made the boy's love all the more wonderful and pure.

I told her that I had always thought of her as Delane and I couldn't think of her as anybody else, which I think she understood.

"It'll be Laurie Gaydon," she was thinking it all over, "when I'm married."

"On the certificate," I agreed, "yeah, but the press boys will call you Delane."

"You can stand all that? The press, the publicity, all the fuss they'll make?"

"Stand it and love it," I told her, "just as long as I can have you," and thinking on to it I was sure I was right, I could stand it, any of it and all of it, and I would be happy to have the chance of doing it.

We talked right through the night into the morning. She wanted to know so many things from me and wanted to tell me all about herself, everything there was to know.

First about me, how right from being a kid, from as early as I could remember in that little town not far from Carson City in Nevada, I had been mad keen on canning and bottling and food preservation. Just couldn't know enough about it, read enough about it, do enough about it. It was me, not Mom, who bottled all the fruit and vegetables we grew and didn't eat, for us and for other folks around. I haunted all the libraries in Carson City, searching for books that would give me more knowledge, and I knew about Appert, the Frenchman, Donkin, the Englishman, about tin-plate, about heat sterilisation, and about bacteria. At home I began to make my own cans, and began to make money too, from my bottling and my canning, and then, when Mom died, I decided to come to Chicago, the growing city where there was so much meat, and so much of it to be canned. How I had set up in a small way, and won contract after contract, because I could make better cans than anyone else, and I still could, and that was for sure.

About my two marriages, what they had been like, and why they had been what they were, failures. It was me to blame, because I had been married to cans then, they were my babies, my everything, and no woman could have competed with them – no, that could have been wrong – Delane could have competed, but I wasn't married to Delane. Now, I had done what I wanted with cans, cans wouldn't interfere with me any more. I wanted this woman now, and the cans could go to hell, except that Norm would keep it all going, and, perhaps, when we went to Europe next year we would fix up mergers over there, but she would be the number one, Delane, and I could see already, she was interested in cans like I was, and in mergers also, but only as second place to a marriage, and I could tell, the way we talked about it all, I was going to have me a partner as well as a wife.

We didn't make love, I didn't kiss her again even, we just sat there, two rational normal human beings, and discussed the things we wanted to discuss. I had never known such peace and harmony, and I was telling myself this was going to be way way better than Norm and Cynthia even, and was happy in a way I hadn't ever felt like at any other time.

She pulled no punches about herself, none at all. I got the full history of her, from her very beginning until now. She told me of her marriages, four of them, and I thought back to the night at Taps' when he and David had talked about the number of her marriages, three or four, and how they had all been failures, failures like mine because she had other interests far greater than marriage, her career, and she told me with complete frankness that, except for the first one, which had been an utter mistake, her nuptials had been to help her on her way up, even the Dennison affair, but she was now ready to be wedded for what a marriage meant, for love, for security, for keeps, and for kids.

We spoke long about kids, and she told me that she could never have any of her own, how they had cut all that part out of her, but she loved kids, and wanted kids, and she would like us to have kids when it all came about.

About four in the morning she made more coffee, and with it scrambled eggs and toast. She didn't ask me if I was hungry, just brought on the eats and said she was peckish, so had brought some for me also. I liked it, the way she had done it and the way she had included me in on it, and it was nice to eat this way, with Delane.

Afterwards we got back on to the subject of kids. She wanted to adopt a lot of them, and have them all live up at High Point.

"Would you like that?" she asked. "Adopting kids and having them up there?"

Yes, I would like it. It wouldn't be that we would have to be there all the time, her father would be there, and Olaf and Martha, the married couple who looked after her father, and who hadn't any kids either, but wanted kids and would welcome them up there, where there was so much room, open country and forest, and mountains and lakes, all the sort of country kids wanted, and wild life.

She sure loved little children. Some of the money she earned went to an orphanage on the west side of the city here in Chicago – this was almost a new part of her for me, until I remembered what Taps had said about her, how she would give to almost anything, and money didn't mean a lot to her. That was something she was proud about, helping with the finances of that orphanage.

"You sure keep it quiet too," I said.

She saw how I meant it, her smile thanked me.

"That part's easy, the new boys and girls don't want to know so much about that sort of thing like they do about other things."

I knew that, it was a great pity it was that way, but that's just how it was.

"Do you like coloured kids?" she asked.

She was glad I did, she thought we might adopt some coloured children, give them a chance in life. I knew she was right about colour. Kids, little kids, didn't worry about colour, they were all kids and they got along. It was only when they grew up and learnt about other things which weren't so much to play at, that colour, and jealousy and enmity, came into human nature. She thought that was why her father liked animals so much. They were all animals whatever their colour.

"Even animals change," I argued, "when they get big they're just like humans, have the same problems, it's only when they're little that they get along."

She guessed I was right, but it wasn't so bad with animals as it was with humans. She knew I would like her father, and knew he would like me. She wanted that I should go up with her and David tomorrow.

"No," I told her, "not this time, you go up with David like you planned. Next time it will be with me."

I was glad to think she was a little bit disappointed about that, but she thought it best, in a way. She had a lot to tell David.

"You going to tell him about us?"

"Yes," she said, "I am."

"How will he take it?"

"I think he will be very pleased, he's very fond of you."

That wasn't what I meant – what I did mean was how would he take losing her?

"He'll be very pleased," she replied, "pleased and very relieved."

I hoped she was right – she assured me she was. She was much more concerned how I viewed her and David. It was easy to tell her how.

161

"I don't want you for what you were," I said, "I just want you for what you are, what you will be with me."

She came over to where I was sitting, went down on the knees again, down to my level. It was nice to talk to her this way, sort of made us both very humble. I was very conscious how lovely she was, how fragrant the perfume of her, but it was just that warm feeling she gave me I got from her, not hot passionate thoughts or anything such as that.

"You're quite sure of that, Danny?"

I was quite sure.

We kept on planning. It was all unwinding before us. I would be down at Midway to see her off on Monday night. By that time she would have told David, and I could tell Norm and Cynthia, but no press, yet. She thought she would be on location in Japan four or five months, no longer than that. Those months would give me time to complete all my plans with the factory, and I could take out the licence for our marriage, here or in New York, or anywhere I wanted. She didn't care where as long as I took it out. Her last marriage had been settled in the proper legal manner, so had mine, there was nothing to worry about. For about six months or so, maybe a year, we would travel, mostly in Europe and England, where I could do the business deals I wanted to make. After that we would come back to High Point, she would tell her father about it all this weekend, and then we could do the family plans we wanted to do. Adopting kids and such like.

She might retire altogether from movies, but might like to make one film a year. Did I mind?

She was pleased I did not mind.

It would take a good story to get her back to movies, but there were good stories now and then, and she was pleased I was that way about it. If she went to make a film she would always want me to be with her. She thought I would enjoy that, and it would certainly help her, my being with her.

"Do you think it will work out, this, for us?" she asked me.

I thought it could. There was every chance because of the way we felt about each other, because we were not children, and because we both knew what we wanted. She wanted me because of my maturity, because I knew what she was, and had accepted her as such. I would go with her, wherever she wanted to go, and do whatever she wanted to do with her. I wanted her because she was Delane, with all the glory, the warmth, the beauty and the personality that went with it.

162

Because I wanted me a wife with all the attributes she possessed to help me run this new world enterprise I was going to build up. I wanted her because I had known for some time I had to stop being a batchelor anymore and get back to being a man again, having a woman to look after, and having a woman to take care of me, and most of all, I wanted her because she wanted me.

I held her in my arms just the once before I took her home. In her high-heel shoes she was as tall as me, and she was the delicacy, the fragrance, the elegance, the charm, of every woman in the world. I kissed her, this kiss stronger, warmer, a man's kiss for his woman, and I could feel the eagerness in that long slim body all the way down against mine.

I could understand now what a woman she was, held tight to me this way, and when she took her mouth from mine so that she could speak, I knew the warmth of her breath on my mouth as well as the heat of all the rest of her.

"Oh, Danny," she said, and I held her so very close that she had to speak into my mouth almost. "I haven't ever had a real wedding before, haven't ever really been a bride, not properly."

I didn't get that – she must have seen I was mystified about it.

"Everything – everything, has always been anticipated before. I wasn't the sort of girl to wait for anything – they weren't the sort of men to wait either." I got it now.

"I can wait," I told her, "for you."

I saw her eyes and I knew I had said the right thing.

"That's how I want it to be, Danny, with you. Everything right this time, like the good story-books – you can carry me over the door-way, and we can have a real wedding night, where things happen for the first time. I sure would like it to be that way with you – for my first real wedding."

It sounded swell, and it was just the way I wanted it really, in spite of the way I was holding her now, which had made my temperature rise by a good hundred degrees. It would be better that way, start things off the right way, romantic, the way she wanted it to be, this time, with me. It made sense.

"That's the way it will be for us," and I could feel the happiness flood all over her, so that I knew to take her back to the hotel before something snapped with me, if not with her, to spoil things. I just couldn't hold this ball of fire in my arms and not be thinking things. I took her home.

163

The dawn had long since lit the sky to the East of the city. It was a perfect morning, cool after the heat of the night, but with the certainty of another hot day ahead. It was so nice to be driving with this woman, and I wished I could just drive and drive, with her beside me, and never stop – well, only stop now and then.

I was wondering what anyone would think when she went into the hotel, although there would not be as many staff about this morning – Sunday, as on a week-day morning. They might think she had been out for an early morning walk, if they thought at all, but, then again, they might not. I pulled up a little way from the front of the block, so she could just walk round the corner and be there. I told her why. She laughed merrily, she hadn't been worrying about it.

"You're so good, Danny." The sun coming up there fast had nothing to compare with the warmth of the brown eyes smiling for me, the cool of the morning nothing to the coolness and the freshness of her, and I knew the coming day would not even bring the heat that she could bring on for me, would bring on for me, someday, soon.

"I'm so happy, Danny, so very happy," she looked it, and cool and languid and easy, but then, suddenly, she changed.

"God kill me if there is ever any man but you."

I could not speak, the ferocity of it amazed me.

"I mean it, Danny, God kill me if any man save you ever touches me again."

I took her in my arms, quietly, and with no panic. I could feel the intensity of her, knew the reason for the outburst.

"Don't say any more," I told her, "take it steady now." She stopped and cooled down, almost as fast as she had boiled up. I kissed her, it was as well the street was empty.

I watched her put on the wig – I sure hated that damn wig – watched her go back to being Laurie Gaydon again.

"Change your mind, Danny," she said, "come with us to High Point – please."

It was hard to refuse. I sure would have loved to go with them, and I knew David would not really have minded my being with them, wouldn't think it strange in any way at all. But I did refuse, because of that inward wisdom which all men have and which told me now to let her be on her own with David, to tell him what she had said she would. She was sorry I would not go.

"There'll be other times," I told her, "just for you and me – have a good time – see you at Midway."

I watched the smartest woman in the world disappear around the corner, and I was proud that she had made a new life possible for me. She sure was a grand sight, even from the back, slim, neat, and like a high-stepping thoroughbred. She sure looked grand, even in that damn black wig.

CHAPTER 31

High Point

David Lander

The drive up there was wonderful. Until we got out of the city the roads were crowded with those who lived outside making for the beaches, where they would join the thousands already burning themselves, and I was glad we were travelling the other way, into the country, the hills and the cool. The heat of Chicago was terrific nowadays, and the prospect of two days up in the hills most pleasing.

I drove carefully for a while. I hadn't driven a lot in the States, Danny's big car now and then, and once I had driven Cynthia into the city when Norm had been too busy to take her in, and it was a pretty frightening business with all the colour whizzing at you on both sides very fast. So I was glad to take it slowly and carefully, at least until I got out of the city and its approaches, to where the traffic lessened, so that I could push along a bit faster. But we were in no hurry and I certainly wasn't racing.

Laurie looked well. She seemed very fresh and said, though she hadn't slept a lot, it had been a very restful night for her. She was absolutely stunning and I thought this mysterious thing which affects all women every month didn't seem to be affecting her much. She was cool and radiant, and once we had got out of the city and I could relax a bit whilst I drove, she was talkative with it.

She knew the route well. It was like a road-map in her brain, something she would never forget. Through Rockford, alongside Lake Le-Aqua-Na for a time, and then the climb into Apple River Canyon itself. It was wonderful country, breath-taking in its loveliness, and now we were climbing, some heavenly views. I wished Danny had been there with us, so he could have driven, which he loved to do, and I could have just admired it all. I told Laurie what I was thinking.

"Yes," she agreed, "he would have enjoyed this, it's a wonderful run. I wanted him to come – knew you would not have minded, but he said no, he thought I just should have this weekend with you."

How great of Danny I thought, and how very typical.

"He would love it up at High Point," she went on, "it will be so cool and restful, a couple of days out of the heat of the city would have been a great change for him."

"I know he would have liked that," I agreed. "He works hard and we've had a hectic time whilst you've been here, Laurie – still you can bring him up with you next time you're in Chicago."

"I'll do that, I'd love him to meet my father, and see High Point," she said, and I could tell she was thinking hard about it. She didn't agree with my point that life had been hectic though.

"That's how it always is in my life, David" – she smiled and then laughed – "well, perhaps not quite, but we never seem to relax at all, and after a time I get very sick of it all and long for the peace of an ordinary life like an ordinary woman."

"That's the trouble, Laurie darling, you're just not an ordinary woman, you're more lovely, more vital than anyone else in the world, and the life you have to live goes with all that."

"You're so nice, David," she told me in the way I liked so much, and she put her left hand on my knee so that I had to concentrate damn hard on my driving, and try not to think, well not too much, of this gorgeous creature sat alongside me, but there was no heat or anything like that in her hand, just a sort of friendly possession, but that was pleasant, and in a way better than the heat and the passion.

"There's a little place just up here we can pull in off the road," she said. "You can drive down to the edge of the peak – it's a wonderful view, we can get out and take a look."

I turned in where she directed, through the high trees along a short winding track with the undergrowth hemming us in both sides, to a small open clearing which seemed to be right up in the sky itself.

"Careful, David," she said, "stop here."

It was terrific, high up, with the blue of Lake Le-Aqua-Na some twenty miles below us to the south-east, and a horizon which could have been a million miles away. As nice as anywhere I had ever seen – the Lake District back home, Scotland, Norway, Germany, anywhere.

"It's just beautiful, absolutely beautiful." I had never been more truthful in all my life.

"It has always been so, right from when I could first remember it

167

– I came here a lot, I would often sit here for hours, just looking, thinking, and admiring this view – that's the lake over there, and the haze is Chicago, sometimes you can see it so very clearly, in the Fall or early Winter, when it's sharp and visibility is good – it's too hazy now, but that's Chicago for sure."

It was so quiet and peaceful up here, and no evidence of other people. We could well have been the only two living humans in the world. I spoke my thoughts for her. She agreed.

"It's always like this – nobody ever comes here but me – Ryker's Peak, it's called. They say the Indians used to kill their enemies by blindfolding them and then making them walk over the top here – I don't know how true that is, but it's the old country tale."

I could believe it, could well think this peak would be able to tell a story all right, like any other part of this great country, or any other country for that matter. How wonderful it would be if a man was able to live through all time and in all history. I told Laurie how I always thought that way.

"It's wonderful country and I love it so." I could see that in her when she spoke. "Not far over there" – she pointed beyond Lake Le-Aqua-Na – "is General Grant's home. You know who he was?" I knew who he was. "And over there" – she was pointing south now – "is the Lincoln monument" – I knew who Lincoln was also – "and that's White Pines Forest. All this was Indian country, David, wonderful hunting country, and I know how the Indians must have felt when the white men kept taking more and more of it from them. I would have felt exactly the same way. I love it all so much up here, when we come back from Japan this time I think I shall come back here for always."

"I don't think I would ever have left," I said.

"You would, David, just like me. When you're young you always want to go off somewhere else, it's when you're old" – she saw what I thought of that remark from her, and smiled just a little in appreciation of my thoughts – "well, when you're older then, you know the real value of places and what they mean to you. It's like that for me now, I'm ready to come up here for always and have somebody take care of me and that's for sure."

Somehow I knew what she was going to say next.

"Would you like to come up here with me, David, for always?"

"No." It was point-blank and without the slightest hesitation. "It wouldn't work out, Laurie. It's all yours, High Point, you're rich, you have money and I haven't. I still have my way to make in the world. It wouldn't be fair, I wouldn't stand a chance at all, much as I would like the first part of it. But soon I would be feeling just like the kept man I would be, and I would hate it, and then start hating you. I just couldn't be a gigolo, Laurie, not even for you."

"You're honest, David, and so right."

"Of course I'm honest, I couldn't be otherwise with you, Laurie, you're so very honest with everybody yourself. I feel you must be honest in this terribly dishonest world. You're everything I would want if I was a big enough man, but I'm not, not big enough for you, and I'm not the man for you – you know that too, well not for – how you people say – for keeps."

Till then she had been just a figure in the forefront of the wonderful view behind her, but I took her hand whilst I was speaking and drew her into my arms. She came to me easily, readily, and now she had become all of the view, so that I couldn't see anything but her, and most of what I could see was warm brown eyes which were very very moist. I held her close to me, she didn't react in any physical manner but just stood there, acquiescent, thinking as I talked.

"What you want, Laurie, is somebody big and strong like Danny. Yes, he'd be the one, Danny. He is big and rich, more money than you, a very strong character who wouldn't worry what anyone or everyone was thinking or saying, if he knew you were right for him, that would be right as far as he was concerned. What's more, he would take care of you in the way you need, by that I mean he wouldn't let you boss him; in fact, he would be the boss because that's just Danny's nature, he's the boss or nothing."

She was less acquiescent now, her body much more pliable and warm, and I had a feeling she was greatly enjoying what I was telling her, it was something she wanted to hear, and badly needed someone to tell her. I could feel my strength rising within me as I held her, so I bent my head down a little to nuzzle it against her cheek, kissing her softly, gently, two or three times, and I knew I was disappointed she was as she was today, or we could have made love up here in this loveliest part of God's world. She let me hold her thus for some time, and with the third kiss, her lips parted just a little, not much, but a little, and I began to think that perhaps she was a little disappointed how things were with her, as I certainly was. She took her lips away still letting me hold her.

"How would I fit in Danny's world, David?" she asked.

I knew just how well, I was enthusiastic about it.

"Absolutely wonderful – you'd be just right all the way. You'd be the luxurious, the elegant, the fabulous, Mrs. Danny Erikson, and after a while, they would all forget you had ever been Laurie Gaydon or Delane, or anything but Mrs. Erikson. You'd be the right-hand woman at the top of his business, and with you to spur him along it could be some business. Wherever you went, you and he, you'd be perfect for him, you could mix anywhere, you'd have everyone, even the women, eating out of your hand, longing to entertain you and Danny. You would be great for him, Laurie, your beauty, your terrific charm, would make him, and Laurie, it would be so good for you both, you're so wonderful and he's such a great man."

Except for my voice it was quiet, with that soft quietness which is all the voices of nature – the gentle sighing of the breeze, sighing through the leaves and the branches of each and every tree, the rustlings low down on the ground, the crying and the whistling of the birds, the calling of the animals, the hum of bees and other winged insects, hurrying, busying by, and somewhere, not far off, there was the lovely chortling, lapping, of water, where I supposed a small stream fell down from this high place to the lake of Le-Aqua-Na, miles down below, and this was one of those never-to-be-forgotten times when I would wish for the world and time to stand still, so that it could be this way for ever.

She kissed me, lips a little more open even, but not fully apart, still nice and nicer than before, and warmer. How long we had stood this way I neither knew or cared – a century, and a minute were as one. She took her lips away again. This was a lovely game, a game I could play all day with her.

"You sure are throwing me at Danny," she said. "Why?"

"I'm not throwing you at anybody, darling," I told her. "I've grown up a lot with you, I think I know what would be good for you, and I certainly know what would be good for him. You have a good look at Danny – before some other lady, with nothing like you have to give him – gets the number one spot with him. If I think highly of him, it's because I have come to know him so well, and I'll never be able to tell you in a million years how highly I regard you."

"No-one ever spoke like this to me before, David. It's so nice to hear and it does things for me."

She kissed me again, warmly but with lips only slightly open, and now I knew how she was kissing me. It was just the way Cynthia

170

kissed me when we kissed goodnight, as we sometimes did, or when I kissed her because she had done something for me. Always like this, lips parted a little way to give something to it, and to also hint she would like to go further with it, but dare not – the big sister kiss, she called it. Laurie was kissing me in exactly the same way, but, of course, it wasn't really the big sister kiss for her, I knew very well why she dare no more today.

"It's time to go," she told me finally.

It was. We had been there a long time and still it seemed that there were just the two of us on this earth, just she and I, with the birds, the animals, the insects, and all the rest that was nature.

"Let me drive, David," she said, as we approached the car. "You can see how beautiful the country is up here."

She must have seen my face what I thought about that.

"Don't worry, David, I'm quite a good driver, honestly."

I took her word for it, and let her drive.

First, however, the wig had to come off. She put it in the small vanity bag she carried, her other cases were stowed in the big boot, nearly filling it.

"They've never seen me in a wig up at High Point" – it was amazing to see Laurie Gaydon vanish and Janice Delane appear just by the removal of this wig, which I thought suited her so well. I couldn't have said whether she looked warmer as Laurie or Delane, and, in truth, the warmth of her was in her eyes, her voice, and in her body.

"Funny, David, Danny doesn't like me in the wig at all – he says he went to meet Delane, and he likes me as Delane."

"Oh, when did he tell you that?"

She was rather confused for a moment –

"Friday, I think – at Taps – or it could have been last night – last night at Cynthia's. No, we didn't speak much there – it must have been when I was dancing with him at the Continental."

"That was a good night, wasn't it, Laurie?"

"It sure was, what I can remember, though I didn't like the afters yesterday. Yes, that's when he told me, down at that party. I'm having a red one, a red wig made for me, how do you think I'll look in that?"

"You shouldn't ask me," I told her. "I'm very prejudiced – for me you're easily the loveliest woman I've ever seen, wig or no wig. If you want my opinion though – you'll look well in a red wig – you would look well in anything – like you look so well in nothing at all."

171

I couldn't resist that and laughed as I said it. She laughed with me. "Do I, darling? Well, you should know." In her good humour, and perhaps because I was allowing her to drive, she leaned over and kissed me. A little bit less sisterly this time. I brought my right hand immediately to her breast, and though she took it away, I brought it back again so that I could hold the lovely contour of her tenderly as I so loved to do, but remembering and not using my hand other than to hold, and human as I am, I could not but think how very disappointing it is at times that women have to be what they are.

CHAPTER 32

Delane Is Home

She was a good driver and, like any good driver should, took it very easily until she had got well settled in and knew the car she was driving. I felt very confident with her. In any case she could not go fast, the road twisting and turning as we climbed ever upwards through deep forest country with sometimes a break in the trees giving a magnificent view for miles and miles. I was happy, it was grand to see this country as I was doing, whilst Laurie was driving well and obviously enjoying it. We did not talk much except when she would tell me where to look for such and such a landmark or a view, and, even then, she herself did not take her eyes off the road ahead, twisting, turning, climbing and climbing.

For many miles we had not seen a sign of any other human beings, nor was there anything else on the road. She told me that quite a few people did have lodges or week-end homes up here, but High Point was really the only permanent residence for miles around, and generally everything was well off the road as High Point itself was.

We came to a fork in the road – we turned left still climbing, the other way seemed to go downhill.

"Just down there, in a little church and cemetery, is where my mother is buried."

It was the first time I remembered her ever mentioning her mother. I made what I thought was the obvious remark.

"You must miss her a lot, Laurie."

"Oh no," she replied, "I didn't ever really know her, she's been dead for almost thirty years now. I'll go and put some flowers on the grave later on, but it's just like taking flowers for someone I never met."

I was silent for a while. There was nothing I could say. I supposed she was right, thirty years is an awful long time, but it did seem somewhat heartless the way she had said it. I couldn't help recalling something Taps had said when he told us about her – good Lord, that was only just a week ago, and yet it could have been an age. Something about not arguing with breeding, and her father not blaming her for her way of life – it was pretty strange. But Laurie herself did not throw any more light on the subject, though she, like me, was silent for a time.

"Not far now, David," she told me eventually. "We drop down a bit here, climb again for about a mile, then we're there, just in time for brunch – hungry?"

I said I was. I'd only had fruit juice, toast and coffee that morning, and this keen, crisp, mountain air, was giving me a good appetite. I asked her something I had been wanting to ask for two or three days.

"Do you often bring people up here?" By people I really meant men. She knew what I meant.

"Oh no, David, never before. You're the first man I have ever brought here."

She understood me very well, understood what I was thinking, thinking and wanting to ask her. I didn't have to ask.

"You'll get on well with my father," she said, "and he'll like you." She smiled and risked a very quick side-glance at me. "Don't worry, David, he won't eat you."

I asked part of what I was thinking then.

"Did you never bring any of – you know – your husbands up here?"

She didn't even flicker an eyelid.

"Never did," she knew that part without having to think back very hard. "My father has only ever met one of them, that was the first one. He didn't want to meet him and, when he did, he sure didn't want me to marry him" – this one I remembered had been Johnny Lamp – a mean little man, Taps had described him, and the marriage had lasted four weeks – "but I knew best" – I was watching her face, she didn't think back to Johnny very happily – "for about three days – then I knew how wrong I had been. The rest my father never met, wouldn't ever come to meet any of them, though I really only gave him notice about the last one – so he'll be very happy to find how much improved my taste is when he meets you, David" –

"I'm honoured," I said, and didn't know how to feel about it.

"I mean that, David, he will like you, you're very much like him in a lot of ways – just you see – oh, here we are."

We came out of a sharp right bend and she pulled up at a high white gate. I could see the name-plate, 'High Point', at the side of the gate, and my eyes caught a glimmer of water through the trees to the right. I opened the gate and, when she had driven through, closed it after her. The house was three hundred yards further on, up a rough drive – long, rambling, two-storied, just as she had told me, clean-looking, brightly painted, seeming to stand out on a ledge with just the sky behind it.

A man was standing at the high white porch in the front centre of the house. The house was about eight feet above the sunken drive, and, as I looked up at him, with two big dogs sat at one side of him, I could see the look of pleasure spread over his face as we came to a stop below him.

I gave her a minute with her father before I got out on the far side from them. The dogs greeted me first, great barking animals, big rough-haired huskies, and I could imagine what harm they could do if they were really trying.

"Down General, down Wisp," her father shouted, they were obedient which was pleasing for me. Laurie brought her father round to my side where I was still not properly out of the car, watching the dogs. Mr. Gaydon was small and slim, but looked what he was, a typical outdoor man. The strong firm grip, as we shook hands, indicated much more strength than the size of him would have had me believe.

"Welcome to High Point, David," the voice was pleasant making the welcome ring true.

"Olaf will bring your bag in," Laurie said, "come and look around."

The house was solidly and sturdily built. It had originally been a square two-storied residence, but extra rooms had been added on the ground floor, all spacious, and with much more glass than had been used in the original house, the outside walls of each room being almost all window. The house had an air of wealth, and I was not surprised to hear that the builders of the newer parts had been Mr. Gaydon himself and Olaf – for them both it had been a labour of love without doubt.

Built some way back from the rear of the house, and approached along a sunken and well-sheltered path, was Mr. Gaydon's workshop. A large place, again built by these two men, and one which served

175

several purposes, not the least important part being a sick-bay for birds and animals. About sixty yards behind that the bluff ended, and there was a sheer drop from here of about two hundred feet to the small lake below. This was part of High Point, and could be got to by a winding path through the trees some distance to the right of the house. It was beautiful to stand and look down at Squaw Lake, as they called it, and on beyond that, almost due west at the rugged colourful country and to another high peak some thirty, thirty-five, miles away.

Inside the house it was just as spacious, and everywhere clean and comfortable. My room was large with a great bay window at the far end, overlooking the country beyond Squaw Lake, though the lake itself could not be seen. The room was well lit, had a wash basin and running water, and was very cosy.

"We have all the comforts," Mr. Gaydon said. "For all my love of nature I am not one to do without the luxuries of civilisation. We generate our own electricity, we have our own heating system, and there is wood in plenty for the burning, whilst we do not need air-conditioning. God provides that for us."

It was terrific up here, the air crisp, cold even out of the sun, and I thought of the heat down in Chicago with the thousands browning on the beaches, and those who were not lucky enough to be there, baking in their apartments or their homes, unless they were rich enough to be part of the wealthy with their air-conditioned homes and air-conditioned cars. This was delightful and I was so glad to be here.

Laurie looked into the room – "Martha's rung the gong for brunch, come and get it – David, you must be starving."

We had wheatcakes with maple syrup, delicate crisp-fried little sausages, and coffee. I ate so much I got in Martha's good books right from the start, and over the meal and afterwards I learned a great deal about Mr. Gaydon, and about Olaf and Martha.

Mr. Gaydon had been fortunate. His father had founded a meat packing business in Chicago, and had hoped his son would carry on the business, when he had not wanted to do so he accepted that and helped him all he could in Mr. Gaydon's one real interest in life, that of becoming a naturalist. Chicago was all right, the lake and the shore, but not the rest of it, not any city, so when his father died, within a year of his wife, Laurie's father, now an orphan, found he had been left rather a large fortune, which he promptly added to by selling the business, part of the deal being High Point. He had never regretted it, not even when he realised the fortunes that had been made in the meat business. Everything had gone well for him also, and he had been able to spend his life doing what he wanted to do.

His writing on American wild life had brought him fame. I had not known until then that this is what he did, and that he was the foremost writer of his kind in the States. I had visualised him as some sort of a rancher or cattle dealer. He had spent a lot of money on High Point which was now in very good order. Though he didn't say it I could sense what was implied, it was all for Laurie and the sooner she came to it, the better for him, for High Point, for Olaf and Martha who both worshipped her, and, to my way of thinking, for Laurie herself. I wonder if he was aware, I kept saying to myself, that she is coming back, soon. I hoped she was going to tell him what she had told me about High Point and children, and I tried to imagine Danny up here; he fitted in very well, and now I knew High Point, I knew what a happy place it could be, with the right people in it.

Olaf and Martha had come to High Point when Laurie was two years old, and were now as much a part of it as Mr. Gaydon himself. Olaf was his assistant, his right hand, his guide and his companion, whilst Martha ran the place, and, I thought, ran the two men as well.

It was funny about Olaf. He had been born in New York, just after his parents had got off the boat which had brought them to the new world. As a young man, he had drifted to Chicago where he had met and married Martha. They had worked together in Rockford, and it was there they heard of Mr. Gaydon, heard that he wanted a cook-housekeeper. They had come up to High Point on foot, camping at night on the way. Mr. Gaydon had hired Martha on the spot, and taken Olaf on as well. He had never made a better bargain, they were wonderful these two; Martha, a great cook who looked after him and the house so well, and Olaf, a tremendous odd job man who never stopped working, could do anything from build a house to binding the broken leg of a wounded animal in the manner of the best veterinary surgeons.

Olaf, who had never hardly seen the country until that day he and his buxom wife had set off to climb into the hills to find High Point, but who was a natural in it. From somewhere he had inherited all the fieldcraft of a Red Indian, everything he did was natural and was right. Without him Mr. Gaydon could not have done half he had done, and, because of the two of them, Olaf and Martha, High Point was a home for him in spite of the loss of his wife and the almost continual absence of his daughter.

There was just one strange thing. There was barely a mention of Laurie's mother. It was odd, and I could not think he had forgotten her, or nearly not known her, as his daughter had. A man surely can not do that. But there was no explanation of her, and, of course, I could not ask. Even when Laurie went off later to see the grave, there was nothing really said about it – perhaps they all regarded it as the grave of a stranger.

CHAPTER 33

Three Wonderful People

I spent the afternoon with Mr. Gaydon and Olaf, two magicians in the magic world of a forest, and I had never thought there was anything like this. The air was wonderful, invigorating, exhilerating, the scenery breath-taking, the blue of the lake, the green of the forest, dropping away and then climbing to that other high peak away there, and the sky a serene blue with white rabbit tails of clouds chasing each other hither and thither. It would be bleak up here in the winter, no doubt, but there was ample fuel for the taking and the cutting, and the stock of wood Olaf had accumulated was mountain high, whilst their stock of fuel for the generator, stored well away from the house for safety, would last six months. In the kitchen it was the same, a vast deep-freeze and cold-store held all these three would require for a year if necessary. Whatever the weather in the winter, it did not really worry them, and they had never really known it very bad, well, not more than for a week or so at a time.

In the forest it was quiet and peaceful, with only the noises of the birds and the animals, the whistling, chirping, shreaking, squeaking and scuffling, and the gentle song of the wind in the trees, to keep us company. Except when they spoke to me neither Mr. Gaydon nor Olaf spoke. They had a perfect understanding of each other, and a nod or a sign to them was as good, better even than the spoken word.

That evening Martha made an oxtail stew which was simply wonderful. We watched her prepare it for a while and saw an artist at work. The oxtails were cut into small sections and browned in butter, then she added celery, carrots, onions, potatoes, peas, beans and some mushrooms, seasoning with salt, pepper and a bayleaf. Laurie brought in a small bottle of red burgundy from her father's cellar, and Martha carefully measured the quantity she wanted into a saucepan, wherein the whole mixture was poured to cook until the meat was done. Then it was thickened, and, just before serving, Martha poured the juice of a lemon over it. I loved it and loved the baked grapefruit we had afterwards, with the fruit halved and spread with spoonfuls of molasses and sprinkled with cinnamon, then baked. Martha got full marks from me for her cooking, and me full marks from her for my eating.

Later we played gin rummy and drank peach brandy, especially kept for such an important occasion as this, so Mr. Gaydon said, and at two o'clock in the morning I was either winning or losing a million dollars, and I wasn't at all worried about it. Neither were Laurie or her father, so we called it quits at the end. After all, what is a million or two between friends?

Laurie woke me just after eight the next morning. I'd had a wonderful sleep. It was grand to sleep under blankets again, whilst the air coming in through the wide open bay window, was pure ozone. I felt as fresh as a daisy.

I ate a huge breakfast, much to Martha's delight.

"It's a pleasure to cook for someone who can eat," she said, beaming at me. "Not like these others, just pickers" – Mr. Gaydon and Laurie, and that finnicky husband of hers – "just pickers, never ate anything properly."

"David can eat for ever," Laurie told her.

"Then David can stay here for ever" – I liked the David part of that from Martha – "good eatin' never hurt nobody."

It was evident that Martha was a rule unto herself. She called Laurie by her first name, and now the same for me, but Olaf called Laurie Miss, and me, Sir. I had to grin at the way Martha had described Olaf as her finnicky husband – does no husband ever get any praise from his wife, but does the wife really mean all she says? I supposed it was ever thus.

Laurie took me down the little winding path to Squaw Lake, and from the boathouse there we got out two single canoes. It was lovely on the little lake, warm in the sun now, but not over warm and certainly not like the heat I had been experiencing down in Chicago. We paddled along the west bank to a large open clearing which sloped down from the woods to the water's edge. We went ashore.

"This is where I'd like to build my own house, David."

"You wouldn't live up at High Point then?" I was a little surprised. I had visualised her being up there, with, if necessary, the already big rambling house being added to.

"No, I wouldn't like to do that, with a husband and children – we could build a grand place, here, build a road through from the house there. We'd be near enough to them, and yet far enough away. I think that would be essential."

She was probably right, especially with Danny, if she was still thinking of him. He would want his own place, and there was room here to build a very big and beautiful home. It would catch plenty of sun, be a little more sheltered in the winter, and, as I saw, when she spoke of it, a lot safer for children.

"I should always be afraid of them falling over the bluff up there, David."

It was a lovely prospect. With money, and there was plenty of that, she could build as fine a home as she desired, and there was no reason why the electricity could not come from the generator already up there at High Point. We wandered around whilst I helped her with her planning, she was so happy and engrossed with it all.

"Go ahead and build it," I told her, "it will be somewhere to come for my holidays."

"Would you come, David, for sure?"

"Of course I would come. I would have to save up a bit first, but I'll come if you ask me."

"We sure will ask you, and we'll send you an air ticket so you won't have to save, could we do that?"

She was using the plural as though it was all fixed, and as though the house was already built.

"I'm not sure I would like the air ticket –"

"Of course you would, David," she interrupted, "if it was Danny and me, it would be just like taking you out for a steak or something like that."

"Oh, no, it isn't like that."

"None of your English snobbery," she was very serious. "I would just love you to come, you know that."

That was much better, even though I still didn't like the air ticket part.

"Would you, Laurie?" I wasn't snobbish, or proud now, even if I had been, just so happy that this wonderful woman could say such a nice thing.

"Of course, David, you know I'm very fond of you. I sure would love you to come."

We were up at the back of the clearing now, almost in the trees, and very close together. I kissed her, she was very soft and warm in my hold, and a tiny way responsive.

"You like to have your own way," I told her.

"Don't say that, David," she wasn't very pleased. "Just say you'll come."

"I'll come," I said, "if you ask me, but no air ticket, and let's not argue about that on such a day as this."

She saw I meant it and tried a different tack.

"Do you really think it could work out for Danny and me, up here – now you've seen it?"

I had no doubts about that, it was an easy one to answer, and to answer in the way would please her.

"Of course, it will, Laurie, it'll be perfect. He'll love it up here, and it's not far from Chicago. He could keep his own place down there so you could have somewhere if you have to go down. There's no doubt you can build a lovely place up here, big, so you can have visitors, and I think you and Danny would make it very popular up here. Then you would be near to your father, so he'll be very happy. Yes, Laurie, I'm certain it could work out for you, but don't forget what I told you – you've got to get hold of Danny before some other smart lady muscles in on him."

"They wouldn't dare," she said, "I'd scratch their eyes out."

I believed she would at that.

I could tell how pleased she was at what I had told her, could feel it in her body, and see it in her eyes and her face. She kissed me, this one more like the Laurie I knew. I drew her back into the cover of the trees, the ground was dry, it was warm here and quiet.

She knew what was in my mind.

"No, David, not here."

I was puzzled, and the way she said not here made it even more puzzling. She hadn't said no, and I had been holding her for a while now, and had known the warmth coming into her. She saw my look.

"We still can't, darling," kissing me again, softly, the big-sister kiss this time – "I'm so very fond of you, David, you're my boy."

I liked being her boy all right, and would have liked being more than that just then. Still, I wasn't puzzled anymore, even if there were other things I was.

Walking back to the canoes she told me she had already spoken to her father about it all. The land was already hers, since that morning, and when she got back from Japan they could start everything going.

"Why wait?" I asked her, "Danny can start everything now, and it would all be complete by the time you got back from Japan."

She liked that and yet she didn't. There was no need for all that speed. She and Danny could live with her father whilst this place was being built. They would like that up there, she thought, and she would like to see all the stages of it. No, she thought it would be best to wait and do it her way.

"You're so nice about it all, David – you've done a lot for me, the things you've said about Danny and me."

"It just can't miss," I told her, "the way I see it, you're just perfect for each other, different enough to be absolutely perfect. I'll tell you what, Laurie, I'll make a bet with you – that it comes off with you and Danny, I'll bet you that air ticket" – I saw the laugh come into her eyes and her face – "to – to," I was thinking hard – I had it – "to a new pair of briefs, you're size and colour, that it comes off, what do you say?"

She was delighted. "Of course, David," a huge smile and a terrific sparkle in her eyes – "I hope I don't win those panties!"

"Don't worry," I assured her, "you won't."

It was a happy day, with Martha putting on another huge meal for me, and it was as well our morning out in the open had given me back the appetite I thought I would never have again after that breakfast I had eaten only a few hours earlier.

"You're a marvel, Martha," I told her, "if you weren't already married, I'd come up and marry you like a shot – how about that?"

"Fine, David," I could see how pleased this big, heavy-breasted woman was. "Maybe if I marry you and the way you eat, we could have had some children – not like old finnicky Olaf out there, just pickin' and never eatin'."

"I hope I haven't started something," I said to Mr. Gaydon as Martha went out.

"Don't worry, David," he said, "it's something she has always thought about, always blames Olaf that there are no children, but it's not his fault, I've had him examined, and Martha won't be examined, says there's nothing wrong with her, and, of course, it must be. Don't worry, they're happy enough, and if she says anything to Olaf he'll crack her over the backside with a brush or something, then she'll be happy."

I thought it best to say no more and could see that, if Laurie adopted children up here, it would make more than her happy. Martha

183

would love it, so would Mr. Gaydon, and Olaf, no doubt, who would have a lot of little boys and girls to teach his animal craft to, and I was very sure Danny would love it. It was funny about Martha though, a great big woman like her not being able to have kids, she would have been the perfect mother. That's the funny thing about nature and about women, those that are best suited to have children don't always have them.

I just loved High Point. It had almost everything, and what it hadn't got Laurie was preparing to bring. Children would love it up here, it was such a wonderful paradise for them. She was perfect on the plans, forgetting nothing. When they built the house they would even build a schoolroom and accommodation for a teacher, and bring a teacher up here to live.

"How many children do you think you'll have, Laurie?"

She wasn't prepared to say, six, ten, a dozen, twenty, it would depend a lot on the children themselves, and, of course, on Danny – it seemed to me that it was now firm in her mind that it was to be Danny, and I wasn't sure how she would go about it. She would only see him for a few minutes at the airport, but I didn't confuse the issue.

She had other plans too.

"There's another big clearing right across the lake from here, David, and I thought once we get up here we might build a lot of log cabins on there, then we could have some of the poorer children from the city up here for vacations, and we could have the scouts and young people like that. We could make a lovely camp over there, and there would be so much to do, fishing, canoeing, everything."

"You're terrific, Laurie, that's a wonderful idea. You ought to get a lot of help from all the authorities for a scheme like that. If more people with money and with land would do that sort of thing, what a great difference it would make for a lot of children."

I was sorry when it was time to leave High Point. It had been so heavenly up there, with Mr. Gaydon, Olaf and Martha, so good to me.

Martha was concerned about my eating right to the last. We had a meal about five-thirty, her own baked ginger scones, full of fruit and just a touch of ginger, smothered in butter, her own peach jam, blueberry pie and cream, and thick, luscious chocolate cake,

"It's just as well I'm going," I said, "if I stayed here with Martha I would be fatter than a pig," saw the look on Martha's face and corrected myself, "fatter than a hog."

"That's fine, David," she said, "hogs is good, just look at the little hogs they have."

She was still at it. I hoped Olaf had a big brush handy outside there in the kitchen.

It wasn't a sad farewell at all. I think they all realised that it wouldn't be long before Laurie came back, and this time, pretty well for good. I could go back there whenever I wanted.

"You'll be welcome at High Point always, David," Mr. Gaydon said.

I told them I would like to come again before I returned to England, but I didn't think I could come without Laurie.

"Nonsense," her father said, "come any time, bring a friend – you'll always be welcome here."

I liked that idea. As we drove down the drive I told Laurie I liked it.

"Perhaps I could come, Laurie, and bring Danny with me so" –

She was fierce. The interruption quite hot.

"No, David, not Danny, when he comes, if he comes, I'll bring him – you come, bring Norm and Cynthia with you, they would like it, but not Danny."

"All right," I told her, "forget I said it."

CHAPTER 34

Ryker's Peak

I kept quiet and concentrated on my driving. At the gate I switched off, braked and put the car in gear, whilst I opened it, drove through, repeated the process and then closed the gate behind me. I didn't look at her, not even at the knees and leg she was showing when I got back in the car. Well, not much more than a quick look and only then so she couldn't see what I was looking at. I drove on down. She was quiet also, that wasn't to be wondered at, leaving up there perhaps, she must be feeling it a bit. I let her think, and thought a lot myself. A few hours more and she would be gone, and it could well be I would never see her again. Well, if that was to be it would be, there was nothing I could do to stop it, and it had been nice knowing her. Nice – it had been wonderful.

"You're mad at me, David," she said, after a while.

"I was mad at you," I agreed, "for a moment, but I'm not now. I've been thinking about it, perhaps you are right, perhaps it would be best for you to bring Danny up here, and best for him."

"I'm sorry, David," she drew closer to me.

"It's all right, Laurie, I should have realised how you would be feeling up there, no need to be sorry about anything, there's been no harm done."

She drew even closer, the skirt of the costume she was wearing, way above her knees. It was an unusual skirt for her, pleated and full, but in her own powder blue colour. Now I came to think about it, this was the same skirt, the same costume, she had travelled up in – easier to travel in, I thought, than her usual tight form-fitting skirts.

I liked her being near to me again, but there was a lot more of her being shown than was good for my concentration.

"Put your skirt down, darling," I told her, "you're getting to be a big girl now."

She laughed, she was happy again, the quick flare-up back there forgotten.

"I never thought you would say that to me, David."

Yes, it was all nice again, and I was enjoying this banter as I always did with her, but I just had to concentrate on this switchback of a road, with the going needing great care in places.

"I wouldn't tell you that if I wasn't driving, Laurie dear, I enjoy looking at your legs as much as any man, but I must keep my eyes on the road, unless you want us to go over the top somewhere – I should think it's rather a long way down some of these cliffs."

She pulled the skirt down a tiny little bit, and cuddled up as close as she could without affecting my driving. She was warm and snug alongside me, making me so content to be with her.

"We've plenty of time, David, you can pull into Ryker's Peak for a while I can put my wig on there."

I was glad she had said it. I was going to suggest we stopped there, though not just for her to put the wig on. Maybe I would never see her again, so I wanted to hold her in my arms just once more, and properly, or as properly as I could under the circumstances. There were one or two things I had to say to her also. There was time to do these things, as she had said, we could spare a little while without worrying or having to rush afterwards.

I remembered the road and slowed down just right, pulling in along the little overgrown track, overgrown as if nature was trying to hide the peak which was so lovely a place and from where there was such a wonderful view.

"You have a good memory, David," she said as we pulled in.

"Not for everything," I replied, "just for the things I like, things I'm interested in. There are very few moments with you I shall ever forget – I'll always have some wonderful memories of you."

"You'll always feel that way about us, always darling?"

"Cross my heart, Laurie," I told her, "I'm so glad I had the nerve to come over to your table at the Statler that night in New York."

"I'm glad you came over, David," she was a wee bit pensive – "not everybody remembers me so kindly as you say you will, not everyone speaks of me in the way you have just spoken."

"Not everyone knows you, the real you, the way I do, Laurie."

She was just going to get out, but that stopped her. She turned back to me.

"What do you really, honestly, think of me, David?"

I held her hand and pulled her over a little further towards me. She was such a nice person, and behind all the beauty, the glamour, and the sex, there was genuine warmth and character – exactly as Taps had told us, and which I had been lucky enough to find in her, and obtain from her.

"If I really told you, Laurie, that wig wouldn't fit you any more" – she squeezed my hand, she knew what I meant by that – "you're the most wonderful girl in all the world, beautiful, lovely, and, as you want me to be honest, the sexiest – no, I don't mean that unkindly, darling, you are sexy in everything you do and you have, without any lie, the most utter female appetite I have known in any woman, not that I have known a lot, but that's you, you are what you are, and you just cannot change it."

I paused a moment to let her say anything she might wish to do. She kept silent so I went on.

"I have enjoyed every minute of you. At first I was terribly scared, not of you, perhaps, but of the loving you gave me, that was in New York. In Chicago it has been so different, I'm not scared of you, and I am very happy to have been a part of your life, grateful for all you have given me, and I will always love you in the way I do love you. I wish, darling, I was mature enough, strong enough, for it to be me you really want, but I know that cannot be, I know it isn't meant to be. But I do know you can achieve the happiness you want so much, Laurie, and I pray it will all go well for you, and Danny."

"I shall remember that for always, David," she spoke slowly. "You always say the nicest things, you do me a lot of good – we two have a lot of lovely things we can remember. I will hope that you can come back and see us again real soon. You will always be welcome, David."

It was nice to hear her say it, and nicer still to know that she meant it. I had got very close to the heart of this woman, just as she was very close to mine, even though we were not for each other it was so lovely to know that, in our memories of each other, it would all be perfect, with never a wrong word or a wrong gesture.

It was just as quiet, as lonely, here at Ryker's Peak, as it had been yesterday. We walked almost to the edge of the peak – the view was really beautiful, and now, in the evening air, much more clear than it had been the morning before.

"That's Chicago, David – you can see it today."

She was right, even with the naked eye and from this distance, it could be made out as a big city, grey and dull beside the shimmering of Lake Michigan, and above the greyness a long flat smoke haze. It was Chicago all right, but I wasn't giving all my attention to the view.

I stood behind her, holding her close to me. I bent my head down into her hair, then on down to kiss the back of her neck, her ears, her shoulders. My hands came from low around her to take possession of her breasts. She, gently, firmly, took them away from her, but back the hands came. I couldn't stop them, didn't want to stop them. She took them away again, but back they came again, and this time they stayed there, just holding the fullness of her, warm, firm, in their soft grasp. She said something which I didn't catch, it may well have been a, "don't, David", but it wasn't very loud whatever it was, and if it was that I wasn't taking any notice. My hands squeezed just a little, and as she moved her head slowly to the right my lips came away from her neck to kiss the corner of her mouth. The heat was rising in her, fast and surely, I could feel it in my hands and in her body against mine. She pressed back into me more now, and my lips found more of her mouth.

"Please don't, David," she whispered, "we can't, not here." But she was still in my arms, my hands still holding her firm, her mouth reached further round for more of mine.

"No, David," she said again, her whisper so low I could barely hear. "We mustn't, we can't – oh, David – darling – no . . ."

I thought it would be cold for her. It was cool up here in the evening air, but I wasn't, nor was she, so I gently led her back to the car. I put her in her side, the passenger seat, almost having to lift her in –

"Move over, Laurie," I told her.

She seemed surprised, she didn't know what to do.

"Just a little way," I went on, "I'm no good on my right side, I have to hold you in my left arm."

She was making funny noises, and I know she kept saying, "No, David", but I wasn't taking any notice of that. I wanted to hold her in my arms again, this would be the last time, and I just had to hold her, kiss her, love her, well, what I could with her this way, eat my cherries – I just had to, for the last time, and I was certain she wasn't really wanting me not to in spite of what she was saying, that was just because she was as she was today, but a little bit of kissing and cuddling couldn't do any harm, and the way I was feeling could do a lot of good.

I got in the car beside her, drawing her back to me, holding her in my left arm, leaving my right hand free. My lips came down and found hers, soft, wet and half open. My right hand found her breast, she tried to take it away, but it just wouldn't leave that part of her. She tried to get her lips away but I would not allow it, my lips, my mouth were too strong. It was me who was demanding now – I had stood up to all her demands, given all that she had wanted, now it was my turn, and I was enjoying all this. Again she tried to take my hand from her breasts but again I was too strong, and now I started caressing, slowly, just a little, tenderly. Suddenly her mouth was wide open.

The sudden ferocity of her surprised me, the heat of her boiled over, and now we were back as we had always been, and her mouth was demanding, so was a lot of the rest of her, like she always had done before.

She was like a furnace, red-hot and moist with it. This was much more than I had expected. I undid things carefully and my mouth found the cherries, both of them in turn, holding them in my mouth, then in my lips, and really enjoying them. She was passionate as I had ever known her, more so even, and when I lifted my head back to her mouth again, I saw there were big blobs of tears streaming down her cheeks.

My wonderful Laurie – she must be as sad as I was that this would be our last ever time together. My poor beautiful Laurie, crying for me, for us. I loved her now with all my heart.

Her skirt had ridden high up her legs, exposing a lot of the bronze. My hand went down, felt the silken glory of her lovely smooth thighs, and went on, and on. My mouth went down for the cherries again, had barely found them when I slowly came upright again to look straight at her.

"You're not – you're not" – it was hard to say – "you're not that way anymore?"

"No,' she said, very slowly, "I'm not that way anymore."

"You don't take long," I told her in my most man of the world style, proud and pleased at what I had just found out.

"No," she agreed, "I don't take long." It was like an echo of what I had said, only much more slowly than I had said it.

"May I, darling – please?" I had never needed to ask her before, but this time it was all fresh again, and I did not want to lose what was so very near.

190

"If you want, David," very slowly, as though she wasn't there, and, as I looked, her eyes flooded with tears again, more than before, and I was so humble that she could feel this way for me. She must nearly love me and I had to be worthy of that, and of her.

The dark came down upon us and we stayed on, it did not seem to matter, nothing mattered save that we two were together and making love. In the end I was far more concerned about that plane down at Midway than she was. We would need to hurry and I would have to drive fast, but fate had other plans.

"I must just powder my nose, David," Laurie said.

"Are you sure you'll be all right?" It was very dark.

"Of course," she replied, "I'll only go a little way – I must."

CHAPTER 35

Disaster

I got out of the car first, standing aside to let her get out, and then holding her for a minute until she got used to the complete darkness.

"Be careful, darling," I told her, and a second later I roared out loud in pain as she slammed the door she had been holding on to, hard on my right hand.

It was excrutiating, made me feel terribly sick, and weak at the knees, but after a time the pain numbed a bit, my hand and my arm, and we put the lights of the car on to see how bad it was. It was bad, my hand a sickening sight and completely useless. She was dreadfully sorry about it, but it was a pure accident, and perhaps had been my fault for leaving my hand in such a stupid position. But there was no doubt about it, she would have to drive.

"Take it carefully going out," I warned, "get used to the lights, then when you think you're all right, push on as fast as you can. You're going to have to drive fast, Laurie, to be at Midway on time."

I was worried about her, she had been in a daze almost for some time, hadn't really come out of it with the accident to my hand, and she was still far less concerned about the time than I was. I couldn't understand her, and I soon had to urge her on again.

"Laurie – you'll have to move faster than this to catch the plane, push on a bit, darling, you'll be all right."

I was sure she would know the way to Midway from the outskirts, which was as well because I didn't. If she put her foot down, we could be there in time, but it was going to be very close. She settled down a lot better and gradually increased her speed. The pain in my hand and arm was back with me, I felt very groggy and sick again

"You're doing fine, darling," I told her, and she was – "we'll do it by ten, but I bet Danny, and Norm and Cynthia will be worried when we're late."

She said something but I didn't hear it. I was having to grit my teeth and fight like the devil to keep from blacking out. I was half that way, in a sort of stupor, when the bang came. I sat up with a start as the car gave a violent lurch over to my side.

"Hold it, Laurie," I yelled, as we hit against something on my side and swerved back right across the road.

I heard her shout, "Oh, David", or "Oh, Danny", I will never be sure which, and in the lights I saw the forest rushing at us. We hit something at her side, a glancing blow, almost turned over on her side, bounced once, then hit something head-on with a hell of a crash.

It was in that very second that I remembered she had not put her wig on, and then I knew no more.

CHAPTER 36

Anxiety

Danny Erikson

It was a miserable Sunday after I had left her outside the hotel, thinking of her all the time, knowing I should have gone up there with them, and just hating the time going by so darn slowly until I could see her again.

Cynthia didn't make it any better for me. I went over for supper with them and told them about Delane coming round to see me, how we talked all night, and what we had talked of. Norm may have been surprised but Cynthia wasn't, that is not until I told her about the invitation to go up to High Point with them, and how I had refused to go.

"That was wrong, Danny."

"How do you mean?" I asked her.

"When she asked you, you should have gone."

I still didn't understand why.

"It was important to her, that's why," Cynthia could see it different to me. "It was important at this time that you should have gone, otherwise she would not have asked you. She wanted you to meet her father, see the place with her, and what's more important, been with her. You were wrong, Danny, you should have gone."

"O.K., O.K., but she'll be all right with David." I reckoned she was being a bit disloyal to him and that was unusual for her. "There'll be plenty of other times for me."

"I do hope so," she said, "I hope so, but I still think you were wrong, not going when she had asked."

That worried me plenty all Sunday night, and about midnight I darn near booked a telephone call to her up there. I didn't though, I was sure she would be O.K.

Monday, I felt better. I did a lot of work, driving Poppy a lot harder than I had done just lately, and feeling better for the work and for that, and it all made the time go by much faster. I collected Norm and Cynthia shortly after nine that night. I wanted to be out at Midway by nine-thirty. Knowing David and his habit of always being in good time, I reckoned he would be at the airport by then. I was strangely excited as we drove out, badly wanting to see her. It had been nearly forty hours since I had last seen her – hell, I had it real bad.

We were there before nine-thirty, it wasn't hard to wait, but when the half-hour came and no sign of them I began to worry. Cynthia saw it.

"Relax, Danny," she told me, "he's not like you, he'd aim to be here at nine-thirty, but when he hits the city it will slow him down a bit – he'll be here, you see."

The waiting got hard work. The minutes ticked away, and at a quarter to ten I wasn't the only worried one.

"They'll have to be here soon or they'll miss it," Cynthia was anxious by now. "You sure it was ten p.m. flight, Danny?"

Sure I was sure, but I asked Norm to check it. Yes, it was ten p.m. all right, and that in itself was something of a relief – Laurie Gaydon was booked on the ten p.m. flight to New York.

She was booked on, but she wasn't there, when they called the flight on to the plane, and she wasn't there when the plane took off. By now we were all a hell of a lot more worried, and I was convinced something serious had happened.

"There's something gone wrong, that's for sure," Norm agreed, "but let's not get too worried. It can't be serious or David would have got in touch with us, maybe they've had a breakdown or a blow-out. Let's not start getting all het-up yet, there always is a simple explanation."

We went and asked about the next flight – one a.m. Yes, they could get her on that, there were a few seats not booked, but would she please reserve one as soon as she came. I sure hoped she would, and soon.

By ten-thirty I was feeling awful, by eleven, I was good and mad, and I couldn't get what sort of a game David was playing at, not letting us know something. I would sure play merry hell with him next time I saw him, and I wanted to see him real bad, and he just had to have Delane with him.

"They won't come now," Cynthia said at quarter-past eleven. 'Whatever it is she won't go tonight now. I think they'll go back to the hotel and she'll travel tomorrow.

I clutched at that. It could be. Perhaps they were at the hotel now – though surely they would have tried to get a message to us. Well, perhaps the message was at the hotel then, that would be it. I drove fast back to that hotel, I sure wanted to know what was going on, but there was no message, the clerk had heard nothing from Mr. Lander and Miss Gaydon had booked out yesterday morning and was not coming back. No sir, there sure weren't any messages.

There was only one thing to do now, that was to go have a drink at Al's. I sure needed it, we all needed one. We had to tell Al what was wrong, he could tell we were worried about something, it must have been very plain on all of us, particularly on me.

He was far from being any help.

"Maybe they gone off and got hitched." He wasn't on to how things were with her and me, and could have no idea of the harm he was doing me.

"No, Al," Cynthia was less excited about it than I might have been. "She wouldn't do that, not with David."

"Who says not?" he asked. "It's just what she would do, has done before. Look at the press she'll get – Delane marries limey or something. It wouldn't surprise me none – them two was really gone over each other."

Now I didn't want any more drink, well not here, with Al coming out with all this stupid stuff. I wanted to be at home where I could get out the medicine I had there, without any damn fool of an Al talking the way he was doing. I dropped Norm and Cynthia home first.

"Not too much whisky," Cynthia told me, "that won't help a lot – don't worry, we'll hear something soon."

"Not too much," I promised.

I hadn't been in twenty minutes when I heard the auto pull into my driveway. It was what I had been waiting to hear – they had come at last. I went out through the porch, it was black outside. They were there all right, the two of them, two figures in the dark.

"Is that you, David?" I said.

It wasn't them, it was Norm and Cynthia. The good feeling I had got hearing that auto left me quick. Something had happened for sure.

"What is it?" I asked.

"Let's go inside, Danny," it was Norm who spoke, "so we can talk."

Inside, as soon as they got in the light, I could see how serious they both were, how white even.

196

"What is it?" I asked again.

"They've had an accident," low and quiet from Cynthia.

"Bad?" I didn't need to ask it, sure it was bad or they would not have been here like this.

"Real bad," she said, slowly and quiet, then suddenly she came out with it.

"Laurie's dead. She was – " she faltered, she couldn't say whatever it was, and I could only stare at her and watch the tears flood her eyes. Norm said it for her, his voice all flat and broken.

"They hit a tree – out somewhere near Rockford. She was killed."

Hit a tree – she was killed – what the hell were they saying?

"We were just going to bed when Cynthia switched on the radio, we heard it almost right off – a special flash – sometime tonight – they went over the bank and hit a tree head-on – "

I wasn't with them. It didn't make sense in my head, a head all gone numb along with my body.

"It's lonely up that way," he was still going on about it. "It was about three miles above Rockford – they only just announced it, so we thought we had better get right on over – thought you might have heard it."

I hadn't heard it, only from them, and it wasn't true, could not be true. No, I hadn't heard it . . .

"They didn't say anything about David," Cynthia was speaking again, "just about Laurie – poor Laurie. Nothing about David."

"You know how they put it over," it was Norm now. "Nothing about David – just Delane – Janice Delane – killed in an auto smash." Yeah – I knew how they would put that one over – "there'll be more details soon as they get more. Do you want we should put the radio on?"

I didn't want the radio on. First I had to have a drink. I got out two more glasses – I knew how to count still and how to do that – and poured them both a stiff shot and myself a stiffer shot. I went in back for the water. No, I didn't want the radio on.

The drink helped. I knew a lot of guys in the Police department, if any of them were on duty, I could get more than the radio would tell us. I knew damn fine what stuff they would put out. There was one guy on duty – I got him after a time, he hadn't heard himself. I told him how important it was he should hear, so he said he would do some telephoning and call me back. I told them, and then put the

197

radio on. We got a flash at once, just as though they'd waited for us to put the radio on so they could let us have it.

They were going to town now just like it always was. Janice Delane, the world famous movie beauty was dead – killed in an auto smash. Stand by for further details. Stay tuned. Keep listening. Just like it always was.

The police guy came on the telephone. He'd got a bit more. The car had gone off the road, hit the tree, it was one hell of a wreck – they'd got her out dead. What time? After midnight, he thought. The guy who was with her was in hospital at Rockford – he didn't know how bad he was –

We got another flash over the radio. They were getting more lurid now, repeating the killed part and the tree part, and some sob-sister going over her recent films and her life – how strange was fate that she had travelled all over the world and had been killed up there near her home.

I poured another whisky for myself, and one more for Norm. It wasn't curing the numbness but it was helping.

"I'm going up to Rockford," I told them.

Cynthia came with me. Norm wanted to come also, but he wouldn't. He would go home, snatch an hour or so sleep, then carry on his normal day – he knew I would want it like that. Cynthia said she just had to come, she wouldn't sleep, couldn't sleep, she would be company for me, and I was glad because she could help to keep that damn numb feeling from being too solid all over me, especially in my head where I would need to be able to think.

We took off for Norm's first, me following them. Cynthia made some coffee, it was good and braced me up a lot. I couldn't eat anything but I sure lapped up that cofffee, and it gave Cynthia a chance to change her clothes. She was practical the way she always is – thought we ought to get some of David's things, pajamas, razor and such like. Norm said no, not just then, whatever he wanted, whatever we wanted for him, we could telephone down for and he would have one of our drivers bring it up, or, if we were still there in the evening, he would come up himself with it.

I drove fast, the roads were deserted and I could get along. We kept the radio on, it was one way of keeping up with the news, even though it was being presented in a way that was doing me no good at all. It kept coming over – every ten minutes or so – Janice Delane – the beautiful, glamorous Delane – killed in an auto smash near

Rockford in her home state of Illinois. Now it was all over the world, in the news flashes everywhere, the early news, the late news, the midday news, she sure was news, and this would be news wherever they showed movies. In the papers everywhere, headlines, pictures, headlines, and soon they would bring out all the magazines to feature her life – she was news, sure-fire news, and this was one time, maybe the last time, she would make it.

Back it came again – Delane is dead, killed in an auto accident near Rockford in Illinois, not far from her home, and all her fans, her public, would mourn her, and maybe four husbands would be mourning her, and maybe not, and I would mourn her too. Janice Delane, the biggest name in films, the number one lady of the movies, killed in an auto smash – near Rockford, high up in the hills in Illinois – she was thirty-two years of age – she had appeared in – they were spilling it all now. The editors, the newshawks, the announcers, they would all have a ball out of Delane.

The first streaks of dawn were lighting the sky over the hills as we got to Rockford. Some of the numbness had left me, and I was thinking of that other dawn, just two dawns ago, when she had been with me, and we had told each other what we would do with our lives. Now she was dead and wouldn't do anything anymore, and I was miserable like hell, sick with it, and wishing I had stayed numb.

We weren't allowed in the hospital to see David. He was sleeping and they wouldn't disturb him. He had a broken collar-bone, the left one, a badly damaged right hand, one of his knees was banged a bit, and his left leg and foot had been twisted badly, and there may be something internal, they didn't know yet. He had been badly shocked when they found him wandering on the road, he was in a bad way when they got him to hospital, so they had given him a shot of something to calm him down. They didn't know anything about the woman – Delane, only that she wasn't there.

We tried the police next. It was dawn now with all the newshounds in the world, or in America, flocking in to Rockford. We were lucky with the police, darn lucky, a lieutenant coming in recognised me and took us in to his office. He had been down in the precinct the factory was in before he had been promoted, we always kept well in with the police down there, he knew me well. I was glad to come up with this lieutenant – his name was Tom Murphy, and from him we got to know plenty.

They were cutting timber somewhere up above Rockford, and the big truck had been going up late at night ready to load up at dawn and bring its load down to Chicago. The driver's mate had seen a figure half-crawling about the road – it was the limey and he was in a bad way. They had seen the smash with the woman still in it – she was dead for sure – it had made the driver and his mate sick to see it, and they couldn't do anything about it, she was trapped inside and all battered up where they had hit this big tree, head-on.

It had been one hell of a job to get the woman out; Murphy had been there and he knew. They'd had doctors and nurses from the hospital, and firemen, and the wrecker-gang from the big auto-place along by the hospital, and the police. One of the nurses recognised the woman as Delane. They got her free eventually, and she sure was a shocking sight, she had really been battered, every part of her, except her face – that was the funny thing – with the driving wheel stove right back into her. Murphy didn't exactly know what her injuries were, the police surgeon hadn't given it out yet, but she sure had been battered, and it was a wonder the auto hadn't caught fire.

It was hard to take it all for me, and for Cynthia I guess. I felt for her, and I knew she would be feeling for me, and she was crying for Delane too. The end part of what Murphy told us was the biggest shock –

"She sure must have been driving fast," he said.

She driving, she couldn't have been. David was driving. That's what I told him, and I was wrong, plumb wrong.

"Look Mr. Erikson, I seen it, and I sure know who was driving. She was, and all that side and the wheel battered in on her. The English guy was on the passenger side, that's why he's in hospital this morning and not down at the mortician's parlour with her, or instead of her."

It must be true, he knew what he was talking about, but I couldn't understand it.

Once they knew it was Delane they had been able to get in touch with her father, they knew Delane and they knew him here in Rockford. He had got down fast, arrived just after they got the body out of the wreck, and he was still somewhere around Murphy thought.

He was a good guy, this lieutenant. He kept us in his office, away from all the newsboys, had coffee sent in for us, went out and was back inside the hour to tell us what more he could.

The surgeons had done all they wanted to do, the morticians had her now. He didn't spare us any of the details, and the only good thing was that she had died quickly from the main injury, or one of the main injuries, a fracture of the skull and contusion of the brain. I hoped they were right, I hoped she hadn't known a lot of pain from the rest of it. Like he said, she had been battered, and the crushing from the driving wheel had done a hell of a lot of harm to her inside. Both legs had been smashed, and about the only thing that hadn't got hurt was her face, that bore no marks from just above her eyes right down, except that the blood had gushed from her mouth and nose. I sure hoped they were right about that fractured skull.

Her father had gone back home. All the arrangements had been made, and the morticians were doing their job now. We couldn't see her yet, even if we wanted to. We didn't want to see her, not yet. He took us out the back way and got one of his men to drive my waggon round to us. It had been lucky for us to have met Tom Murphy, though all of what he had told us had been hard to listen to.

Cynthia waited outside in the waggon whilst I had a shave and wash at the local barber shop. The barber could talk of nothing else but the smash – he sure would liked to have seen it – I could have killed him with his own damn razor. We drove back to the hospital.

CHAPTER 37

World News

While we were waiting at the hospital we called Norm and told him a little bit of what we had found out, and that we were waiting to see David. It was just on twelve o'clock when we did get in to see him and I'd done a lot of talking to make sure we got in. The hospital staff were having one hell of a time with all the press boys and the camera men – this limey they had there was the most wanted man in the world just at now.

I was more glad than ever Cynthia was with me when we finally got in to see him. She got more out of him than I would have done on my own. He was half-lying, half-propped-up, with a big bandage down the left side of his face where he'd been gashed, he was strapped up on his left side, and his left leg in supports. His right hand was bandaged. What we could see of him, except for his eyes, was darn near as white as the bandages.

Cynthia kissed him and I could just say, "Hi, David." We took it easy with him, like the doctor had said we should, let him ask the questions and Cynthia gave him the right answers. I was glad Cynthia did the answering. They hadn't told him about Delane yet, but Cynthia knew how to answer when he did. She told him straight out, as it was probably best to do. He knew already, I was sure, and what Cynthia told him was only confirmation.

She let him recover a bit, then, slowly, easily, she got his story out of him. He would have to get it out for the cops, and they would be in next.

We'd heard a bang, like a tyre, he thought. He felt the car lurch, first over to his side then back to hers, felt it bounce, almost turn over, heard her shout something – he looked straight at me – it could have been she shouted, "Oh, Danny". He didn't rightly know, it may have been, "David", he would never know, but she had shouted, then there

202

came this crash and next thing he knew was that he was in bed, and he thought she must be dead, had known it almost, before Cynthia had told him.

We didn't stay too long, they were watching him closely, still weren't sure of what had happened inside, and it was only after we had left him I realised we hadn't asked him why she was driving. Cynthia hadn't thought to do so, and I had hardly spoken. We couldn't go back and ask him now, but I sure would have liked to have known.

"What now, Cynthia?" I asked her, we had done what we came up to do.

"Do you want to go back down to Chicago, Danny?"

"Why, what else is there?"

"We're half-way up, let's go on and see her father."

I thought it a bit early, and, in any case, I was a bit scared of meeting him.

She didn't think it was too early.

"Let's go," she said, "if he doesn't want to see us, he'll tell us."

We rang Norm again to tell him what we were doing, and to say he should bring some of David's things up to the hospital. We would meet him there at seven that evening. I drove round to the police station to tell Tom Murphy what we were going to do. He wasn't in, but they would give him the message, and make sure he knew where I was if he wanted to get hold of me. I asked them about the route to the Gaydon property – that was easy – High Point – they all knew it, a lovely place up there, right on the main route, I couldn't miss it.

We drove on up. We didn't need the radio now and we hardly spoke. Cynthia had taken all this very badly – Tom Murphy hadn't pulled any punches, and I knew Cynthia must be feeling the same way as me about the manner in which Delane had died. Then she had been shocked when she had seen David. He was a great favourite of hers, and she must be feeling hard for him, how he was going to take it when the full realisation of it came to him, if it had not already done so. Then she had been solid for me and Delane, I knew that for sure. She must have seen a lot in us for each other or she would not have told me what she had, nor Delane either, Saturday night after supper when the two women had gone out back to do the chores. Like me, Cynthia had taken it hard.

I drove as fast as I could up the twisting, winding, climbing road, glad it required a lot from me because that stopped me from doing a

203

lot of thinking of Delane. Other times, I guess, we would have thought how nice it was up this way, but not today, there was nothing nice about the world today. Cynthia let me in through a big white-painted gate, with the name-plate – High Point – alongside it. At the top of the rough drive was a lovely sprawling house, high up above us down here on the drive.

It was so quiet up here, not a soul to be seen. I had the feeling we should not have come up, it was as though we were not wanted, but I was wrong, and Cynthia soon proved right. As we sat there wondering what to do, a small elderly looking man, escorted by two huge dogs, came down to see who we were. That's how we met Mr. Gaydon.

He was glad we had come on up. He knew who I was, knew who Cynthia was. He was very nice, a bit reserved, but at the same time quite friendly, and very composed, hiding his grief well. He had been wondering what I would do, and had been thinking of calling me on the telephone. He had heard all there was to hear about me from Laurie – that was the first time he had mentioned her name, had made any reference to her – and I was welcome. Cynthia was welcome also. We went up to the house.

There was a peaceful air up here, a quiet atmosphere which suited the day, it was a relief to find this after the rushing about we had done. Neither of us had slept all night, probably Mr. Gaydon hadn't either, and, in spite of my shave and wash, I was feeling jaded now.

The woman, Martha, big and friendly, was waiting for us. There was still no outward mention of what had happened the night before and the tragedy it had brought to this house, to them and to us. I was pleased when Martha took Cynthia off for a rest. Cynthia could do with it, I knew, and it gave me the chance to talk to Mr. Gaydon the way I wanted to.

His heart was broken all right, he didn't try to hide it so hard with just the two of us together. Martha's heart was broken too – she had loved Laurie so much and Olaf's heart broken – his man, Martha's husband, off now somewhere in the woods where he could be sad and be with the birds and the animals he loved. It was terribly tragic, but that was how it had to be, and sometimes hearts were meant to be broken. He accepted it as it was, without blame on anyone or anything, and now I was real glad we had come up right away as we had done, real glad I had this chance of talking with him. I think it did a lot for him and for me.

There had been a long distance call for him from New York earlier on, he told me. From the film company she was under contract to. They had wanted his permission to do all the arrangements for the funeral. He thought they had been very good about it and he had fallen in with most everything they wanted. The only thing he had insisted on was that, after the big affair down in Chicago, and he had had to accept that – there would be a much more private ceremony up here, and her body would be brought up, and she would be buried in the family grave, a mile or so down the road, where her mother already lay.

He was going down to the funeral parlour in Rockford that evening, and, after he had been down there, the film company would take everything over until they brought her back up here after the funeral down there in the city was over. I think he wanted me to agree with it all, and I did. It was what she would have wanted for sure. When she was Janice Delane she belonged to the world, and to me. I never thought of her as anyone else, found it still hard to get used to her the way they all called her up here, and the way Cynthia called her, and David. For me she was Delane, and I agreed with the funeral down in Chicago. The press boys, the television, the radio, the camera men, still wanted her – the world knew her, and would want to know everything. That was the way it had to be.

Martha made us eat, all three of us. When it was ready I ate well, so did the others. It was our first meal of the day. Olaf came back and we met him, he could not keep the sadness out of his eyes, and it was most noticeable that Martha never mentioned her name, though no doubt, she had talked to Cynthia a lot.

Early that evening we drove down to Rockford, Mr. Gaydon in with us, and Olaf and Martha following us in the big house waggon. Norm was waiting for us at the hospital, but we couldn't see David. He hadn't had a good day and was sleeping now – I guessed they had given him another shot. They still didn't know how bad he was.

I had been in several funeral parlours before, to see my own folks and other folks, but never felt the way I did now. The morticians had finished and done a good job. The parlour was heavy with the scent of flowers and, in the light of the four big candles, Delane looked perfect, just resting there. A little of the beautiful hair which that damn wig had covered so often when I had been with her, was showing out of the veil on the top of her head, covering anything bad there was to cover, her warm brown eyes were closed for always, but her face was unspoiled, and she was lovely in death as she had been in life. I knew she would have been glad of that. We stayed there a long time, the two women softly crying, and me with my eyes wet and a great lump in my throat, and all of us with our thoughts and our prayers for her.

The film boys were waiting when we came out, and the camera men all ready. We said our goodbyes to Mr. Gaydon, Martha and Olaf and drove back to Chicago, me following Norm and Cynthia. I couldn't help thinking that about twenty-four hours before she had been on her way down – she hadn't got as far as this though.

CHAPTER 38

So Close To Happiness

The funeral reminded Chicago of those other funerals way back, when they buried the big gangsters, and the press boys in the manner of their talk said it was even bigger and better than the biggest and the best Chicago had ever known before.

There were flowers blocks high, in spite of her father asking for donations to the orphanage she was so interested in, rather than flowers, but there were some big donations also.

There were movie stars, the big names of the world, and big people from the stage – glamorous women and rugged handsome men. There were producers, directors, camera-men, writers, everything – Americans and foreigners. There were the children from the orphanage, children of all colours, different ages, big and little, but all dressed the same in their white shirt and shorts or white blouse and skirts. There was the general public, there in their thousands and tens of thousands.

Her public, the ordinary men and women, white, black, brown and yellow, who loved her and loved her movies, who, if they were girls or women, played the parts she did with her, and if they were men, young or old, played opposite her and all of them were the man who got her in the end. Her public, the people who paid their money at the box-office, so that there could be women like Delane, movies like she made, and funerals like this.

The news coverage, the radio, the television, it was all terrific, and all over America other folk would be listening and watching, all mourning her with these thousands here in Chicago, where it seemed that the entire city had turned out for her, even this early in the morning for which it had purposely been timed, to avoid the sweltering heat of the sun. Outside America, they would be listening, and later they would read all about it, and see the pictures of this last fantastic farewell appearance of Janice Delane.

The family mourners were few, just her father – there were no other living relations on his side that he knew of, though there might have been some on her mother's side – Martha and Olaf. Martha, all stiff and starched and proper in black, in spite of the heat. Then there was Norm, Cynthia and me.

Al had told me he sure would not be there, he hated all funerals, and he hated this one where such a lovely woman was going out before her time, but I knew he had sent a whole heap of dollars to that orphanage I had told him about, in memory of her, and because he had liked her so much and she had liked him. Taps felt the same as Al – no funerals for him either, but, like Al, he had sent a big donation. I knew that somewhere along the route Poppy would be watching, and for sure she would be weeping for Delane, and for me.

There were three lots of flowers on the coffin. A wreath from her father, a big bunch of mountain wild flowers from Martha and Olaf, and twelve red roses with a card, "David", that was all.

Cynthia had bought them for him, and had told him she would when she had last seen him. Cynthia had known about his red roses for Delane the day after the ball game when he had bought some for her as well. She remembered these sort of things like all women do, and had told me how she would just get the twelve roses to put on the coffin.

"What about you, Danny?" she had asked.

I had told her, there would be no flowers from me. I had never sent her anything when she was alive, had known better even than to offer to buy that gold outfit for her the day I had taken her and Cynthia down to the city, and there would be no flowers now. But I made a vow to be sure that the orphanage got a lot of things it wanted. If she knew about that she would be happy and not mind there had been no flowers from me.

They hadn't let David down for the funeral, and would not allow him to be up there at the graveyard near High Point. Cynthia had said she didn't think he wanted to be there, and I kind of agreed with her. Last time we had seen him, yesterday, he had still been very low, miserable, and still shocked. He was in some pain from that bang down the left side of his head, and they still would not let him put any weight on his bad knee and leg. He'd had a belly full of the cops, had told his story about a hundred times, he reckoned, and that hadn't done him a lot of good, but he had been lucky in that the hospital authorities hadn't let the press boys get at him. The one good thing we had learned yesterday was that they were sure there was nothing wrong inside him, physical that was.

It was a much smaller procession that drove out of Chicago and up to Apple River Canyon. Still plenty of camera-men but only a few mourners. There wasn't a great deal to do at that little place up there when we got there, just have the parson say a few words over the coffin, and then watch it lowered down into the ground on top of the remains of her mother, and Delane had gone.

It was so quiet and none of us could speak, only the parson who had come all the way up from the city with us, to say the words he had to say, and the rest of us, the mourners, could cry, the women openly and the men inwardly, whilst the camera-men went about their work, and overhead the sky was all serene, with a gentle breeze sighing its melancholy dirge through the trees to give sad music to we little group of mortals up here in this wonderful part of God's country, vast, open, colourful, lonely country, gathered here to give Him back one of His own flock.

All down the years I shall remember it, the beauty of it and the sadness of it, remember how we did not want to leave her there, even after we had looked down and sprinkled our handful of earth atop the coffin, were reluctant to leave her, though we knew she was back with her mother again. What the others were thinking I didn't know, but some of them would be as sad as me, more sad maybe, and it would take a long time before we could stop feeling that way.

Martha took it worst of all. It wasn't outward that you could see, and I would not have known it myself had not Mr. Gaydon and Cynthia told me how very much she was suffering. Olaf too, took it badly, and the most composed of us all was her father, who had accepted it like he said you must accept these things, and, like it says in the Bible – God's Will be done. Me, I was still numb with it all, a terrible, depressing numbness that I found hard to shake off.

In the immediate days and weeks after the funeral I spent a lot of time up at High Point. It threw a lot of extra work on Norm down there, and I knew we'd have to think fast of getting him a really good deputy, but I had a lot of things I wanted to go over with Mr. Gaydon, and it was nearer to Rockford being up here, so I could go in and see David almost every day, most times taking Mr. Gaydon down with me.

Cynthia and Norm came up at week-ends, and, like me, were made very welcome at High Point. It was lovely up here, a pleasure to be out of the oppressive heat of the city down there, something I knew Norm and Cynthia appreciated as much as I did, and I was sure that at this time it was a good thing us being up with them for these three, Jim Gaydon, Martha and Olaf, who would otherwise have been very lonely.

David recovered well, he was young and tough and the physical side of the smash would soon wear off him, how the mental side of it would affect him was up to him. He had nothing to blame himself for – there was no doubt she had been driving – why, I could not bring myself to ask him, and I had my own legal boys handle everything for him that they could handle.

I had written a long letter off to his boss so that he would know the full story – I could guess some of the newspapers over in England would get as sensational about it as some did here in the States, so I wanted him to be in the full picture. I pitched in a bit for David, so they would know back there how good a boy he was, and how high he was in our regard, and how well he had done. Mike Govern agreed there should be no change in the arrangements for him, and Poppy got him all fixed up on the Queen Elizabeth for about mid July. I thought he wouldn't go back to the factory anymore, but spend the rest of his time with us just getting fit, and I meant fit in his thinking as well as everywhere else.

The cops didn't worry him much, my legal boys saw to that, and the Press didn't go for him much either – Cynthia said that was because he wasn't a Prince or a Duke or a Count, and I thought by that remark she was getting over the whole affair well. It was something we all had to get over, me, Jim Gaydon, all of us, and most of all, David, who had been with her when it happened, and would take a long time to forget it.

Cynthia told me how she felt about it all.

"It's hard to believe it still, Danny. You both had so much to give each other – I'm perfectly certain you would have gone well together. I liked her a lot, we got on famously, would have been very great friends. I got very close to her, she had so much in her life, and yet she had missed such a lot, and she was so close to getting those things with you, and then this. She didn't deny anything, she'd led a pretty hectic life, and there had been a few men concerned with her, yet she was sure, Danny, when she had you all that was over, and she would have been just for you. I believed her, she was so sincere, so truthful about what had gone before. It was impossible not to believe her. It is so hard to understand."

Of the four husbands she'd had, there had been flowers from only the last one – Dennison. I talked a lot with Jim Gaydon about them. He'd known only the first one, Johnny Lamp, and he'd tried hard to stop that one, but couldn't, it was like it always was, you just couldn't stop her when her mind was made up. It was something she had inherited from her mother, and her mind was made up about this man, even though her father thought she knew it wouldn't work, and she went through with it. It hadn't worked out, right from the start, but she would never admit she was wrong about it, and he thought he had made it worse by opposing it.

He hadn't seen a lot of her for a long time after that, she was too busy making her career into what it became, but he heard all the stories of her, and there had been plenty to read about her in the newspapers and the magazines, she certainly made a lot of news. The hot magazines always loved her, vivid photographs of her and all the gossip of her men – they must have loved her, those magazine editors, they never lacked for news and scandal about her.

I asked him one night what had been in my head to ask him for a long time.

"How do you think she and me would have got on?"

"I've been waiting for you to ask me that one, Danny," he told me, a wry smile about his face. He was beginning to smile again a bit now, we all were, except for Martha.

"She told me all about you, and I liked what she said. She was keen on it, Danny, and that was good. Once she got keen she gave all her time to it, and – I think – she would have given all her time to being married to you – "

I butted in. "We'd sort of agreed she could do one movie a year if she wanted to" –

"Yes, she told me that as well – she might have wanted to, for a year or so, but she would have faded out, I guess – I always thought she would fade out when she was right at the top – that was always her intention – she would have done that, especially with you. She was so keen, Danny, on what you and she were going to do together – she was happy to think she could help you doing what you wanted, and she was more than happy that you were as keen as her on having all the kids up here and building the places she wanted to have."

"Which we're still going to have," I interrupted.

211

"Which we're still going to have," he agreed, it hadn't put him off his trend of talk. "With all the things she and you were going to do, she would have had plenty to keep her occupied. That's why, I'm sure, she would have given up the idea of the movie a year – she would have travelled with you, been kept busy up here, had the full life she wanted and was used to having, but a better, fuller life, the sort of life she had been looking for.

"Then, it had to be with somebody like you, Danny, I'm sure of that, somebody big in the world, big as her, bigger than her, somebody she could lean on, somebody who could boss her, like her father never did, like no man ever did. Make no mistake, Danny, it wouldn't have been easy for you, nor for her, you're both very set in your ways, and there would have to have been a lot of give and take on both sides, and I think you both could have done it."

Even though it was sad to hear all this, with all that might have been, still I was glad to hear it and to know it. She had been sure we could have made a go of being married, I would have tried my heart out to make sure of it, Cynthia had said she thought we would be just right, and I had a lot of time for Cynthia and the things she said, and now her father was confirming it all – we couldn't have been wrong.

Jim Gaydon hadn't finished.

"You see, Danny, where you impressed her was that you were like her, had started from scratch and done what you wanted to do, built up this big place you have. That was a big thing with her – she'd done that herself with her own life – yes, I know it helped a bit her having money – I always gave her what she wanted but it wasn't only that – she had talent, and she had guts, and that got her to the top. Just like you, Danny, you've known it all, the struggle, the heartbreaks, and that would have helped a great deal. She told me about your place, when you took her round, and believe me, Danny, I never thought things could mean all that to a woman, especially a woman like her, but they meant a lot to her, you meant a lot to her because you had done all that."

I saw how he meant that – Cynthia was right again, it was as she had said, gain her respect and all the rest would follow – there's a hell of a lot in it, without respect there cannot be love.

Jim Gaydon and me did a lot of the things we wanted to do to bring into being all she had been planning. We set up a trust fund for the orphanage down there in the city, and, with the donations that had come in, and with the way my legal boys went about it, there wouldn't be a lot for that place to worry about in the future. Now we were concerned to double its size, and we were looking for new property so we could move it to a better part of the city, in any case there was no room for extension where it was.

We got out all the plans for the children's home we were going to have built at the side of Squaw Lake – this would be part of the orphanage down in the city and the children would come up in turns to live up here for a while. A little way along from this we would clear a lot of the timber, and build a little hospital and convalescent house, so that the sick children could be up here all the time. Right across the lake, in a big clearing, we would build up a bigger place – a camp like she had wanted, so that we could take big parties of children and young folks up there, and give them a vacation away from the heat of the city.

We had so many plans, and the great pity of it all was that the person who was really responsible for them, the woman who had first created all this and got us so interested, wasn't here to share it with us as she should have been. It was so very sad that part, for all of us, and, hard as I worked at the planning, that was always in the back of my mind. It always would be, like her memory, her image, would always be with me, and there wasn't a day, hadn't been a day, when I didn't bitterly regret that I had refused the invitation to come up here with her and David. Cynthia had been dead right about that also. How I wished I had come with them, I would have done the driving, and she would have been still here.

CHAPTER 39

Now I Know It All

It was funny about that driving part. Much as I wanted to do, I had never got around to asking David why he hadn't been driving. Not that he could have prevented anything happening if he had been driving, and I knew for sure a blow-out could cause a hell of a lot of concern even to the best of drivers. I had never had one, and I didn't want one either, but it was still queer she was driving and not him. I badly wanted to know why and yet I just couldn't ask him. He had never said why when we had been talking, and kept right off it all. I knew he couldn't be blamed for that, it was something he badly needed to forget.

There was only one bit of planning Jim Gaydon wouldn't hear of me doing up here, and that was to build a small house, cabin or shack, of my own. I had thought hard about it, spoken to Cynthia and Norm about it. We could have used it, shared it, and we liked the idea of it. I had even got as far to enquire about land higher up, or just down a bit, but I sure got a beefing from Jim when he heard about it.

"There's no need at all, Danny," and I could see he was genuinely upset about it – "there's plenty of room for you here. I sure would be annoyed if you stopped coming here, any of you stopped, it's something we never had this company, and we like it a lot. Martha likes it, and she would be real mad at you if she knew you wanted to build on your own. Olaf too, you know you're one of the family, Danny, let's leave it that way."

We left it that way, for the time being at any rate. I knew what he said was very true. We were welcome up there, all of us, me, Cynthia, Norm, and David, and the best of it was how Martha and Olaf had accepted us. Martha was great, couldn't do enough for me, and loved Cynthia being up there – it must have helped a lot, we knew how much she had been affected by what had happened.

I got along well with them all, and me and Olaf got to be proper buddies. He took great interest in me so that we would spend hours together, and, after a time, a lot of the knowledge I'd had when I was a boy back there in Nevada started coming back to me, and it pleased him a lot that I could learn to do things so quickly under his guidance. He had looked upon me as a city gent, which I was, but though I had lived a long time in the city, I had been a country boy and had known as much of the country as any boy, and a lot of it I remembered now.

It wasn't that I neglected my business, no sir. I went down for a couple of days and more in each week, and I got through what I wanted to do a lot quicker these days, and passed a lot more on to Norm, taking a lot of the duties he did from him, passing them on down, giving him more time to do my things. Poppy knew how I was feeling about it, and did even more than she had done, and that had always been plenty.

I took her up to High Point for a couple of days while we worked on a special report I was doing to send over to Mike Govern in England about a place we were looking together for in France or in Germany, or somewhere on the continent of Europe. She loved it up there, and, like Cynthia, was soon a life-long friend of Martha's, except that Martha fed her too well and she was taking too many calories.

It was great for Martha to have these city ladies up with her, especially when they got on so well like Cynthia did with her, and Poppy also. Martha was amazed at the way Poppy could write down everything I talked about so fast – she hadn't heard of shorthand – and how fast she could use a typewriter, to her Poppy was just marvellous.

It was that same way for Poppy with Martha. Poppy loved everything Martha could do around the place, and that was sure plenty, like bake and cook, bottle fruit and vegetables, cut meat – better than many a butcher, make wines, all sorts of concoctions, and enjoy all this work so much.

It sure was great up there – I walked miles with Jim and Olaf, through the forests, and up and down the high hills. So did Cynthia and Norm when they came up at weekends, and we would be out in canoes on Squaw Lake for hours, so that I got very fit, fitter than for a long time, and we all got very brown from the sun, whilst the pure air up there must have been doing all sorts of good things for our lungs.

It was surprising how quickly the accident and the funeral dropped out of the news. It was all Delane for a week or so afterwards, with special issues of all the magazines about her, with all her photographs and all the stories of her brought back again, but then they dropped her. That was the way of it always – there was a new glamour girl now for them to point at, not as nice as Delane maybe, not her reputation either, but they could soon build all that up. New photographs on the magazine covers, new old poses, showing all they dare, new names, new gossip and new scandal. Delane had gone but the press were still there, and there was always some new woman just waiting for the limelight, there always had been, and I guess there would always be.

We knew her company were rushing out the new movie of hers, the last one she had made – 'The Searing Heat' – the gala opening night would be in New York, and the film and that night would bring her back into the headlines for a while. They wanted Jim Gaydon to go to the big night in New York, but he wouldn't go. They were good about it though, they had fond memories of her, and all the money from the night would go to the sort of places Delane would have wanted, and we would see that some children's homes and such like in New York would benefit.

I went to New York with Jim to help him settle her estate. It was a complicated affair, and I knew he was glad to have me along. There was the money she had earned and the battle with the tax boys on that, and then there was a settlement from two of her husbands, a small one from Parker, and a bigger one from Dennison. Jim hadn't known about these, but she had used them in the manner she'd used a lot of her money, for the kids she was so concerned about in Chicago. We were about a week in New York, which gave me time to do some things on my own line as well as help Jim with her affairs.

I took the chance to call on Lily Lee. She was doing well in New York and the Latin Quarter had extended her contract. She sure looked well and was glad to see me. She had read in the papers about David being in the crash, and she wanted to know all about it from me. I took Jim Gaydon to see her do her show, it was the first time he'd ever been in a place like the Latin Quarter. I think, in his own way, he enjoyed it. Lily came and sat with us between her shows – we'd delayed eating till then, and she ate with us.

Jim liked her and the three of us got on well. She was easy to like, Lily, and the fact that she had come up a bit in the world since leaving the Casanova Club, and was becoming quite a name with one of her new records spinning up towards the top twenty, didn't make one bit of difference, she was as she had always been, a darn nice girl. She had more poise now, was even more elegant, but that was natural, she was learning fast and earning good dough. Whatever happened she would remain much the way she was, and that was sure nice.

She spoke a lot of David, and I told her he would be coming through New York soon on his way home to England. Perhaps I would drive him down and see him off.

"Do that, Danny," she said, "I'd like to see him again, bring him in to see me."

I promised I would, promised a night at the Latin Quarter. I would like it, and it would sure do David a lot of good.

When we got back to High Point David was out of hospital, so the next day Jim and I went down to the city and collected him. Jim wouldn't have it any other way – David was to go up to High Point and convalesce up there.

"I'd like it, David, and I just won't take no for an answer," he said, and it must have been wonderful for the boy to know how much Jim liked him.

It wouldn't be lonely for him at High Point, and we wouldn't give him time to mope, and he would have been a lot worse on his own down in the city.

He was getting over it, young bones mend fast, and, except for the stiff way he used his arm and a slight limp, he was O.K. again. O.K. outwards, and I think he was a lot better inside. He had to go down for treatment on the arm to Rockford once or twice, so I drove him down, and while he was in the hospital, went in and saw Tom Murphy and invited him up to High Point, telling him about all we were going to do up there.

When Norm and Cynthia came up at weekends it was great for us to be all together, and yet that was the time it was hardest for me, probably for the others as well, that was the time when I missed her most, missed the way I knew she would have been about all that was going on. We tried not to show it, all of us, and it was easier to mention her name now, not that I ever did – I would never get used to it – for me, she was Delane, for ever.

It was getting near the time for David to go home. I had made up my mind to drive him down, so that we could spend his last night in New York, and then, the next day, I would see him on the Queen Elizabeth. He had got used to High Point, and it wasn't hard at that,

217

the way Martha mothered him, and Jim and Olaf spoiled him, and was pleased that he had not had to go back to the factory. He was getting very fit again, was soon as brown as any of us, brown as Olaf, and, like us all, began to talk of her without any outward signs of worry.

About ten days before he was due to go off, Norm and Cynthia took him to Niagara Falls on their long promised short vacation. I went down to Chicago for two days so that Norm could be away, coming back to High Point on the Saturday afternoon.

That night Jim told me about her mother.

I hadn't asked, I had never even thought about her, and it just came up naturally in our conversation after we had eaten the king-sized steaks Martha had cooked for us, and settled down, just us two men, with the bottle of peach brandy Jim had got out, as he quite often did after our evening meal and when we were talking.

It had happened a long time ago, all this he told me. Over thirty years ago, but he could remember it as though it was yesterday, told it me as if it had been that recent, and this was the first time he had told it to anyone in all those years – well, told the truth that was.

It was unexpected and mighty interesting, told in his soft clear voice, in the quiet of that big comfortable room, with now and again a murmur of a snort from one or both of the two big dogs sleeping at his feet.

When he had first come to High Point, he had lived here on his own for some time. He didn't mind, he could look after himself, and it had been pleasant, with the birds, the animals, this lovely place and his writing, he didn't think he was missing anything. Women had never interested him, he had barely known any, or wanted to know any, and he had no thoughts then of getting married.

"That's how it always is, Danny," he said, "then somebody comes along, and no matter what you think about it, nature settles it for you."

He had taken a vacation in New York, a vacation cum business trip, because he had finished his first book on the wild life of this part of the country, and he wanted to have it published, if necessary, he was prepared to pay the cost of having it published himself.

In New York he had stayed at a little hotel – a boarding house really, run by a widow woman and her daughter. The daughter was young, about his own age, sturdy, well-built, attractive, lovely complexion, smooth skin with not a hair anywhere, ripe and ready to be

218

married so she could get away from the drudgery of the life she was living. They had gone around together a lot, to the museums where he spent much of his time, and in the parks.

He had told her all about High Point, the big house – it was big even then – up in this lovely country. A house in which he lived all on his own, a house which was waiting for some woman to come up and run it for him. She liked what he told her, was always asking him questions about it, and the more he told her the better she liked it.

"She knew I had money, Danny, and that helped. It couldn't help but impress her that I could buy her things and not worry about the dollars I was spending. She'd had a hard life, and in me she was the escape from it. I was just what was required to take her away from the drudgery into the life she had dreamed about."

The way he told it, there was no doubt about what it meant to her. Out of all this he would take her, as she had long prayed, if she did pray, somebody, one day, would take her, away to a wonderful new life. That's just the way it always is with girls, at the start.

"I told her she could always come down to Chicago or even New York on vacation, if she got tired of it up at High Point. I had money and a short vacation would always make her want to come back up again – you know how it is, Danny, how easy it is to say such things when you're young, and the sap's rising, and this was the first time my sap had ever risen."

I knew how it was all right – easy to say things, very easy, if you don't always mean them.

"When I told her that, loving this place the way I did then – still do – I never thought she would want to go back to the city, any city, New York or Chicago. She didn't want, at first. She liked it up here nearly as much as me, then Laurie came along and it was all O.K., and we were happy. But then she did want to go off, just for a week's vacation so she could see her mother, and that was no harm."

He had his eyes closed, he was right back in those days he was talking about, and it was all still very clear in his memory.

Then it got that she wanted to go down into Chicago, just for a day, then a day or two, and that nearly every week – just to see the city and the stores, that was all. I couldn't blame her, Danny, she was a city girl and she missed the city – missed it like I would miss the country, and I know how much that would be. It was easier for her to be away, Olaf and Martha had come up then, and Martha could take care of Laurie, and that meant she could go off even more."

He sat up a bit, opened his eyes and looked straight at me.

"Now I found out what it was, Danny, it wasn't High Point she didn't like, in fact I think she did like it up here. It wasn't that she missed the city all that much, she did miss it a little, but most of all she missed men. She was all sex, full of it, and now she had come to full womanhood she couldn't get enough of it. She didn't want just one man like me, she wanted ten men, and another ten after that, and now I knew what she did in the city, she went round the stores and the shops in the day time, and at night she went round the joints and taverns, she loved them, and for why? Because that was where there were plenty of men."

We had another glass of brandy, it was good stuff and you could hold it on the tongue and know how good it was when you let it slip down, and feel the warmth and the aroma and the taste of it.

I was thinking a lot and I knew, or I was getting to know, what Taps had been meaning when he had spoken of Delane and her breeding. Like he told us, he had met Jim Gaydon when Jim had gone down to try and stop that first marriage, and he must have been told some of what I was hearing tonight.

"Sometimes she would come back to see Laurie and to see me – she was away now far more often than she was here. It's a queer thing, Danny, but I think she did love me, in a way, and I knew she loved Laurie, and when she came back here she liked it again, for a time, then the itch, or whatever it was would come over her, and it came up fast and often, and off she would go, for more men."

"Martha hated her, by this time Laurie was Martha's baby – Martha couldn't have kids. So Laurie was hers, and she just hated Janice – that was her name – hated her coming back. Olaf hated her too, but only because of how I was affected when she did come, but I didn't hate her, Danny, didn't hardly blame her, people are what they are and they can't help it. I should have been more careful, made sure about how she would stand it up here at High Point, but you know how it goes, Danny, you don't always think of those things – "

I knew how it went. I hadn't thought of a lot of things when I had married Ellen and Joan. This was the first time I'd heard her mother's name – Janice. I was learning a lot.

"One time she came back and she made a discovery. There was a big timber camp up along Sundra rise – that's about six miles from here. It had been there for years but she hadn't known it. First thing she knew about it was when one of the men up there – a great big man named Harry, that was all we knew him by, came here with a dog that had been mauled badly in a fight – they'd told him about Olaf and I down at Rockford. We kept the dog awhile and he kept coming, first to see the dog, then to see her. I knew it and I did nothing about it. I should have done, of course, but how can you stop a raging torrent of a woman like her?"

He wasn't really asking me, and I couldn't have told him how.

"She didn't have to go down to the city now, she had what she wanted up here, rough and tough and raw. One day Harry took her out to the camp, and she saw some of the other husky men out there, and, after a while, she threw Harry over. It's easy to say it now, Danny, after all this time, she went the rounds at the camp, there was all sorts of trouble there, fights, murder – like I told you, she was all sex, and they fought over her like – well, you know."

I knew what he wanted to say – humans and animals aren't an awful lot different at times.

"It was my fault – right from the start, and now Olaf and Martha hated me for allowing her to come back here when she came. I should have stopped it, Danny, but I never did – she had all she wanted from me, money, everything except one thing, and it was the money part that upset Martha – she was using my money to get what she wanted – it was me to blame, not her."

I waited for him to go on.

"It had to stop and one day it did. She had been home a couple of days she knew how Martha and Olaf were about her, but it didn't worry her, and sometimes I used to think she had come back to rile them, not to see Laurie, certainly not to see me, unless it was for more money."

I waited again for him.

"One evening Olaf and I were up there on the bluff – there's a part where you can get down a bit and we had been setting a bird down there, one that Olaf had been treating for a damaged wing. We thought it was ready to be set free, so we had put it on this ledge, we'd done it before with other birds. Laurie was with us, she was about three and liked coming round with Olaf and with me.

"Janice came out from the house to see what we were doing and to take Laurie in. She told me she hoped I would go in soon because she wanted money, she was going off again. It was the first time she had ever said anything like that in front of either Olaf or Martha, and I saw the hatred flare up in Olaf's eyes. I knew then it was time to do what I should have done long before, so I sent Laurie off with Olaf, and spoke to her."

I was picturing it all, and seeing it as it happened. He was a good talker, Jim, and I could get the hang of all he was saying and meaning.

"I talked sensibly to her, Danny, but sense wasn't what she was interested in. I annoyed her because I'm not hot-tempered, and she was so mad that I could talk to her this way and not myself get angry about it – she was used to men fighting for her now, and I was just talking. She was really mad and she told me why she had to go off, because I wasn't man enough to be what she wanted, so she went looking for real men – of course, she was right about me, no one man would ever have done for her."

He was very fair, this man, and I had often seen how a person who can talk cooly often riles another person. I could see him talking to her up there at the edge of the bluff, see her, losing her temper, see it all . . .

"I knew she was right, but still something had to be done. I remembered she was my wife, she was Laurie's mother, and soon our daughter would be old enough to have some idea of what was happening. I remembered the hate of her in Olaf's eyes, and I remembered how Martha hated her, and then, for the first time, I remembered Harry, and I thought of some of the men she had been with, so I got hold of her and I told her it had to stop.

"I have strong wrists and arms, Danny, always have had, and, in spite of the fact that she was bigger than me, really stronger than me, I held her easily. I think she liked it, my getting hold of her like this, appealed to her in some way, but she didn't lose any of her temper, it was like the sex of her, hot and fiery and raw."

I wouldn't have any more brandy when he offered it. I was too interested in his story, didn't even like the break in it.

"She said what would I do if she didn't stop, and I told her. Told her unless she gave me her promise to stop it all, I would push her over the cliff there and then. It was so stupid really, Danny, her promise would have been worthless, and I knew it and so did she."

I could see that, a promise wouldn't have been anything for her to make, if she was like Jim described her, and she must have been, then nothing was sacred for her, only sex. It was funny how this grand man could have gone all the way down to New York as he had done, and picked a she-cat like this one for his wife. Like I already well knew, fate is such a funny thing and plays some strange sort of pranks, not that it was a prank for him, but it was the way of fate.

"I held her easily, right at the top there, I can remember it now exactly as it was then, held her there while she raged and screamed, and all the time I think she enjoyed it, there was a bit of something left in me after all."

I knew exactly what was coming, it was all unfolding for me, all this that had happened so very long ago. He had told it in such a clear way, built it all up so that it was fascinating to hear, and the climax so very obvious to me. I knew a lot of things now, and one thing I did know was why they had never talked of her mother.

"Do it then," she told me. Do it then! She knew how very safe she was – Push me over – how very safe . . . "

It wasn't easy for him to tell this part, he was living it all over again. His eyes were closed and for him the years between were as nothing.

"You wouldn't dare – you haven't the guts." She was loving it almost, she knew me so well, and she knew she was right, knew I wouldn't dare. She was screaming at me – Do it then – Push me over – and she knew I couldn't.

For a moment I thought I had been wrong about the climax –

"Go on, Jim Gaydon – if you dare." She laughed in my face, she was so sure of me and herself. "Do it, damn you – go on, do it." She was so sure I couldn't do it – but I thought of Laurie again, and how she was growing up so fast, and of the way Olaf and Martha hated her, and of Harry and the other men – then I thought of Laurie again . . . "

I was right, it was as I had known it would be.

"I thought of all that, and I looked at her, and I heard her screaming – Do it then – Do it – so I pushed and let go of her and over she went. As she went over I saw her face, and even then she still didn't believe I would do it, had done it."

I had been so right.

"It's all of two hundred feet there, Danny, and I knew she would hit once or twice on the way down, knew also that when she finally hit down below she would be dead."

Just like that, told as if it was yesterday and not all that time ago. If there was any remorse or anything like that in his voice I could not sense it.

"We said it was an accident," he went on, "said that she had slipped over looking at the bird we had put down on the ledge – there was nobody to say that it wasn't. The police came up but they did not bother so much in those days – it looked like an accident, we said it was an accident, so, for them, it was an accident. There was no publicity about it, why should there be, it was just a silly woman slipped over a ledge and fallen and killed herself. It was so easy for us – Olaf and Martha backed me up – there wasn't a lot known about Janice or her ways, it was really so simple to cover up the way we did."

"Martha and Olaf – they knew what you had done?"

"Of course they knew, Danny. Martha saw it all, and as we all said, Janice had been looking down at the bird and suddenly she had gone. Martha and Olaf had no regrets, even if I had."

"Did she ever know?" I asked. I meant Delane of course, that was the name I knew her by. Jim knew who I was meaning. It didn't seem strange to him that I hadn't used her name.

"No, she never knew, to her it was always an accident. Only I knew, and Olaf and Martha – I don't think Janice ever really knew, I often wondered if she did before . . . "

I knew what he meant – before she had died in the fall. There was no remorse and there was one thing that puzzled me, why a man as honest as he was had not told the truth about it – but he hadn't quite finished.

"God knew what I had done. He knew it wasn't any accident – one day I will have to answer to him. There wasn't anyone alive, save Olaf and Martha, who would understand why I had done such a thing, and Olaf and Martha thought I had done right, so did I – so I'll wait and see how God judges it."

I didn't know what to think about that, I didn't really need to. It had waited over thirty years, it could wait a little while further yet for sure.

"I think, Danny, that is one of the reasons I have grown even fonder of God's creatures, and though we have never spoken about it, I'm sure Olaf feels the same way. We do all we can for His creatures because we think we owe it to Him."

We sat in silence for a long time, doing our own thinking. This was why they never spoke of her mother up here. I could suppose she had been brought up knowing her mother had been killed in the accident, and never allowed to talk about it or think back to it. Just when I thought it time to call it a night, Jim spoke again – he had been thinking hard about what he said, I could tell that by the way he said it.

"Though I did what I did, Danny, I never really blamed her for her way of life – it was in her and it came out."

He thought a few seconds more.

"I never blamed Laurie either for anything she did – a lot of what was in her she got from her mother. I often thought that, if nothing had happened to Janice the way it did, there would have been nothing to pass on down to Laurie – that sound funny?"

He didn't wait for an answer, not that I could have given one.

"The last time Laurie was here – when she spoke about you, and told me what you two were going to do, she was different. Maybe I'm wrong – what is it they say? Heat is never cold – but the way she spoke, everything she had left was for you – I like to think of it that way."

I knew a lot more about Delane now. Knew why he didn't blame her for anything like Taps had said, it was in the breeding. She had inherited from her Mother, the way all children do, and she couldn't be blamed that it had been what it was. For both of them, she and her Mother, it was in them, and it had come out the way it did. I hoped what we were about to do now for a lot of children would help Jim in the repayment he had to make for what he had done up there on the bluff. Because of what he had told me, I sure knew a lot more about Delane, and like Jim, I would never blame her for anything, couldn't and just wouldn't – how could I? Like he had said – heat is never cold.

CHAPTER 40

Time To Go Home

David Lander

I was going home, and I think I was glad. It was hard to know just then, when there were so many goodbyes.

I closed the big white gate of High Point and got back in the car beside Danny. He drove on down.

My last two days up there had been quiet, and rather sad. Norm and Cynthia had been with us, as they always were, and, like Danny, they liked to spend all their week-ends up there, out of the heat of Chicago, and in the friendly atmosphere of the big house, with Mr. Gaydon, Olaf and Martha.

It was natural that my last visit up there should have some sort of effect on them all, on me as well. There was so much that might have been, but then, there always is, right through life.

We'd spent a lot of time looking at the drawings for the big place they would have built on that clearing on Squaw Lake, where she was going to have her own house built, and the drawings for the hospital and convalescent house a little way along, where the work of clearing the trees had already started. They were wasting no time, but that was typical of Danny. It had all to be ready for next spring, and it would be, and the big camp they were to put up across the lake would be ready too.

Danny and her father had got very close, and Danny had thrown himself wholeheartedly into all the planning. He hadn't really needed to drive me down to New York as he was doing now. I could quite easily have gone by train, my heavy stuff had already been sent on, but he said he wanted to be in New York anyway, and would like to see me away. He liked driving, would drive anywhere and never be tired. I knew if he had been up with us that time, the accident would never have happened – well, not the way it did.

So we left them up there, Mr. Gaydon, Olaf, Martha, Norm and

Cynthia, and I was a bit sad about it. They had all been so good to me, and I would remember all of them so very well. It had been hard to say goodbye.

During the previous week I had spent three days down in the city, staying with Norm and Cynthia, and saying all my goodbyes down there – Al, Elmer, Taps, and during the full day I spent at the factory, all those I knew there, especially Poppy, and Marcia. It had been a quiet time for us all, and not a bit like the riotous farewells I had once envisaged.

I knew Danny was spending less and less time down in the city, leaving much more of the running of the business to Norm. He could manage it all right, but I knew, had things been different, I could have been a good help to him, and I would have had a very fine job there. But things weren't different, they were as they were, and we couldn't alter that, much as any of us might want to.

Yes, I was going home, and I had a dozen pairs of seamless stockings somewhere in my bags to prove it. For a certain young lady who had written me such a nice letter when she had heard all about what had happened, and knew I was in on it, which cheered me up a lot, much more than the one Mr. G. had sent, even though that had been very nice too. Jenny's eyes would sparkle when they saw the stockings, and I badly needed some eyes to sparkle for me – I'd seen enough sad ones in the last few weeks.

I couldn't think I was heartless about it. I wasn't. I knew what it had meant to a lot of people, and I knew what it had meant to me. I'd had a hell of a lot of time, lying there in a hospital bed, to do nothing but think of it.

I didn't really remember a lot of it, though the last few seconds of it would remain imprinted on my memory for ever. It had been a burst tyre, the experts had confirmed that, and she was going so fast we really hadn't had a chance. It might easily have been the same if I had been driving, and it might have been me – not her – that hit.

It was a funny thing that my right hand was the slowest to heal, wasn't even better yet. All the rest of me had mended, except the hand, and, if she hadn't slammed the door to on it, and, if she hadn't got out, and if I hadn't, and if we hadn't gone in there in the first place. There were so many ifs.

I felt very sad about her and Danny. She had got so keen on him, suddenly, and yet not suddenly. A week is ample time to know each other really, when you are both mature and worldly-wise. I still think she and Danny would have made a go of it – they knew what they were doing, he knew what he wanted, and so did she – it would have been all right.

I had been awake long through many nights in the hospital, thinking of her, of us, and of her and Danny. There was so much to think about – that last time we had spent together up at High Point, she had been strange then. I knew she had talked a lot with her father about what she wanted to do, she and Danny, and she had been very much away from me, apart from me even when we were together. Yet, in that last hour with her, we had been somehow closer to each other than I had ever known it before – it was so hard to explain, so very hard. It was as though, just this once, she had given herself to me – other times, she had taken me. I'd spent a lot of time wondering why, and still didn't know the answer, still didn't know if I had my facts right, if she had given herself to me, she had, and yet, even then, she hadn't seemed to be with me – she was the enigma of all women, and I would never solve the puzzle of her.

I would never know either who it was she had shouted for almost at the last seconds of her life – it could have been my name, it could have been Danny. He was a lot in her thoughts, and it might well have been for him – whoever it was, Danny or me, it had been her last living thought.

I had thought such a lot about her, lying there in the hospital. She had been a wonderful, beautiful, thrilling woman, and I had been very lucky to know her as I had done.

If it had not have happened, the smash, I would have said goodbye to her at Midway, and then perhaps, never have seen her again. Well, maybe I would have done. Danny would have brought her over to England and I would have seen them, and she would have said, "Hi, David", and she would have been Mrs. Danny Erikson, and I would have just said, "Hello – Laurie", just like that. It was strange too to think how it might have been.

"Steady a bit, Danny," I said, "there's a place just down here I want you to pull in."

He was surprised. We had barely spoken, he never did talk a lot when he was driving, liking to give all his attention to it, and I had been thinking.

I wanted to talk to him now, just the two of us, for the first time for a long while. He had been with me in hospital this way, just us two, but it had been strange there, now we could talk.

228

This was it, he pulled in as I directed. Laurie had been right. I have a good memory, and this was somewhere I would never forget.

Danny was still surprised as we moved in, very slowly, through the overgrown track, on to Ryker's Peak – more surprised still at the vista which opened to us.

It was just glorious up here today, in the clear air of the morning. The view was just as it was in my memory, in my memory for always. Down there, Lake Le-Aqua-Na, a beautiful blue, and further away, Lake Michigan itself, a lighter blue, dancing and shimmering in the heat down there. Chicago there in the distance, with the smoke haze overhead. Fresh and glorious up here, the little white rabbit tails of clouds chasing each other in the blue overhead, it was wonderful, and just like it was when I had been here with her, only this time I was with Danny.

I hoped now, after I had talked to him, and after we had pulled away again, the growth would seal in the track so that no other humans would ever come here again.

Danny was enchanted with it, as I had been, was still.

"This sure is great," he said.

I pointed it all out to him, just as Laurie had done for me, told him what she had told me about the Indians blindfolding their enemies and making them walk over the top –

"How do you know all this?" He asked.

I told him how I knew, how this was a place Laurie knew, and that we had come in here on our way down from High Point that night, and how she had described it for me.

"You came here – that night?"

He was thinking hard, and I was matching his thoughts. I purposely hadn't told him we had also been in here on our way up to High Point. I wanted to talk to him, but, no matter what he asked, he would only hear what I wanted to say. I had thought about what I would tell him for a long time. All the thinking I had done in the hospital had been for this, only I hadn't known it then. I knew what he was thinking, and I knew just what I was going to tell him, just what I thought he should know and nothing more.

"We were early," (that was true anyway) "she wanted me to see this place." That was true also, but it had been on the way up she had first shown me. "She wanted to stop somewhere and put her wig on, she never wore it at High Point." That was true and something he hadn't known.

"I sure hated that wig," he told me.

"I knew you did." He was surprised again. "Laurie told me that."

"We pulled in here to talk." That was true, even if what I had wanted was more than talking. "We hadn't been together a lot up at High Point, she'd been with her father such a lot, and now, there were some things she wanted to tell me."

I saw how interested he was. I expected it this way. In the last few weeks I had seen how he was about her, and now I was so very glad I had given such a lot of time to what it was I had to tell him.

"When she had shown me the view up here, we got back in the car – she'd been different up there at the house, Danny, it's hard to say how." I had to be a bit cruel now but this was how I had to do it. "But I think she wasn't so interested in me the way she had been, and though we had grown apart that way, we had become much better friends, if you see what I mean."

He saw what I meant, I was watching him close. I had to, I had to be one move ahead of him all the time.

"At first I hadn't been very pleased – you can't blame me for that." I hope he didn't blame me, I could have said more but I wouldn't rub it in. "But then the real friendship with her very quickly developed, and it was so wonderful, she was such a great girl" – the agreement was plain in his eyes – "that I liked it, liked it a lot. It made a big difference to us both, and it meant that we could talk, talk properly."

I let that sink in a moment or two, but I went on quickly. If I looked around me too much, thought too much, there were too many things, too many memories, that could spoil what I was doing, and I didn't want it spoiled, it had to be this way, for her, and for him.

"We talked a lot about you Danny – that was why we came in here – I knew that after we'd been here awhile" – that wasn't exactly true but it was only a white lie – "she told me how in the time she had known you it had done something for her, something that no other man had done. You see, Danny, nobody, not even me, had ever thought of taking her round a can factory before, nobody, not even me, had ever treated her like an ordinary woman, with a brain and an opinion and a business sense. Everybody, me even, had known her for what she was on the outside" – this was cruel also, but very true – "a sex symbol, and all we thought about with her was just sex."

He was following it all, just the way I wanted him to do. He wasn't asking any questions, just listening, and he was, I think, liking what he heard.

"You were different with her, Danny" – now I had to be human with him for a minute – "now, don't let's have any mistake about it, you'd have got around to those sort of things with her the same as anyone else – she would have wanted it from you" – he still knew everything I was meaning – "but it wouldn't have been the begin all and end all with you, as it was with the others – that was all they had wanted from her."

He was with me all the way, it was going much better than I had even anticipated.

"Of course, you would have wanted her that way, she would have wanted you" – a little bit more cruelty, though softened down for him – "and I think with you Danny, she had found what she wanted." I couldn't miss the light in his eyes then. "There would have been no more Delane, she would have been Mrs. Danny Erikson, and Mr. Erikson would have been enough man for her, because, with you, Danny, she would have shared all your interests. She would have been in on all you were doing, been head of the company with you, knew you would ask her things, knew you would do things for her, the company, the children up here, there would have been so much to share with you, Danny, and it would have taken a lot from her to share it, so she would not have had time for anything else."

He was a very happy man – I could see that.

"If you want my opinion, Danny, the main reason for her being what she was – you know how they said she was" – he knew, just as well as I did – "that was because every other man she had known wanted to share her bed with her." That was true and really they couldn't be blamed, I knew that for certain, but I didn't have to tell him that part. "Nobody ever thought of sharing her life. Then she met you and you were what she was looking for. With you there could be a lot of sharing, business, children, everything, and you were a man she could respect, look up to and be glad of, and I honestly don't think, Danny, she had ever felt that way about any man before."

I had done it, as I had wanted to do it. Because of her, because she would have wanted me to do it, and because of him. He was pleased, I knew, and happy. But there was just one more thing I had to tell him, something he had wanted badly to know, and hadn't ever asked me.

"We talked so much about you, and about the way you would make your life, that we stayed on a bit too long. Then she wanted to powder her nose – I said I'd keep my eyes shut, although that didn't matter, it was dark then. She got out on her side, the passenger side" – that was true and I emphasised it. "I leaned over to tell her to be careful" – nearly true – "and she banged the door on my hand." I was watching his face again, saw relief in it, it was rather strange, it wasn't that important she had been driving, or was it? "It was awful, Danny, she just had to drive."

"You don't say," he said, and it was just a straightforward expression, not disbelief in any way.

I did say, and I made it very clear.

"It hurt like hell," and that was true, and it was hurting now as I was saying it, as though she had just slammed the door on it.

"We looked at it in the lights, and it was bloody awful. I felt so sick, and the hand got numb, and we knew she would have to drive."

That part was true, and, with my hand hurting again so strangely, I could tell this part with great feeling.

"By the time we realised that, we had wasted a lot more time – she didn't powder her nose, didn't even remember to put the wig on. She was so upset about my hand, and it wasn't her fault really, I should have had more sense than to put it on the door like I did."

All the time I was talking I was remembering it all so very clearly.

"She was going to have to drive very fast to get to Midway in time. I knew that, but I told her to go carefully until she got used to the car – you know how it is? She went very slowly, I wouldn't let her go fast until she had got used to the lights and had driven a mile or so. She was worried about my hand, and about how late it was, and the hand was hurting like the devil, and I was feeling very sick. It must have been awful for her, but she did well. Then I made her speed up a lot, and she drove and drove – until – "

He knew until when.

"That was how they knew her down at Rockford, she hadn't got the wig on and they recognised her right away. I didn't tell them who she was – nobody asked me. It was such a simple thing, Danny, her slamming the door like that, otherwise I would have been driving."

There was no more to say, he knew the rest, and what might have happened could only be imagined. He knew it all now, at least he knew all I wanted him to know. I was glad we had talked like this, glad and very relieved.

We went out along the track and back on to the road. I looked up at the rabbit tail clouds – up there, wherever she was, I thought she would be pleased. It's funny how you think these things.

We drove on down – down the road she had driven me that night – along the stretch where the tyre had burst, where we had lurched, swerved, bounced, and then hit the tree. It was here I had been found wandering along the road, dazed and with no real idea of what had happened, save that we had been in a terrible crash – just here, along this stretch of road.

Through Rockford, where I had been so long in hospital. Rockford, where she had been taken when they had finally got her out of the wreck. Through Rockford and on down.

We could go on thinking, Danny and I. He would have a lot more to think about now, but his thoughts could be more pleasant perhaps, because of what I had said up there at Ryker's Peak – I hoped so at any rate.

I was going home. We would skirt Chicago, on to the Northern Indiana Toll road, through to the two hundred and forty-one mile long Ohio Turnpike, which continued into the Pennsylvania Turnpike, an unbroken super-highway between Chicago and New York. Somewhere along the way we would stop the night at a motel, and tomorrow we would be in New York. Tomorrow night we would see Lily Lee at the Latin Quarter – which would be very nice and the next day I would board the Queen Elizabeth.

I was going home. I was glad that last evening I had driven down to the little cemetery with Cynthia – only the second time I had been there – with those red roses for Laurie. I was glad I had told Cynthia about talking to Danny, very glad indeed. Cynthia knew what I should say – women know about those things. Cynthia certainly did.

I was going home.